CONSTANTINE HUNG HEAVILY IN DARKNESS, AS QUIETLY AS POSSIBLE.

The light was from far up the shaft. He could hear machinery clunking, grinding; felt the whisper of rising air lifting the hair on the back of his neck. He waited, dangling in a void, his arms aching.

The gripplers came. He could hear the fingers snuffling inquisitively around in the chamber he'd just left—he could picture them clearly, in his mind's eye, four-fingered hands, like something on toads, tip-tapping their way along the floor, bloodhounds with their smellers in their fingertips, picking up his scent. . . .

His arms throbbed; he felt like his shoulders were slowly, slowly dislocating.

He could hear them coming closer now, tippity-tap, slither, tippity-tap, slither, closer and closer, looking to grab his wrists, perhaps to fling him down the shaft to their fellows, where the other gripplers would pull him apart or, maybe worse, impregnate his skin with fungi that would send their roots worming into his flesh, his veins, and finally into his brain. . . .

JOHN CONSTANTINE™ HELLBLAZER™

SUBTERRANEAN

A NOVEL BY

JOHN SHIRLEY

BASED ON CHARACTERS FROM THE VERTIGO/DC COMICS SERIES

POCKET STAR BOOKS
New York   London   Toronto   Sydney

An *Original* Publication of POCKET BOOKS

 A Pocket Star Book published by
POCKET BOOKS, a division of Simon & Schuster, Inc.
1230 Avenue of the Americas, New York, NY 10020

This book is a work of fiction. Names, characters, places and incidents are products of the author's imagination or are used fictitiously. Any resemblance to actual events or locales or persons, living or dead, is entirely coincidental.

ISBN-13: 978-1-4165-0344-6
ISBN-10: 1-4165-0344-7

This Pocket Star Books paperback edition December 2006

10 9 8 7 6 5 4 3 2 1

POCKET STAR BOOKS and colophon are registered trademarks of Simon & Schuster, Inc.

www.dccomics.com
Keyword: DC Comics on AOL.

Cover design by John Vairo, Jr.
Cover illustration by Tim Bradstreet

Manufactured in the United States of America

For information regarding special discounts for bulk purchases, please contact Simon & Schuster Special Sales at 1-800-456-6798 or business@simonandschuster.com.

For my heroes
Jamie Delano and Mike Carey
Hellblazers

Special thanks to everyone at the
Voices From Beyond Hellblazer forum
(http://hellblazer.ipbhost.com/index.php)

Farewell my freends let playne simplicity
Be stil your guide to lead you in your race
So shal ye neare approch to Unity
And evermore obtayne from him his grace
For double dealers, false and treacherous men
Wil quickly be entrapt in Errours den.

—Robert Fludd (1574–1637)

"Sometimes, mate, the only way out of the devil's claws is double-dealing the devil's way, and right brisk, too ..."

—John Constantine (1953–?)

From the Servants of Transfiguration

Dossier on John Constantine

Top Clearance: Eyes Only

John Constantine, a working-class British magus, is rumored to be a magical adept by some, a con man by others. He may or may not be problematic to the SOT. He was born in 1953 in Liverpool (making him a "Scouse") to a family that can be charitably called "working class" and this class association has marked his personal style. According to hospital records he was a twin, but his brother was born dead, asphyxiated by an anomalous loop of umbilicus. The magic symbolism of this seems ambiguous, to say the least. Additionally, Constantine's mother died in childbirth. His father, Thomas Constantine, apparently blamed the infant JC for this. Thomas was incarcerated for stealing women's underwear, at which time the boy and his sister were sent to live with an aunt and uncle, a rather troublesome pair, in Northampton. John Constantine's relationships with family members have been rocky at best.

In 1967, he was expelled from school. Eventually he moved to Portobello, London, where he was involved in some of the more extemporaneous "rock and roll" scenes extant at the time. Constantine is reported to have had scores of occult adventures—possibly *misadventures* is a better term—but our researchers find it difficult to separate out fact from legend. It does appear that Constantine had a particularly nasty interaction with a demon invoked at Newcastle, leading to an extended sojourn in Ravenscar mental hospital. Despite the notorious sadism of Ravenscar's staff, he seems to have emerged from the hospital with his sanity largely restored, all things being relative.

Constantine seems to be almost entirely without conventional financial support. We have no record of his taking money for an occult investigation or activity. He appears to make some of his very modest living through supernaturally enhanced gambling.

Our researchers are unable to discover precisely when and where Constantine learned about the Hidden World and gained a proficiency in ritual magic. We note a number of Constantine's ancestors with a reputation for the supernatural (see SOT files, *The Inquisition*), hence he may have inherited some magical ability. He also seems to have actively explored the supernatural from fairly early in childhood, quite on his own initiative. As an adult, he may well have had inspiration from some other well-known figures in the uncanny realm, including the voodoo priest known as "Papa Midnite" (see dossier entry, "Papa Midnite: an authentic personage"). There are rumors that Constantine was involved with the (mythical?) elemental known as the "Swamp Thing."

His abilities are not known for certain, but John Constantine is understood to be capable of limited telepathy, precognition, astral projection, and the successful invocation of elementals, demons, and angels. There are persistent tales of his having visited Hell itself, somehow walking away more or less intact. However, he does not seem to have been allied with Hell's supervisory denizens, nor is he regarded as a diabolist. Indeed, in recent years Constantine has been known to seek out white-magic spiritual adepts in a bid for improved control over his abilities.

Constantine has his weaknesses, including bouts of drunkenness, but is to be regarded as a dangerous adversary. He is not without allies and is influential amongst aficionados of so-called chaos magick. E.g., there are at least two "alternative Tarot" decks which include an image of John Constantine as one of the face cards.

SOT operatives interacting with Constantine should keep in mind that he is cunning and treacherous. Our psych profile on him suggests that he is not without loyalty and some peculiar code of ethics evolved according to his own lights. Unfortunately we have no reason to believe his loyalty could ever extend to the SOT. He must be regarded as a loose cannon, at best.

If the opportunity arises, John Constantine's elimination would be advisable.

Dossier Addenda

About a year ago, John Constantine interposed himself into our War Lord project, causing the destruction of several principle Servants—including Dyzigi—and, more disastrously yet, derailing the ritual invocation of the War Lord

N'Hept, thus effecting the undoing of the Grand Transfiguration. The meticulously planned and prepared-for world war and Apocalypse did not come about.

Since that time, the halls of the SOT have been overcast by a cloud of disappointment.

The Council has held our own Hierophant Magister, Mac-Crawley, responsible for this fiasco, and has summarily assigned him to a new project that will bring about our revenge against John Constantine and set the stage for a new Transfiguration.

MacCrawley has been advised that he fails this undertaking at his own peril.

Prologue

A fine misty rain fell on a street in an Irish city, on a late Saturday afternoon; it fell too on a man of middle age, walking along, hands in his trench coat pockets, a Silk Cut trailing smoke stuck in a corner of his mouth. The asphalt was worn away in places to show the old cobblestones underneath; a drunk snored in a doorway; a taxi careened by, a bus rumbled and squeaked and hissed and was gone . . . and a boy rattled by on a skateboard, shouting, "One side, gobshite!" at John Constantine as he slouched slowly down the sidewalk.

Constantine was only faintly aware of all this. His mind was retracing the journey he'd taken from London to Wales, thence to Ireland and a heroin-addicted neo-druid on the outskirts of Belfast who had given him directions to a crumbling monastery on the Irish west coast—where a policeman had fined him for "vandalism." He'd been digging under a cornerstone, marked with a complex interlacing of crosses, looking for a stone artifact, more pagan than Christian. Which, sod it, someone else had gotten to before him. The box was there—plundered.

Knew it was likely to be a waste of time, he thought.

Squandered two hundred quid looking for the bloody thing. Threw away valuable time that could be spent fleecing sheep in the casinos, or drinking meself into a stupor. Ought to go to the dock—wasting more time wandering about.

Then something did catch his attention as he turned a corner—a familiar smell, a familiar noise. Guinness and sawdust, cigarette smoke, the *ka-chunk* of darts, a jukebox playing Flogging Molly, a band he rather fancied. It was a pub—a "boozer" the locals called it. Just the thing to cheer a man up . . .

Constantine went in, there was never any doubt of it, and found an empty stool. He ordered a Bushmills with a Guinness to the side, and had knocked back the first and was partway down the second when he saw her in the booth—and she saw him at the same moment.

"Oh shite," he muttered.

It was Kit. Dark, wavy hair—she was wearing it longer now; slender; a humorous intelligence in her eyes; dressed today in a green military jacket twice too big for her, which looked odd with her ankle-length dark purple dress—never seen her in one of those— and high-top sneakers. *Going for a piecemeal look,* he decided, *nothing goes with anything, and that's the statement.* Perhaps it was a way of saying "I'm not here to meet men, so sod off." Even wearing this hodgepodge, she was beautiful—a simple honest beauty.

She was looking back at him, reproachfully and wryly at once. He crossed to her, smiling, almost bowled over by a heavy-set drunk with tattoos up and down his arms who was dancing thumpily to Flogging Molly, and making the floor shake.

"Careful, you were almost run over by our human lorry," Kit said as he walked up. "How are you, John?"

He noted a second purse, opposite her in the booth—she was here with one of her girlfriends. Did that mean she was available?

What are you thinking? You performed a spell to drive her out of your heart. You sent those feelings into your demon counterpart, in Hell. What are you doing, gaping at her like a schoolboy at the leggy substitute teacher? Those feelings are gone!

"Well I'm gobsmacked," he said. "What a gormless bastard I am. Here you are. I just stopped in for a quick wet . . ."

"Did you now?" Her Irish accent was modulated by her time in Britain. "Don't take me for an eejit, John. Just happened to wander into my favorite boozer, out of all the pubs in Ireland?"

He looked around and winced. He had been here before. He'd been blocking all that, he realized. He hadn't walked here at random at all. Probably—

Probably his whole journey, his ostensible search for the Curse Stone, had really been about coming here, to this pub. He'd been aching with loneliness—and Kit had been the only woman he'd gotten close enough to, to really ease that ache. He had more in common with Tchalai on some levels, but that hadn't worked out. He'd unconsciously gravitated to this pub to regain what he'd exorcised.

"How's . . . every last little thing, Kit?" he asked, knowing he sounded feeble.

"I've got a new job, working in an office, but apart from that everything's as arseways as always. Still—I haven't got the divil to worry about, or not any more than most, these days . . . and it's been a bit of a relief, that, John." She said it not unkindly, and with a look of sympathy. But she'd left him because he'd been unable to leave magic alone, and her meaning was clear. *I'm better off without you and your Hidden World.*

"You know—I really could give it all up," he began. "I mean, if you were to consider . . ."

"It's good to see you, Johnny," she said. "But no thanks, love. I don't mind a man who comes with baggage. They all do. But *your* bags—open those and anything might come out. It's just . . . good to see you."

He nodded. "Right. Well. I was just . . . in the neighborhood. Can I buy you a drink—for old time's sake?"

"No, thanks, love, I'm off the drink. Water for me. I was drinking too much. You might think about the wagon yourself."

"Think about it all the time—got to stay alert for it. Only way to be sure I can avoid getting on it, thinking it's a bus."

She smiled. "Same old John. Oh, here comes my friend—she's telling me her troubles, John. Her husband—"

"Right. I'm off. But . . . I suppose I was hoping to see . . . you know, see how you were. Can I send you a letter sometime, Kit? Just to say hello. I don't reckon you have the same address."

She looked at him for a long moment—the gentleness of her pity made him want to tear his hair—and then she fished in her purse, found a pen and paper, scribbled an address. "You can write to me, John—just a hello letter." She handed it to him.

Her friend, a slouching, red-haired woman with a black eye, was hovering at his elbow, so he smiled and winked at Kit, and made himself turn and walk away.

And out the door. The rain had intensified, and he let it run down his face. Best that way. So no one would know. He hated to show weakness.

He lit a cigarette and walked toward the docks, thinking, *Oh the glamorous world of magic. Doesn't it just get you all the best.*

1

SOME MIGHT CALL IT SHAMBHALA—AND SOME MIGHT CALL IT SHEOL

Setting out on his mission, eager to follow the stranger, Duff Duffel heard the soft-headed boys sniggering at him as he left the only surviving village pub in Tonsell-by-the-Stream, Cornwall. "Dee old Dee!" called the boy Bosky, as Duff clutched his old Navy coat about himself in the late afternoon May drizzle and shuffled past the alley where the young wastrels clacked their dice and their skateboards. The boy Bosky wasn't such a bad sort; he had to give the old man a jeer or two, but he was never one to call him a stinking old drunk, like that Upson fellow. Duff gave the jeering no more thought than he gave the chattering of squirrels in Smithson Wood. He knew the locals thought him daft, called him Daft Old Duff, wrote him off as a senile guzzle-guts, and he cared not a speck, because in his time he'd seen marvels and dreams come to life, indeed he had. His soul had left his body and flown to the Palace of Phosphor; he had bestrode the rings of Saturn and he had seen dryads dancing in the circles of stone.

He belched a memory of the three ales he'd drunk—drunk them watching the stranger in the pub—and he picked up his pace, beginning to wheeze in keeping up with the interloper, who was now fifty yards up the lane, heading for the edge of the village. Mr. MacCrawley was this burly, sharply dressed toff's name—so the pub keeper had called him, when he'd settled his bill for the drinks and two days renting the little flat out back of the pub.

Now this MacCrawley was striding away down the lane, but Duff had seen him in the smoky pub clear enough: a stocky man, wide-shouldered, with iron gray hair cut short, almost bald; black tufted eyebrows, pale gray eyes, and a jutting block of chin. He wore a fine Savoy Row greatcoat, the color of fog, and shiny new black shoes. On an index finger was a ring with a great red cabochon, on which was carved a symbol few would know: a dragon with its body curved into the shape of an *S*, twining the letter *T*. Duff knew that crest, for he had been the apprentice of a true magician in his time. Duff's drinking and whoring had caused Master Scofield to turn him out, but it was Scofield who came a cropper—for he vanished into the Deep Barrow, and never did return. The magician was dead, surely, while Duff still tottered about, drawing the dole and getting by on odd jobs, doing his little castings now and then, just to keep his hand in, but afraid to go far with it. If a spirit did answer his conjuring, it was only to laugh at him.

Duff passed the flower and gift shop—it would

scarcely survive, were it not for the American tourists, buying supposed "Celtic pendants" and the like—in the window of which was a placard advertising the "Flower Show and Jumble Sale in Aid of Preservation." Up ahead, MacCrawley had turned the corner. "He's off to that barrow in the wood, he is," Duff muttered. "I knew it, too, did I not? I did!"

Duff hesitated about following MacCrawley into Smithson Wood. He had only a half pint of whiskey on him in his old Navy coat, and he was not sure so little drink would see him through a visit to the barrow, a place he had not visited these twelve years and more.

Still, it was Duff's mission to protect this village from the likes of MacCrawley—from those who bore that sigil on their rings, and the dire disembodied who served them. Old Duff was not appreciated for his efforts, no not by half. More than once he'd driven away those harridan mists who fed on the bone marrow of old men and women, so that elders could not fight the sicknesses that came and died of pneumonia. The villagers laughed at him, as he ran through the village waving switches of ash wood at what they supposed were scraps of fog, but Duff forgave them, they didn't know better, and more than one of them had given him the price of a bowl of soup and a drink on a cold night.

So Duff made himself plod onward, after MacCrawley; made himself continue on into the lengthening shadows of the wood.

-→==◎==←-

"Who is that MacCrawley bloke then, Skupper?" asked Butterworth—a middle-aged, moonfaced man with a thick crop of long, dyed-blond, permed hair, looking up from snooker as the landlord of the Sleeping Plowman returned from the bog—the landlord sniffing his fingers, as he always did. "I've seen him coming out of His Nibs'—twice he was there not twenty-four hours past. What's he up to?"

The landlord, "Skupper," a gloomy man of no certain age, greased-back hair, pitted skin, and a red nose—for he tippled right along with his customers—only growled in response, running his beefy hands down his stained apron, slipping his substantial girth behind the bar like an eel fitting into a hole too small for it.

"Come on then, Skupper! I've got a right to know! I'm on the committee to save this here pub—"

"Don't want to save it," Skupper growled, pulling a lever to gush draft into a glass. "Want to sell the buggerin' bog-hole."

"—and if he's buying up property round here from Lord Smithson, why, we have a right to see to preservation—there's preservation laws! It's hard enough keeping some semblance of tradition, with the foot-and-mouth driving the piggeries and sheepmen out of business. How many farms selling off to developers, and the like! The only other pub already turned into flats! And fox hunting banned, so Lord Smithson can't go out anymore with his hounds!"

"Here, you're one to talk of tradition, Butterworth," said Harry Garth, a cadaverous man with white hair and a deeply lined face, and a cap he'd had so long it was scarcely more than a rag, though he had money enough from selling his dairy to buy any number of new caps. "Wasn't so long ago you were trying to get us to host a bloody rock festival!"

"Wasn't long ago, he says!" Butterworth retorted, chalking his cue furiously. "Why, that was twenty-five bloody years ago! I was scarcely more than a boy!"

"Was I you, Butterworth," said Skupper, scowlingly wiping out a glass with a rag that might be making it dirtier than it had been before, "I would not ask over-much about MacCrawley and Lord Smithson. If they is doing deals, Smithson won't take to anyone poking their great beezers into 'is business. They're in some kind of lodge together too, like the Masons or the Oddfellers, for they both got the ring—and them as in lodges is tight."

"He's right," said Garth. "You run your tourist shop at the sufferance of 'is Lordship. Turn you out whenever he pleases!"

Butterworth scoffed—then pointed his cue at the back door, where Garth's teenage grandson, Bosky, was furtively reaching through to a forgotten glass of whiskey on a table, trying to snake it out without being seen. "Here, Garth, your grandson's at the whiskey again!"

"Bosky!" Garth roared, coming out of his booth, waving his cane. "Cease and desist, boy, or I'll tell your mother, you—"

Bosky snagged the whiskey glass and ducked out with it, tittering, followed by an ashtray thrown by Skupper. "Garth, you'd better keep your grandson out of here or I'll have the rozzers on him!"

Outside, Bosky knocked back the whiskey, shuddered, tossed the shot glass into a pile of crates and led the way out of the alley as Finn and Geoff came complaining after him, asking why he hadn't shared the drink. "Because it wasn't enough to share, you pillocks! Come on, let's go to the wood and smoke up what I got in my pocket!"

"You what?" Geoff chided him. "You said you had nothing!"

"Almost nothing. It's not much more than a crumble . . . Let's cut through Mrs. Bushel's yard . . ."

They were running much of the time, vaulting fences, dodging bulldogs—two bulldogs, one old and fat and one young and sleek, in two yards—and pounding up the lane, skylarking, trying to trip one another up. Then they veered off the road onto the familiar path into the Smithson Wood, his Lordship's land, as so much was hereabouts, Geoff tapping at his iPod to try to get it going, stumbling over the mossy stones as he frowned down at the device. "Forgot to charge the bloody thing . . ."

Bosky led them through the intermittent shafts of sunlight slanting through the branches of the alders, the ash trees, the English oaks. The thin cloud cover, sometimes drooling rain, only reluctantly let the sun through . . .

Not a quarter mile more and they'd reached the place some called "the barrow," an old pile of stony hummocks taking up most of a clearing. They liked to smoke the green that Bosky got from his cousin in

London here, and many of the stones were marked with their graffiti.

"You reckon any of those mushrooms could be magic, like?" Finn asked, kicking at the circle of toad-stools around the great tumble of gray stones. "I mean—ya know—psychedelic shrooms."

"Oh you'd hallucinate a treat, right before you died!" Bosky hooted. "Those aren't shrooms, you git, they're toadstools. Here . . ." He passed the little brass pipe to Finn, a pale, athletic boy—or he had been, once—with white-blond hair, nicknamed for his Finnish ancestry.

"Shite you've crammed a lot of old joint-ends in there—we're smoking paper. Too harsh—"

"Oh stop your whining, Finn," Bosky said, climbing up on the rocks. "Hey—there's someone's coat laid over one of these rocks! Crikey that's a fine coat too!"

"Here, this big rock's been moved—" Geoff called. He was a bespectacled boy with pale skin, freckles, red-brown hair trailing over his collar—the one who'd excelled in school before they'd given all that up. "Look—a tunnel!"

"Stay away from that tunnel you little fools!" a voice croaked from the edge of the clearing.

Startled, they turned to see Old Duff swaying in the waist-high weeds just this side of the screen of ash trees. "Ha! Old Duff!" Bosky crowed. "Is this your coat, then?"

"Not a chance it's his!" Geoff snorted. "It doesn't smell like whiskey—and it's too fine for him. Some-one with money left that coat there!"

"Money? You reckon?" Bosky picked the coat up

and immediately began poking through its pockets. But he found nothing much—only a meerschaum pipe and a leather pouch of tobacco.

"I should put that coat down immediately, but gently, if I were you," said a rumblingly silky voice from the tunnel's mouth. Stooped over, MacCrawley emerged, dusting himself off. Cobwebs clung to his elbows. He stepped away from the tunnel and to one side—rather hastily—putting out his hand toward Bosky, who silently handed the coat over. And then the pipe and tobacco.

There was a raspy, breathy sound coming from the tunnel now. And an unpleasant smell. Like nothing Bosky'd ever smelled before. Something that smelled dead—but not.

"Run boy, get away from there!" Old Duff shouted.

"What has he to fear, Old Duff?" MacCrawley asked, lofting his eyebrows theatrically. "That tunnel leads to a glorious sight—some might call it Shambhala! 'Course some might call it Sheol too!" He chuckled creakily.

Never taking his eyes off Bosky, MacCrawley put the coat back on and then pointed—while still staring at Bosky—at the Finn. "You, boy! Come here!"

"Sod off, you old poof!" Finn said to MacCrawley. "I'm not going to—"

"Oh but you will, my lad!" MacCrawley interrupted, turning toward Finn and making a curious hand motion, as if he were reeling something invisible toward him. Finn's eyes glazed, and he stumbled toward MacCrawley.

Bosky stared. "Finn?"

The raspy sound from the low tunnel entrance became a whipping noise, and Bosky turned to see a long, hairless, gray-black, rope-muscled arm stretching out. There were only four fingers on the hand, fingers shaped like those of a toad but longer than a man's, and they tapped at the ground as if tasting, sniffing it. On and on the arm stretched . . . impossibly far, two yards, and three. And still it stretched out, with a crackling sound, its elbow switching back and forth double-jointedly, the fingers trembling as it reached for Finn's ankle—

"Finn! Get back!" Geoff yelled, climbing up toward him. But Duff was there then, dragging both Geoff and Bosky back with surprising strength.

Finn came out of his trance as the long prehensile gray fingers closed around his ankle—he screamed as it jerked him off his feet and dragged him as fast as a frog sucking in a fly, down into the tunnel. In a moment he was gone—they heard only his echoing shriek.

"I disturbed the grippler," MacCrawley remarked, rolling the small boulder—and showing no significant effort—to cover the hole again. "It was coming for me—had to give it someone. Would have been awkward, otherwise." He gave the boulder a final push and then turned to the boys, who were backing away, aghast.

MacCrawley grinned wolfishly, showing a mouthful of blocky yellow teeth. "Now off with you—back to your little hovels—you wouldn't want to miss the fun." He reached into his trouser pocket and Duff expected him to pull out a magic wand, but instead it

was a large black metal revolver. MacCrawley
pointed it at them. "You heard me—and that means
you too, old man! Get back to the village or I'll find
you and your families and put bullets in the whole
lot."

The boys needed no more urging; they fled, the
old man puffing along behind them. They went by
the shortest route, across the fields, following the
cow paths.

⊷═◉═⊷

The rain had started to fall with more decision
before the two boys arrived at the outer reaches
of Tonsell-by-the-Stream. They were still running,
pounding across the old stone bridge arching over
the Hillcrease River, which was in fact too small to
be rightly called a river. Just on the other side,
Bosky pulled up short, breathing hard, leaning forward, hands on his knees. "Oh Christ, I've got to
stop smoking."

"Bosky . . . what're those?" Geoff asked, wiping
rain from his eyes and pointing.

Bosky looked at what he supposed were ordinary
surveyor's stakes, the sort one sees in fields marking
a place for building, only what was hanging from the
stakes wasn't the usual soft plastic streamer. He
walked over to it to be sure—the stake had been
driven just atop the grassy bank of the river, on the
village side—and Bosky confirmed for himself that it
wasn't a plastic flag; it was, yes, a streamer of skin
and hair, *human* skin and hair, because part of the

face was there too, hanging from a knot of the brown hair still in the torn-away scalp. It was missing its eyeballs, but the sockets and nose and upper lip were there, a bit leathery but recognizable, like a mask made of human skin. Rainwater ran over it, made the skin look like it was sweating. There were curious little runes scrawled on the stake, running down its vertical length. Looking at the skin, Bosky's stomach contracted, and he backed away, gagging.

"Fuck me! There's more of them, Bosky!"

Bosky looked up to see there was a line of the stakes, at the top of the grassy bank, each about seventy-five feet from the next, following the outer edge of the town, along the river.

"We're awake, aren't we, Bosky?" Geoff asked hoarsely as the rain began to slacken, the wind picking up to make the hanks of hair and skin snap and wriggle. "I mean—with Finn being grabbed by that thing—and then this . . . it don't seem . . . real."

"I don't know anymore, mate," Bosky said.

"You reckon Finn's dead?"

"I don't know that neither. But I'm going to go home, check on me mum."

"Yeah—I'll check on me uncle . . . Then we got to call the coppers and tell them about these fucking stakes, man. Somebody's been up to no good—"

"And what do we tell them about Finn, then? Eh? How do we explain that? They'll laugh us out of the fucking door, mate."

"I know but . . ." Geoff broke off, just shaking his head.

They started for the nearest lane—it ended just

before the riverbank, at a metal guardrail there with a dead-end sign on it—and they had just climbed over the guardrail when they heard Old Duff shouting wheezingly at them. He was finally catching up.

"Boys! Don't go into the village!" he called from the other side of the bridge. "Stay outside the markers!" He pointed at the grisly stakes. "You mustn't—"

But the sight of the old madman only set loose the terror that they'd just managed to keep under control till that moment, and they both turned and ran, wordlessly, toward home . . . into the village.

⊷═◎═⊶

Old Duff stopped to catch his breath in the middle of the bridge. He leaned against the rail, wiping his forehead where sweat was replacing rain, and squinted at the stakes. When had MacCrawley put them up? He had accomplices, maybe Lord Smithson himself, or Smithson's man Pinch.

A cracking sound came then, and just beyond the stakes the ground was splitting open.

The earth shook, the bridge beginning to splinter and split under Duff; stones fell from its balustrades to crash into the river. He had to cling to the bridge to keep his footing as the sundering ground split in a lightning-shaped crack between the shallow river and the edge of the village, all the way around—cutting the village out from the rest of the world the way a man cuts the core from an apple. The crack opened wider, becoming a crevice, then a ravine—one that traveled all the way around Tonsell.

Screams and plaintive calls rose up from his home-town. Trees and houses swayed. Dust plumed—an old yellow pickup truck, attempting to drive from the village, pitched into the widening abyss, blaring its horn, the sound diminishing pitifully as the truck vanished into the darkness. Old Duff could only watch helplessly as the ground supporting the village shuddered and slipped, down, down, not rapidly and not slowly, inexorably lowering the village into the earth, as if it was on a giant, unstable freight elevator of bedrock. Down went the rows of cottages and brick houses; down went the pub and the village hall; down went the gift shops and market; down went St. Leonard's church, its steeple the tallest structure in the village. Last to vanish was the cross atop the steeple—shadow drew over it like a dark blanket drawn up over a dead man's face. Down the village went—and out of sight.

Where the village had been was a great yawning pit, rimmed in dirt and rock, sending up dust and smoke. Birds, once part of the village life, now abandoned it, pigeons and sparrows and others, flapping up in their panic to escape, and they fled just in time, for in a moment even the pit was gone as sheets of bedrock shrugged and crept forward from both sides of the opening to close it up. The bedrock came to-gether like clasping hands, but crunching into one another, closing the pit off from above, sealing the lost village away deep underground . . .

There was only a great roughly round patch of raw earth and gray stone then, where the village of Ton-sell-by-the-Stream had been.

The ground ceased trembling; the bridge had cracked and crumbled at the edges but substantially held together. Old Duff still clung to its stone sides so hard his fingertips bled. He gazed at what was now a great stony scar in the ground where the village had been removed . . .

Smithson Manor still stood, on the far side of the scarred earth. It was a sprawling eighteenth-century structure of stone and timber, the double-peaked main hall three stories high. Its many windows seemed to gaze down in shocked silence at the convergence of roads once meeting at Tonsell-on-the-Stream, now ending abruptly in a raw field of stone and dirt.

All was silence, except for the unconcerned gurgling of the Hillcrease River, and the squawking of ravens wheeling overhead.

2

ANOTHER GHASTLY COCK-UP?
MUST BE CONSTANTINE DONE IT

"So Kit won't have you back?" Chas said, annoying Constantine by saying it with a certain *serves you right* in his voice.

Constantine signaled the barman for another drink. "G and T, mate," he said. Mention Kit, and he instantly needed a fresh drink. Why had he sought her out in Ireland? At the sight of her . . . it had all come rushing back. Maybe not his love for her, entirely—but a heart-wringing affection, and a profound nostalgia for the time they'd spent together.

I don't mind a man who comes with baggage. They all do. But your *bags . . .*

It still hurt, so that now he turned to Chas, who was working his way rapidly through a tall bitters; Frank William "Chas" Chandler, cabdriver and sometimes unwilling Constantine chauffeur. "And how about you and your Renee, then? The wife welcoming you back with open arms, is she, Chas?"

Chas clacked his glass down and turned a cold glare at Constantine. "Right. That's the end. How long's it been we've known each other? Since 1969, that's how long. Fucking hell! To think! Thirty-five years!"

"Nearer thirty-six," Constantine mumbled, addressing himself to his drink. And privately regretting his remark about Renee.

"Driving you around for free—no, not just for free! It cost me hundreds, thousands! Losing fares because of it—"

"I did you a favor, once," Constantine reminded him. "Cut you loose from something wicked . . ."

"If you want to call arranging for my mother's death *a favor*—"

"She was a monster! And all I did was do away with that demonic monkey of hers—but she was so tied into that foul-smelling primate . . . Anyway, you thanked me, you said you were free, free at last, sounded just like Martin Luther King—"

They both broke off, realizing the Cutter's barkeep was staring at them with narrowed eyes, having heard something about arranging deaths and mothers. "Not what it sounded like, mate," Constantine said. Though it was just what it sounded like. "Just an old wheeze."

The barman shrugged and went to serve a group of rowdy, rather muddy rugby players in uniform, fresh in from an afternoon's match.

"Thirty-six years of nightmares," Chas went on, his voice low, "is enough gratitude anyway, Constantine."

Constantine glanced at Chas, then noticed an empty beer pitcher and a shot glass beside his mug.

Constantine had arrived only a few minutes before. But Chas had been drinking for a while; Constantine guessed he was past the convivial glow of early drinking and on into the sullen bit. "Come on, Chas," he said, keeping his voice mild. "It's not as if you haven't had some rewards in all of it. You got to see things other people only wonder about. They wonder if there's life after death—you know it! The veil was lifted for you, mate, and—"

"Did you say *rewards*, John? Would that be when me family was kidnapped, when the serial killer was after us—or when I was fucking possessed by some bloody damned demon—"

"Redundant, that is," Constantine interrupted, mostly to himself. "'Damned demon.'"

"—and nearly beat my Renee to death!"

The barman was staring at them again. Constantine shrugged at him and hooked a thumb toward Chas, then tapped his head and winked. *Just humor him.*

The barman went back to refilling a bin with ice, but he kept watch on the two middle-aged men at the other end of the bar: Constantine with the deliberately spiky blond hair, the ratty trench coat, and the wry expression, and Chas, the slightly bigger one with the dark, accidentally spiky hair, the slight paunch, and the stolid, angular face—with a pug's nose, for it had been broken in its time—beginning to show the ravages of too much drink.

"So," Constantine said, "your Renee hasn't forgiven you yet?"

"Forgiven me? She won't let me near her! She's staying with Geraldine. Won't even come to the phone when I ring up! And that's your doing, mate."

"That demon taking a ride in you wasn't something I arranged—you were just the handiest horse in the stable, like. Not my fault, Chas. Christ the cry is always, 'Another ghastly cock-up? Must be Constantine done it!'"

"No it's never your fault, is it John? But it always turns to shite when JC comes round. I don't need the aggro. I almost got up and left when you sat down here and I believe I will now."

Chas got up and walked out.

Constantine shrugged and gave Chas the finger in the mirror behind the bar. But Chas never turned around to see it—so that Constantine found he was giving himself the finger. He sighed and ordered another gin. His hand trembled as he pushed his empty away and he knocked it over, spilling a little ice on the bar. He looked down to see that one pyramid-shaped piece of ice was moving across the wooden counter, sliding slowly but definitely moving. He supposed it was moving from the vibrations in the bar caused by the rugby players thumping the wood at the other end as they compared exaggerations. He watched gloomily as the piece of ice moved . . . and then more closely as it moved a little faster, up and down, right and left, leaving melt in a trail that spelled out letters in water:

You are summoned t

He smeared it away with his hand before it could finish.

"Not me," he muttered. Could be someone contacting him—could be his stressed-out imagination. He shook his head. Not going to answer that telephone.

That's when the rugby players decided to play "We Are the Champions" on the jukebox. And the barman turned it up loud.

"Fucking *Queen,*" Constantine muttered. "Sod it. That does it for me."

He got up, slapped some money down on the bar, and walked unsteadily out the door.

It had just stopped raining. The evening streets were slick, making iridescent petrol rainbows; the gutters gushing after the heavy downpour, a rain so recent that people passing still had their umbrellas up, though the only dripping now was from eaves and shop signs. He walked along, thinking he might go back to the card room, play some poker. He'd about run out his string in Garcy's, however—they knew he was cheating somehow. They didn't know he was using telepathy, but then they didn't care how he was doing it.

No, he couldn't face all those glum card players, the dealer's air of exhausted boredom. So he simply walked, without caring where.

In Constantine's coat pocket was a letter to Kit, in an envelope that was sealed, addressed, stamped, ready to mail. He'd been carrying it around all day. Kit had turned him away, in Ireland, three days earlier. He'd written the letter on the boat across St. George's channel, on stationery bought in the ferry gift shop. He took out the envelope and looked at it, remembering what he'd written.

Kit, I know you think I don't value you, but that's all wrong . . . You have a love for life that gives me hope. When I'm with you, life means something. There's nothing I wouldn't do for you—only before, I didn't know that. I know it now. It's like Lou says at the end of "Coney Island Baby": I'd give it all up for you. Just say the word and I'll turn my back on this other life. I'll get a square job, just so you'll have me. Can't remember the last one I had. Haven't got one yet, but just say the word. The Hidden World, all that, it's drawn me for a long time—I guess when you grow up a Scouse kid, your da in jail and your mum looking at you like she thinks "He'll end up there himself," and you feel you're at the ragtag end of things, you jump at the chance to get away from this world into another, into the Hidden World. You go from no one to someone at the casting of a spell. It becomes an addiction. But there's such a thing as recovery from addiction and you're what I need to bear the world, not magic or drink, and if you'll give me another chance . . .

⋆═◉═⋆

"What a load of bollocks," he muttered now. He'd meant it all—but him sounding like a poncey greeting card, it'd ring all false to her. And ringing false or not, she'd turn him down. What woman in her right mind wouldn't? He had no real career, he just got by a week at a time, sometimes a day at a time. He owned no property, and more important, yeah, he had baggage, tons of baggage. And she was right: in some of that luggage there were demons, literal demons, just waiting for the clasp to be opened.

It was hopeless. Like everything else. You lived, you died, you forgot who you were, and you were swept into the sea of consciousness. There was no point in any of it, except being part of some vast multilevel chess game played by entities who might well be as baffled about their own origins as human beings were about theirs. And Kit just wasn't going to take him back.

He crumpled up the letter and tossed it into the stream hissing down the gutter; watched it sweeping along, turning this way and that.

"I put a spell on you, 'cause you're mine"— sang an elderly, ragged black man, teetering along the sidewalk nearby.

Fury flared in Constantine and he strode over and grabbed the old man by the lapels. "Right—put a spell on you, is it? Who sent you? Which buggered spirit? Just tell 'em to belt up and clear off!"

"Ooh, you're right bladdered, you are!" the old man said. "Let me go, old cock, I was singing an old song, that's all, I didn't mean nothin' by it!"

Feeling foolish, Constantine let him go.

"S'all right, mate, I've had a jug or two meself tonight. Got any baccy?"

Constantine lit a Silk Cut for each of them, and the old man wandered on, taking up his song, *"I put a spell on you, cauuuuuuuuse—"*

"Synchronicity," Constantine muttered. He drew deep on his Silk Cut, looking at his crumpled letter stuck on a beer can in the gutter stream, like a ship becalmed. He kicked at the beer can to set the letter free, and watched it swirl away down the roadside. He found himself following it, unsure why he didn't want to completely let go of it. Maybe once it was gone, that really was the end. He'd give up on himself completely then, somehow. Nothing else to do anyway.

So he followed the drifting letter, crumpled roughly into the shape of a boat, as it sailed around the corner, expecting it to slide into the rainwater drainage grate. But a sudden gushing in the stream pushed the crumpled letter spinning past the grate and on down the street. The street sloped down a slight hill here, enough so that the letter, carried almost urgently in the strong stream from the heavy rainfall, was thrust up the slight bellying of the cross street and across, down the next street. He had to stride more quickly to keep up, and the letter was swept around another corner up ahead. He hurried to the corner, turned, and saw the crumpled letter swirling up to a sewer grate in front of a vacant lot. He almost cried out *Stop!* when the letter went into the sewer grate at the lot. But down it went, gone for good.

He walked up to the sewer grate, looking at its shadowy mouth. It gurgled, the sound echoing, tumbling, hissing, seeming to form recognizable syllables: *Consssstannnntine* . . .

He shook his head, looked up at the vacant lot. It was as if the drifting letter had been bringing him here. A building had been knocked down and mostly carted away here at some point, but someone had run out of funds and the new one hadn't been erected yet. The lot was overgrown with weeds, and a single, small, leafless tree still stood toward the back. Under the tree was the crumbled edge of a concrete wall, all that remained of the structure that had once stood here. Constantine shrugged, flicked his cigarette butt after the letter, walked into the lot, the weeds making his pants wet from the knees down, and crossed to the concrete wall, kicking bottles and disintegrating pieces of cardboard out of his way as he went. Seemed like an apt place for him to fetch up, somehow. The lot was the remains, after all, of a broken-down ambition, overgrown and decaying.

Constantine sat on the broken wall, as if it were a bench, and took out his pack of Silk Cuts—but there were only three left. He put the fags away and wondered what to do with his life. He felt the depression like a thick hempen rope around his neck, heavy and tight. He could almost feel the bristles. He could barely breathe. What was the bloody point of anything, when you had to face it alone? He'd kept company with the French sorceress Tchalai for a while last summer. But with Kit he was able to let go, feel himself—feel like an ordinary man. With Tchalai, the Hidden World was never far away. Seeing he wasn't going to get serious, Tchalai had shrugged and said she had no interest at her time in life in fixing her identity around a man anyway. She announced she would sell her building in Paris and go to a retreat in Tibet. *My soul needs to grow, John . . .*

"Right," he muttered now. "It'd be stunted, hanging about with me."

He looked up at the sky, hoping to see a few stars, or the moon. But there was nothing but the cloud

cover, reflecting the dull glow of the streetlights, like
the ceiling of a cavern. The sight gave him a shiver of
premonition . . .

He shook himself and lyrics came into his mind
from a song he'd performed with his punk band Mucous Membrane, what was it, twenty-five years ago,
or more? He'd written it himself but not thought of it
in decades.

> No I
> don't know where it is I'm going
> and I
> don't really know what to think
> But I
> will wake up calling for another drink
> And no
> no bastard is going to take the truth from me
> and no
> no bastard is going to force me to believe
> some lie
> some lie that'll make me buckle under
> some lie
> like a fly crawling up his sleeve . . .
>   No lies! Won't believe your lies
>   No lies! Won't believe your lies
>   Going to come up with better, much better—
>   lies, lies, lies . . . of my own!

Couldn't remember the bit after that. Some bollocks about not wearing ties, maybe, mostly because
it rhymed with *lies*. But he was wearing a dark green
tie now, though it was on crooked and needed laun-

dering, and he was glad to have it. His only silk tie—
Kit had given it to him. Kelly green . . .

"Oh bloody hell."

He almost wept then. *Come on, Constantine, stop
your whingeing, get your game on, get it together.*

Or get a drink.

"That's always the solution," he muttered, in an
outburst of self-contempt. Beyond the overgrown vacant lot, a silver-blue mist was rising from the wet
streets, whirling itself into a ghostly shape that was
like a man in a robe, an old man with a beard . . . an
electric-blue robe . . .

The Blue Sheikh.

What would he think of me now? Constantine wondered. He'd be bloody disappointed. Treated me like
a son, he did. He'd want me to meditate now, lift myself up above all this "identification" with the dark
side of things.

Worth a try.

So in memory of his erstwhile mentor—dead now
a year—Constantine sat up straight on the stone
wall, closed his eyes, and brought himself into the
meditative state taught him by the Blue Sheikh. Bring
the mind back to silence in the present moment, to
the uncarved block, to pure sensation, the pure
awareness of now. Find the field that contained consciousness, the current from the universe that sustained it.

A longing to be free of his body came over him. To
soar free again, astrally projecting above it all . . .

He detached his consciousness from his body
with the inner movement he'd learned—long ago,

he'd learned it, but the Blue Sheikh had helped him
improve it—and he was suddenly drifting above his
body, a yard, two yards, over the vacant lot, looking
down at himself sitting there; his body anyway, just
sitting there, breathing but unoccupied, hands on
knees.

Looking at the nicotine stains on his body's fingers; at the corner of his lip where he habitually
shoved the cigarette. The creases in his face more
numerous than the creases in his battered old coat.
The gray hairs showing at his temples; the stubble,
forgot to shave this morning. A few hairs growing out
of his nostrils, his ears. A single age spot on the back
of his right hand. Dirt under his fingernails. A
chewed-up thumbnail. The youthful hair style, like a
man trying to pretend he's still in his twenties. Pa-
thetic. The habitually glum set of his features . . .

*Christ, no wonder Kit wants nothing to do with you.
Who'd want to look at that, day in and out?*

But he knew it wasn't his worn, shabby appear-
ance that bothered her. More like it was his worn,
shabby soul.

It seemed to him that his body, sitting there on the
bench, was a monument to lost possibilities.

The depression seemed to congeal in him then, to
thicken and grow heavier and denser, so that he was
weighted down, his gloom dragging him back down
toward the body, so that he fell back into that sad,
aging man seated with his eyes shut on the broken
wall in the ugly little vacant lot . . .

And with a thump he was back in his body, his
eyes snapping open.

"Oh fuck me," he murmured.

"You'd be the one," said the hazy figure, stumping toward him through the weeds.

Constantine blinked, clearing his eyes. "What?" It was another old tramp, slogging his way. Wanting a cigarette, the price of a drink. "Bugger off."

He was an old white-haired, white-bearded man with a red nose crisscrossed by broken veins, tiny foggy blue eyes, wearing a tattered black sailor's jacket from the Royal Navy. "My name's Duff," the old geezer said. "I've come for you."

"Right. So you're like the Grim Reaper except you're the Grim Tramper, eh? Come to take me to the land of the terminally pissed?"

"Close—come to take you to Salisbury Plain, I have. To Tonsell-by-the-Stream—or where Tonsell used to be. The military boys have kept it out of the papers, but you might've heard the rumors."

"Right you are, rumors that a lot of bloody hippies have been overrunning Stonehenge again, down that way. Got a drink on you?"

The old man stared at him, shrugged, reluctantly fished a pint out of his coat and passed it over. Constantine took a long pull and almost gagged. "Crikey, what's that, lighter fluid?"

"It's whiskey, that is. My second cousin Basil makes it. We'd better be off, got a long way to go."

"Thanks for the drink, mate. Take it back and kill the weeds in your lawn with it, if you've got a lawn. I'm off to the pub for a real drink."

"We haven't got time—I've cast the knucklebones, with the claws of a hawk, and seen it all from high up, and that's how I seen you. Saw you in my mind. Go to London, said the bones, follow the stream there, once you're out the underground, the water in the gutter will take you to 'im, he'll be alone on a stone wall—and there you was. I don't know who you are, but you're the one to help—the rain told me so, too."

Constantine was beginning to suspect there was more to this old man than rum or lunacy, but he wasn't having any of it. He wasn't going to listen to messages written by ice on the bar or sent along through old rummies in vacant lots—because he knew the messages came from the Hidden World and he wanted no more messages from anywhere that didn't have a postal code. Not in this lifetime.

"Here's a fiver," Constantine said, tucking the bill in the old man's coat pocket. "Get yourself a drink—somewhere I won't be drinking. I'm off."

Constantine lurched up from the wall—still a bit unsteady from the whiskey and having been unbodied—and staggered across the vacant lot to the street. He was distantly aware the old man was following him, so he headed uphill, where he figured an old geezer would have a harder time following, and soon outdistanced him. He couldn't stomach the Cutter again, so he popped into a liquor shop and bought two pints of Bushmills. If he got good and drunk it'd numb him to the psychic impulses from the Hidden World. It was like taking the phone off the hook. He managed to get one of the pints down not twenty steps from the shop he'd bought them in, and was just getting a good start on the other—the empty was still in his right hand—when the bobby came rolling along.

"Here, what's all this?" the round-faced, mustachioed bobby demanded, tilting his helmet back with his nightstick, just as Constantine chucked his empty pint bottle after a cabbie who'd ignored his hail. The bottle smashed on the street.

"The bashtard shaw me standing there and fookin' ignored me!" Constantine said, slurring the words and sending a rude gesture after the receding black cab.

"Look here, turn that other pint over, mate," said the copper, putting his hand out, "you've had quite enough. He didn't pick you up because you're scarcely standing, you're swaying . . . Now let's have it."

"Oh you want it, do you?" Constantine asked, slapping the bobby on the shoulder with a false bonhomie. Then Constantine grabbed the cop's collar, jerked him close, his other hand shoving the open pint bottle, tipped over, into the top of the bobby's trousers. Irish whiskey gurgled onto the bobby's private parts.

Constantine was just wondering what that sensation was like when he felt another sharp sensation—the bobby's nightstick cracking him on the side of the head.

⊷⇒◉⇐⊷

Constantine woke in the company of two old friends, pain and disorientation. He could see a concrete corridor slipping away beyond his upturned feet. After a moment, a pressure at the back of his neck

suggested that he was being dragged by the collar—
and he could see he was sliding along past a row of
holding cells. Moments later he was dumped unceremoniously in a drunk tank. He rolled on his side,
found himself staring into a puddle of half-digested
meat pie, and, fortunately, lost consciousness again
before he could add the contents of his own stomach
to it . . .

When next he woke, he made the mistake of sitting up. This sudden movement drove a broken ice
pick from one temple to emerge from the other—
that's what it felt like, anyway. He felt his head with
his shaking hands to confirm that there was no ice
pick, only a lump on the left side of his head. "Oh . . .
fuck me . . ." he muttered.

He got to his feet, found the cell's only sink,
washed his face, drank a little water—and threw it all
up along with everything else in his stomach. Then
he made himself drink a little more.

⋄≕⊙≕⋄

"They're going to charge you with assault," Chas said.
"That filth wanted to ask for a 'on Her Majesty's pleasure' for you . . . Christ, why I ever came, let alone
bailed you out . . ." He had just picked Constantine up
and was driving him away from the police station.
"You smell like a pig wallow, by the by."

"Why you ever bailed me out . . ." Constantine
growled, pausing to swallow four aspirin with tea
from the Styrofoam cuppa the desk sergeant had
given him, and put on his cracked sunglasses against

the morning light, ". . . why you bailed me out is, I reminded you of the time you came to me howling they were after you because you drove a car for a loan shark's hitman—"

"Right, fine."

"—and got yourself up to your neck in dead bodies—"

"All right, you already—"

"And who came to your rescue, why the bloke you sent to the devil last night—"

"Right, right, you already guilted me on that. And you're right, I'd not have come but for that. I owed you one. But then, John, does that make up for getting me possessed and what happened to my Renee?"

"I'm also the one who got you unpossessed," Constantine reminded him. "Christ on a bike, it's that old geezer again!"

The old man—Duff, he'd said his name was—rushed out in front of Chas's cab, waving his arms, hair wild, mouth agape to show a snaggle of stubby teeth.

Chas hit the brake with an inch to spare, so that the old man had his hands on the bonnet of the car, either side of the hood ornament. "You! You're the one!" the old man bellowed.

"He was outside the hoosegow," Chas said, "marching up and down and mumbling. Who the fuck is he?"

Constantine grimaced. "I'm not sure . . . Wants me to go to . . . I think it was Cornwall . . . said the Salisbury Plain . . ."

Old Duff had come around to Constantine's side of

the cab, was banging on the window. "We've got to go! There's no time! They may already be dead down there!"

"If he's going to take you out of town," Chas said musingly, "maybe you should go. They're going to charge you and put you in the cooler for a month, at least. The cop says you attacked him. *More* than a month, probably. You were on probation, you remember, after you threw that garbage can through the window of the sweet shop . . ."

Constantine sighed. "You reckon Cornwall is far enough?"

⋯⊙⟜⋯

"Can't believe I let you talk me into this," Chas said, rolling down his window as they came to the crossroads. "Need some fresh air in here with you two fragrant beauties along."

"Three hundred sixty quid talked you into it," Constantine reminded him. "Most of me dosh." Chas was done giving Constantine free rides.

Chas shrugged. "Truth is . . . I wanted to get out of the city myself. Living alone in that flat. Plumbing don't rightly work. Water dripping, dripping. Pipes making daft noises. Don't know how my Renee is. Just had to see something else . . ."

"I need me a drink," said the old man in the back.

Constantine glanced back at him. The old man's hands were shaking, clutched against his round belly, and his tongue was snaking in and out of his mouth. He was getting the DTs, right enough. "Just saw a sign said Tonsell-on-the-Stream, two miles. Ought to be a pub there," said Constantine.

"'Tisn't anymore," said Old Duff. "That's my village, the one I told you about."

"Oh right. Sunk into the earth, you said. Half buried or something."

"No—it's all gone. You'll see."

Constantine grunted noncommittally. On the way here Duff had told them about the boy pulled into the Deep Barrow, and MacCrawley—a name that had gotten Constantine's attention, making him think he would be wise to take a pass on this whole venture— and the vanishing of the village. The latter was hard to believe. But then Constantine had seen even stranger things come about.

Hard to believe, is it, mate? the old man had told him. *Not if you know this region—not if you live round Tonsell-by-the-Stream. Haunted, and always has been. Crowded, it is, with dark spirits, so that they run off most of the good-uns. Why, men have been vanishing hereabouts for a good hundred years and more. Some into the barrow—anyhow they was always near there when they went missing. Many vanished, none accounted for. My old master, Scofield, he said he had found a way to the palace hidden under the barrow, where a great treasure was to be found, and he never come out . . .*

Scofield. Constantine had a grimoire the man had translated from Latin. A magician of some power; long missing, presumed dead.

Chas waited for a lorry to pass, then drove through the intersection just as the clouds unloaded dump trucks of rain. It came slapping hard down on the windshield, and Chas rolled up his side window and turned on the wipers. "That's the heaviest piss-down I ever saw," he marveled, slowing the cab. "Wipers can barely keep up . . . Tropical-like, it is."

"I got to get me a drink," said Old Duff.

Chas sighed. "We'll stop for a drink at the inn there. Don't expect they'll let the old man in—but you, John, can hit their loo and clean yourself up some. Nice sponge bath—or wet-paper-towel bath, any gate. I'll bring him out a drink." The "inn and public house" sign was barely visible through the silvery curtains of rain.

⊷≡◉≡⊷

Cleaning up in the inn's WC, grateful for the soothing cool of the water on his still-throbbing goose egg, Constantine thought: *Now's the time to ditch the crazy old bastard with his knucklebones and hawk's claws. He's near his home, he'll be all right.*

He'd come this far with the old geezer mostly out of a kind of inertia—and, like Chas, from wanting to get away from London. Or was that the reason?

He looked at himself skeptically in the mirror of the WC. "You know better, you bastard," he told himself. An addict doesn't know he's relapsing into his addiction till well along in the process. *You swore off magic, and you're out here looking for it again, like a bugle-addict swearing off cocaine and then accidentally-a-purpose wandering into just the neighborhood where it's sold.*

He sighed and shook his head. He was here now. May as well look at Tonsell.

Was that what the cokehead said to himself? *Since I'm here, may as well see how me old bruv the dealer is doing . . .*

There were other reasons to leave this alone, apart from fear of feeding the addiction. His enemies were at hand. He had gone out of his way to hide himself from them—several conjurations it had needed, one requiring two pints of blood from him and a shot glass of semen. And *then*—

He winced at the memory.

But it had worked. He'd hidden himself in a magical fog—and it might be that MacCrawley had found another way to locate him.

Constantine returned to the car, ducking his head against the rain—it had slackened but still fell steadily—and they drove on, the old man easing himself with the six cans of ale Chas had bought in the inn. The windshield wipers chuffed with pendulum regularity, and the rain drenched the car, ran in sheets over the road, so that the cab tended to skate a bit at sharp curves. The air in the car grew muggy; the seconds and minutes seemed to pile up with a weighty tedium, and Constantine made up his mind that he was going to ask Chas to turn around.

But then they swung round a curve and had to slam on the brakes.

There was a roadblock ahead, military men and cops in slickers holding up STOP signs and making fierce gestures. Beyond them the road curved through a stand of trees. "The village was beyond those trees—but it ain't there now," the old man said. "That's why we're being stopped."

Chas waved to the cops and turned around, the cab skidding a bit and heading back down the road the way they'd come.

"I know a way through," said Old Duff. "There's a path through the fields . . ."

"What, the way it's pissing down out here?" Chas snorted. "Not bloody likely. You'll be up to your arse in mud!"

"He's right, Duff," Constantine said. "Bucketing down mad out here, it is. We're going to let you out at that inn and go our way—maybe take in the seaside, down to Brighton, eh Chas? Weather couldn't be any worse there."

That's when they hit the flooded-out section of road—and spun out, to stop immovably in the mud on the road's shoulder.

"Bugger me blue!" Chas swore.

They got out of the car, their shoes squelching in the mud beside the pool of water, heads ducked against the continuing rain. The water was from a blocked culvert that ran under the road here; a stream ran from the culvert, on the other side, where some of the water was still getting through, and into a deep ditch that angled into a ravine edging a wood . . .

"We can try to move it," Constantine said.

They had a go, two or three times, their fingers slipping off the rain-slippery metal of the boot, their feet only jamming farther into the mud. Finally they gave up, angrily kicking mud off their feet.

"Won't budge," said Old Duff. "Means you have to come with me, it does. Across the fields!"

"Not a bloody chance!" Constantine growled. He sloshed into the pool of water, washing mud off as he waded across it up the slope, back the way they'd been going. Sticking out his thumb to hitchhike in case anyone should come by . . .

The pool of water on the road rose up, becoming a wall of water wobbling gelatinously—and it hung over Constantine for one long threatening moment as he turned to stare. He refused to be impressed or intimidated by whatever magical entity was trying to contact him and managed to say, "Didn't I see that in a Charlton Heston movie? You can do better than—" before the wall of water crashed down on him, knocking him off his feet, rolling him like a log in surf off the road and down into the ditch. He fell shouting face-first into the water rushing from the culvert, and was tumbled arse over elbow a few times; then he caught a projecting tree root and pulled himself up out of the water, sputtering, coughing. "Chas!"

"Right here mate!" Chas shouted in disgust. "It got me too—naturally!"

Constantine turned his head to see Chas clinging to a root beside him. "Where's the old duffer?"

"I don't fucking know and I don't fucking care. That was some of your supernatural bullshit, John— which arsehole demon's hacked off with you this time?"

"Don't rightly know." Though Constantine was beginning to suspect who was behind this. He remembered the talkative ice in the bar, the sewer grate gurgling his name. This tropical-style heavy rain . . .

He pulled himself up onto the bank of the ditch and turned to help Chas up. They were a surprising distance from the road—they could just make out the headlights of Chas's stuck cab through the trees, up above them. The rain had eased up some but it was still a thoroughly wet world.

"Road's back that way," Chas said.

"No use, Bruv—we try to go any direction this thing doesn't want us to go, it'll slap us down. You can't fight it, mate, when it's got a whole element to throw against you. You know what old Lao Tzu said: 'Nothing in the world is as soft and yielding as water, yet nothing can better overcome the hard and strong—'"

"Fuck your Low Zoo! Just lead me wherever we're going so we can get this over with and I can get to a dry hotel somewhere!"

"Right—well, it wants us to follow the stream, I reckon. Let's go."

It wasn't a cold night. It was one of those rainstorms that seemed swept from warmer climes—it may indeed have been tropical—and if it weren't for the way his wet trousers were chafing his goolies, Constantine would have found it all strangely refreshing. Walking through the wood, in the thinning rain, the light from the moon breaking through the cloud cover, gleaming on the wet tree trunks, turning their drips opalescent; the exhalation of rising mists, smelling of soil and living things . . .

"Here, John—are we going the right way? Look!"

Chas pointed at the water. "It's changed directions on us. It was flowing the other way before."

Constantine saw fallen leaves traveling along the stream, back toward the road. "You're right—whatever lifted us up and dropped us down here was flowing against the natural current. Which confirms . . ."

"What?"

"Well, nothing's well and truly confirmed yet."

"I'm knackered and hungry. Worried about me cab. Maybe I'll leave you to it . . . Chances are it's you this thing wants."

Constantine nodded, putting on an expression of indifference, though he wanted Chas along. A funny old world, he sometimes called it, but it felt like a lonely old world lately. He made a show of patting his coat, wondering if his cigarettes were dry. He had gotten three packs, and they were still sealed up. He opened a pack and lit a Silk Cut with a Zippo lighter, sheltering it against the drizzle with his hand. "Off you go, Chas," he said, the words accompanied by a stream of exhaled smoke. "Cheers."

Chas stuck his hands in his pockets, started off toward the road—and the stream surged up again, water spouting, hissing warningly . . .

"Sorry—it wants you to go with me!"

"Well it can fuck off! I can be up this bank and into the field before . . ." He let the bravado trail off as the water fell back, as if it were discouraged. "There, you see—you're not the only one with a little mystical authority . . . ummm . . . John? What's that?"

Constantine was already peering at the strange, rolling shapes in the creek, trying to make out what they were. Three of them. They seemed cylindrical, in a shabby way, spinning down the creek to them. "Logs or . . ."

Then the shape flopped an arm into view. Another drifted nearer, and he saw it was a human body. A dead man.

The reek of death rose from the creek, and so did the dead. The three bodies twitched and flapped and thrashed in the water—and then sat up. All three turned their rotting heads toward Chas and Constantine at once. Two men and a woman. The men were badly disintegrated, as much bone and ragtags of slimy-dripping clothing as flesh. One of them had his eyes, but they had gone milky; the lower half of his face was chewed away.

The woman was naked from the waist up. One of her breasts had been nibbled into a mere socket of flesh. Her face, though bloated and purple, was mostly there, apart from the eyes. Patches of blond hair remained on her scalp.

"John . . ." Chas seemed frozen on the spot, gaping, his hands stuck up under his armpits in some irrational defensive posture. "Did you . . . conjure them things?"

"I bloody well did not! Look like drowning victims, I reckon." The drowned would naturally be subject to the will of the water elemental. The girl, it seemed to Constantine, was too well preserved—despite the earthworks wriggling from her ears—and he suspected some enchantment had brought bits of her back together. This was no mere haunting. It didn't seem likely they'd all drowned in this creek, either.

They'd been brought from some far place. Squinting, he perceived the faint violet glow of a controlling enchantment about them.

The three drowning victims stood up, and, as if choreographed, took a splashing step toward Constantine and Chas—who, as if choreographed, each took a stumbling step back.

"John—do some . . . some fucking exorcism thing or something!"

Constantine winced. He hated exorcisms—people had tried to cast out nonexistent demons from him, in the past. "I've gone out of my way to not learn those rites . . . I'll see if I can think of . . . of some kind of banishment spell or . . . fucking hell, I don't know . . ."

The woman, standing in front of the other two drowned corpses, reached out a shriveled hand toward Chas. She spoke—the voice, a teenage girl's voice filtered through a dying frog, came from the water as much as from her. *"Frankie . . . Frankie Chandler . . ."*

"Oh my God," Chas blurted. "Cynthia!"

He staggered back, fell against the bank, stared up at her in shock.

"You . . . left me . . . the abortion . . . nothing but . . . the Thames for me . . ."

Constantine was long past surprise at visitations from the dead. But this one had him curious. "Chas—who, uh—?"

Chas covered his mouth with a shaking hand, staring at the dead woman. "She . . . before I met you . . . got her knocked up and . . . she was Catholic and I practically strong-armed her into an abortion and then I . . ."

"You left me."

"My mother made me, Cynthia!" Chas blurted. "You don't know what she was like! She wasn't a natural human being! She said she'd kill you if I didn't break off with you! Oh God . . ." He put his face in his hands and moaned.

The shorter of the drowned men spoke, then—he had bits of skin stuck to his skull, like tissue stuck on shaving wounds, and a few of his teeth remained. He seemed to have an eel for a tongue. *"Constantine . . . this one . . . Chandler . . . must go with you . . . He must go with you . . . or he goes—with us!"*

And the drowning victims took a shambling, threatening step forward, extending their bony, oozing claws . . .

"Jesus wept!" Chas spat, turning to run—and tripping over a tree root. "Shite!"

"Chas, there are lots of drowning victims," Constantine pointed out, helping him up. "The spirit behind this can call them from all over. You can't go your whole life avoiding rivers. They might come out of the fucking bathtub drain, mate."

Chas turned and grimaced at them, then looked reluctantly at the path along the creek into the increasingly dismal-looking woods. "Right. I'm going with Constantine! Tell . . . tell whoever it is I'm going with him!"

"No!" Cynthia hissed. *"Chas—resist her! Don't go with Const . . . an . . . tine! Come . . . with . . . me . . . instead!"*

"I . . . what?" Chas gulped. His voice shook as he

went on, tears in his eyes. "Cynthia, darling, my sweet, I am truly sorry about what happened to you, I'm dead sorry—oh shite I shouldn't put it that way—I'm . . . *very* sorry. But I can't go with you!"

"Someday . . . you . . . will!"

Then she lifted her head and gave out a violent shout of disappointment—so violent that she fell apart with the reverberation of it, her head falling down into her rib cage, which fell into her hips, which tumbled between her legs, which crumbled into the water. The drowned men turned away and fell sighing into the creek. They sank into the ooze and vanished.

Chas sat down then, just sat there for a full minute, head in his hands, hyperventilating. When he'd quieted, Constantine gave him a cigarette. They smoked in silence for a couple of minutes more. "I can see why you didn't tell me about her," Constantine said, wishing he could think of something more helpful to say.

"That one was me mum's doing," he sobbed, ". . . and my own cowardice! I thought I'd put it behind me . . . then it comes up out of the bloody slime . . ." He turned a glare at Constantine. "Would be behind me too, was I not with Mr. John Fucking Constantine, the magnet for all things hellish!"

Constantine stared gloomily at the cherry of his cigarette. "That's me, innit? Sorry, mate."

Chas shook his head and wiped his eyes. "Fuck it. Come on . . ."

He stood up and looked at the stream. Which simply flowed on as before—and they went on themselves, trudging along the creek, but against the direction of its flow.

Another mile and the ground began to rise, as the woods grew denser around them, until they were stumbling through a thicket. "Bloody thorns!" Chas muttered. "And I thought heading out of town with you would be better than my comfortable little room! I was daft!"

At last they came to a hillside covered in vines and boulders. The stream flowed from a crack in the hillside shaped like an inverted V.

"Now what?" Chas demanded.

As if in reply, the hillside began to groan.

"Strewth!" Constantine muttered, as the crevice in the hill groaningly opened wider, wider . . . invitingly wider. An ethereal blue light shone from the crevice now; it gave off a scent of dissolving minerals, of fungi and rot.

"Oh no, not me!" Chas declared, laughing bitterly. "I'm not going in there!"

The water began to surge upward, pillaring; the hill groaned and growled warningly.

"Oh do come on, Chas!" Constantine said. "We're already wet. In for a penny, in for a pound."

"In for a pound of flesh you mean!"

"No doubt—but we're stuck." He didn't want to go into the cave, either—mostly because it intrigued him so. He wanted to struggle with that addiction, turn his back on it. Find Kit and tell her: *I was on the edge of plunging in again—and I turned back. I left it alone. I can give it up, Kit* . . .

But the water began to churn restlessly. He knew

what that meant. "We've got to go in," he said at last. "It's that or drown—it'll come after us."

"But—if I go in the water . . . she was in there. She'll pull me under . . ."

It took Constantine a moment to realize that Chas meant Cynthia. "She's gone, mate," he said gently. "I'd feel her if she was about . . . she's moved on. At least for now . . ."

"I don't want to go in there, John. But if it's that or . . ." He shuddered.

"Fuck it—come on!" Constantine climbed down into the stream, which flowed well above his knees, tugging his trench coat back with it.

He slogged onward into the crevice, only having to duck his head a little. Cursing under his breath, Chas came sloshing along behind him into the curiously well-lit darkness.

3

BLOOD WILL OUT . . . AND OUT AND OUT, ALL OVER THE FLOOR

Lord Smithson shook his head with an air of sad disappointment. "This disrespect, MacCrawley, makes me wonder at your sincerity. You do not use my title when you speak to me—that is bad enough—but to put me off in this blackguardly way—I can only say: *Tsk!*"

MacCrawley raised his bristling eyebrows even more, and his grim visage showed a glimmer of amusement. "'Blackguardly,' Smithson? I was just thinking that your attitude was very eighteenth century—expecting me to spout the M'Lords and so on—and then you use that quaint adjective 'blackguardedly'! But that's not enough—you set about *tsk*ing me! What a prat you are!" He chuckled, moving a little closer to the fire burning in the grate of the high-ceilinged, drafty, dusty library of Smithson Manor. The room smelled of musty books and old wood. Rain hissed down the chimney now and then, and pattered against the tall peaked windows.

A liverish, tweedily-dressed jowly man of early middle age with hooded eyes and a weak chin, Smithson repeated his melancholy head-shake, clasping his hands behind him. "And a lodge brother too! *Tsk!* Consider the oath you took as a member of the Servants of Transfiguration, MacCrawley! You are not to betray a fellow in the SOT! You promised me immortality if I were to deliver the village to you! Do I need to remind you of—"

"You are not going to speak to me of penalties, are you?" MacCrawley interrupted, his voice low and freighted with warning. "You are a sixth-degree initiate. I am a thirty-third-degree initiate. If I choose, I can have your head taken from your body and stuck on the topmost spire of the nearest cathedral. None of the Servants of Transfiguration will question me, nor ask my reasons."

Smithson stared at him aghast. "You—a thirty-third! Rubbish. I have no proof of any such hierophantic heights!"

"Rubbish, is it? I would offer you proof, but you are not initiated enough to recognize it," said MacCrawley dryly. "You may ask SOT Command if you like. As for promises, you shall have your immortality. I merely told you that I will provide it in my own good time."

"But that might be years, decades! I could die before then!"

"No. It will be sooner. In fact, within days. When I have time to take you to the Palace of Phospor, in the realm of the Sunless."

"Take me to the—" Smithson's eyes bulged and his

mouth dropped open and stayed open. "You don't mean I have to go *down there!*"

"Oh I do," said MacCrawley, smiling as he went to the minibar in the corner near the fireplace; a recent addition, the minibar looked out of place in the room filled with centuries-old furniture and yellowing paintings. He hummed Stravinsky's *Rite of Spring* to himself as he poured a large snifter of Smithson's best brandy. He didn't offer Smithson any.

It struck Smithson that MacCrawley had a deucedly proprietary demeanor, as if this were now his manor and not Lord Smithson's.

"See here, MacCrawley—"

"I was wondering when you were going to say 'see here.'"

"—you may be at a higher level of initiation in the lodge, but blood will out, MacCrawley—"

"Yes," MacCrawley murmured, under his breath, "it will out and out, all over the floor."

"—and the whole point of my achieving immortality is to protect that sacred bloodline. It is for Albion's sake!" Smithson insisted.

MacCrawley drew deeply on the snifter, sighed in appreciation, and said, "For England, was it? So you relegated hundreds of Englishmen and women to the realm of the Sunless for England? Self-deception is so very amusing."

"The only deception here is yours, sir!" Smithson said sharply, striding to the window, and keeping his hands clasped behind him, as did the figure of his ancestor in a painting on the wall. He stood at the window, dramatically silhouetted against the afternoon light, gazing out through the old, distorted glass at the blurred garden, blurred even more than usual by rain. "You were all hail-fellow-well-met when you first came here, MacCrawley! Butter wouldn't melt in your mouth! 'My intention,' you said, 'is to give you exactly what you need and deserve, your Lordship!' Those were your words! And now your tone is quite different. Disquietingly different. And there are military men tramping through my garden, yes, and banging on the door, asking me questions. 'We suspect terrorists have undermined the village somehow, your Lordship—may we inquire as to your political sympathies? Have you ever been personally conversant with the IRA?' Imagine! Me, conniving with the Irish! What a revolting thought!"

"Ach, and how do ye feel about the Scotch, then?" MacCrawley asked, allowing his accent to emerge.

"Why they're not much more—that is, I respect them, of course! But you said you'd handle the inquiries! All I had to do was give you access to the churchyard, and the village morgue, so that you could get your nasty little bits of human flesh from the locals, provide you with a few other items—you said nothing about having to deal with government investigations!"

"They're as baffled as can be, 'your Lordship,'" said MacCrawley. "We have nothing to fear from them. We pulled up the stakes before they arrived, and that evidence is ashes in your furnace. No witness remains who can connect us to the event. Except your man, Pinch, knows—and perhaps—"

"—he is fiercely loyal to me!" Smithson said, turning furiously to MacCrawley. "He knows very well

what I am about! Britannia is sickly, it is dying because it is run by politicians!" He began pacing up
and down, hands still clasped behind him. His butler
and factotum, Pinch, an old man in grossly outdated
livery, with white hair, a long nose, and a cynical
gleam in his eye, appeared at the door and waited till
his Lordship's diatribe ran itself down. "The time
must come—and will come!—when royalty returns
to power! I am in line to the throne—far down the
line, yes, but should I live long enough, that succes-
sion will eventually come about! My personal as-
trologer has seen the inevitability of it! When the
great international economic depression comes, all
present governments will fall, and only those with
enough gold and diamonds will maintain their for-
tunes intact! We of noble lineage have not failed to
set aside some portion of our wealth as imperishable
treasure! That money will buy power, sir! And those
with the ancient bloodlines will emerge as leaders
once more! The people will recognize their natural
superiority—and in relief, *they will greet their King!*"

Pinch cleared his throat.

"Ah! Pinch!" Smithson said. "There you are! Tell
MacCrawley that you understand the importance of
what I've done!"

"Certainly, M'Lord. One assumes it had to be
done." His voice was carefully modulated, his expression completely neutral.

"The villagers, if there had been time to explain,
would have willingly sacrificed themselves, I'm sure!"

Pinch fixed his gaze on a spot in the Turkish car-
pet. "I'm sure of it, Your Grace."

"Come, Pinch!" MacCrawley said, putting the empty snifter down on the minibar. "You know damn well government only keeps the aristocracy around for the tourists these days! Most particularly the royals."

"It is not my place to say, sir," said Pinch. "But I have served his Grace for thirty years, and have learned to accept his wisdom in all things."

"Well said, Pinch!" said Smithson. "There you are, MacCrawley! Ah—was there something, Pinch?"

"The military gentleman is here again, sir."

Smithson groaned. "Not again. Well, I shall have to speak to him. Tell him I'll be there in a moment."

"Very good, sir." Pinch buttled out.

MacCrawley hooted softly to himself. "What an anachronism!"

Smithson looked at him with narrowed eyes. "Mr. MacCrawley. If you continue to—"

"No sir!" MacCrawley snapped, taking two strides to loom over Smithson, who shrank back from MacCrawley's glare. "I will not continue! I will say just this: when you took *your* oath to the Sons of Transfiguration, Smithson, you vowed to put the lodge above all personal concerns, and to accept its hierophants as the ultimate rank in all the world. You vowed to submit to their will, sir! Your hunger for some shortcut, some means to push yourself to the forefront of power, led you to seek shortcuts in magic—only to discover that you were consigning yourself to our control! You have made your bed, sir!"

"Now . . . now . . ." Smithson stammered, backing up. "I . . . I submit to a certain amount of . . . of ritual and, ah, precedent but—to say that your lodge—"

"*Our* lodge, Smithson!"

"—that the . . . that our lodge *controls* me . . ."

"Oh but it does! As you will discover, Smithson, if you try to breach your oath! As for your great con-voluted plans for the empire . . ." He snorted. "You've convinced yourself a worldwide economic collapse is coming? I have news for you—a collapse would not be convenient for our grandmaster! After our failure to create a new world, we decided to throw in with the powers that be. That is, the pow-ers of *this* world. Eventually we will make them sub-mit fully to our will. In the meantime, we have invested heavily in munitions and chemicals—and a collapsed economy will simply not be permitted. We would lose money. So you can abandon that little fantasy now. And as no worldwide depression is coming and as you have several millions in liquidity in your London account, you will not need the gold and diamonds you have alluded to. I assume you have them in that Swiss bank vault of yours—I myself will require them!"

"What!"

"Or would you like me to speak to the authorities about the young lady you got with child, and tried to have killed? A young woman, one Kathleen Murphy, second-generation Irish immigrant. She now lives in London, vividly remembers the thugs you set about her, barely escaped with her life, is paralyzed from the waist down—and I could easily—"

"So now you blackmail me!"

"Very perceptive of you."

Smithson went to the bar, poured himself a cognac, his shaky hands spilling a third of it. "How did you find out?"

"Why, from your own mind, which leaks like a sieve! I have located the lady—and there are other secrets—"

"Enough! Keep your voice down!" Smithson glanced worriedly at the door. "The rituals we took part in, to give the village to . . . to those beneath . . . they bound you, as well as me! Your promise was heard in the ritual!"

"I will keep my promise. You will make that vault available to me. And when the trap has closed, and I have my quarry as well as the power promised me by the Sunless, I will see to your immortality."

"Quarry? What quarry?"

MacCrawley looked at the rain on the window. "A certain disgusting, foul-mouthed, treacherous little Scouse, who fancies himself a magician. And he is just magician enough to hide his whereabouts from us. Every time I sent someone to kill him, they ran into some sort of spell of concealment—one that conceals him only from his enemies. Couldn't find him. But that spell will not function in the vault of the Sunless. And I have seen to it that what passes for a local wizard will bring him here. Constantine cannot resist siding with the underdog . . . and I shall take the Scouse with us, when we go . . ."

"When we go. MacCrawley. I'm . . . I'm not sure I want to go down there. What if . . . suppose . . ."

"You *will* go, if you want your immortality, Smithson. It awaits you there. I will take my leave now. I shall go out the back. Continue to bluff your military men—then make arrangements about the gold. And do not deceive yourself as to who is master here. It is I, Smithson. And I alone."

Smithson watched with a down-spiraling heart as MacCrawley picked up his best decanter of brandy, corked it, tucked it under his arm, and sauntered whistling out the side door.

"John—I can't feel my feet anymore! They're dead as mackerels on ice!"

"I think we're almost there, Chas," Constantine said. His own feet were going numb, too, in the increasingly chill water of the cave. They had been sloshing through it for nearly an hour, through a long, luminescent, guano-reeking cave. He couldn't make out where the light was coming from and supposed it to be generated by magic. The walls were chiseled with time-worn druidic figures, the signs for water and for star . . .

"Now how can you have any notion of 'almost there' if you have no idea where we're going? Unless maybe you do!"

"I do and I don't." The blue-white glow had increased in the last few minutes—and so had a sound of crashing water. "Sounds like a waterfall ahead . . ."

Thirty sloshing strides more, and the tunnel widened out into a spray-cloudy gallery, its ceiling fanged with stalactites. In this cavern a waterfall about thirty-five feet high cascaded into the shallow pool that fed the stream. The light here seemed to emanate from the pool—and now to coalesce, to organize itself into the shining outline of a woman. Suddenly ice formed on the surface of the pool, crackling as it came, and rose up to enclose the glinting light— which was like sunlight playing in seawater—and in seconds a beautiful, translucent figure stood there, a ten-foot-tall woman carved out of ice, with her long hair formed of water running from the top of her head like an overflowing fountain. Constantine recognized this being: it was the powerful water elemental he'd summoned, and contracted with, on the Mediterranean Sea, a year earlier.

"Fuck but she's beautiful," Chas blurted.

What a charming turn of phrase, the water elemental said, her voice resonating in their minds.

Startled, Chas took a spasmodic step back and stumbled, and fell on his ass in the water, where he sat up to his chest in the stream, gazing at the radiant living ice sculpture as she spoke on.

Her head turned, with a slight creaking sound, to look from Chas to Constantine. **John Constantine. I saved your life when your own kind would destroy you; for you, I struggled with N'Hept. You gave your oath that you would serve me in return when the time came. And the time has now come. You are doubly summoned: your enemy has summoned you here, too. You have tried to refuse the lure; the fish turning from the hook. But you cannot refuse me.**

"Just out of curiosity, what happens if I do refuse to fulfill my part of the bargain, O Lady of the Sea?" Constantine asked. If he could just turn his back on all this . . . for Kit.

He assumed that the elemental, being old school,

would kill him for reneging on his oath. This was as good a place to die as any. He'd had a vision once that he would one day die by drowning. The circumstances were blurred in his recollection—perhaps this was that fatal circumstance. Being a water elemental, wouldn't she kill him that way? There were worse ways to go. A couple of minutes of discomfort and it was all over . . .

I have seen into your heart, John Constantine, she continued. **I have seen that you are not averse to your own destruction. Your anger at yourself might even lead you to accept a terrible, prolonged death. You may presently have occasion to discover if you are genuinely ready to die.**

There might be another way out, though. Constantine had other magical relationships—he might rush out of the water, get to high ground, before she destroyed him and Chas, and summon the elementals of the earth. After all, he was surrounded by rock and soil in this cavern. He could even feel the earth elementals somewhere in the background. They might block her. But that'd be just another act of magic, wouldn't it? A betrayal of his determination to let it all go. Still—it could be the last one, to get him out of this ugly little adventure she was planning for him. He had to act quickly . . .

But the soul within you whispers to me, the water spirit went on, **that you are loyal to your friends—and your friend has no wish to die . . .**

"Right enough I don't!" Chas said, guessing what the elemental had in mind. He turned to crawl from the chamber.

The ice of the water elemental's lower body extended, so that the water around her ankles instantly froze, and crackled as it spread in a peninsula that reached out to encompass Chas. Ice encased Chas's legs, his waist, his chest.

"John! Help me!" he shouted.

That's all Chas got out before the ice enclosed him entirely, locking him in a crystalline sheath, freeze-framing him in a crouch with one arm uplifted, his mouth open. Staring. Glinting coldly.

"Here, release him!" Constantine shouted. "He has not given his oath to you, Lady!"

He has come to this sacred shrine, where of old I was worshipped—for I am not merely an "elemental" as you call it, I am a queen—some called me the Lady of Waters, and all men who enter the domain of water are rightly mine. But my power is limited by the massing of stones, the looming of mountains, the bony grasp of the earth. So I brought you both to this chamber, so that you would know my power, and I saw to it that your friend came along—I whispered to him in his flat, in the dripping of water, till he was ready to come to your aid. He is my guarantor, John Constantine. Your friend is in a state of enchantment now, a stasis in which he sleeps, unharmed. You will do as I ask, or the enchantment will end, and the sheath of ice will fill with water, and your friend will drown for all eternity in my world. Just as he dies, he will be revived only to drown again, and so it will be, forever. I give you five days to do as I ask— to fulfill your oath to me—or on the sixth day I will draw him into me, to drown forever.

Constantine sighed. He was outmaneuvered—and checkmated. And after all, he had given his word to her. An oath was a powerful thing—if he didn't fulfill it, he'd pay the price someday. "Bugger. Right. What is it you want me to do, then?"

Behind the falling water is a passage, leading downward, ever downward, to the realm of the Sunless. Here rules the Gloomlord, the King Underneath. He has sent his gripplers to a thousand repositories of poison, and brought the poisons, in their containers, to his world. He mixes them and sends them out again, through the underground rivers, to poison the sea. Thus is it that whales and sea lions wash up, dead on your beaches, in ever greater numbers, harbingers of the sickness to come. I sent one such whale up the Thames as a warning, not long ago—but the warning was not heeded.

Repositories of poison? Constantine thought. Then he realized. Toxic waste; discarded nerve gas canisters; nuclear waste.

"What's this Gloomlord bloke poisoning the sea for?" Constantine badly wanted to light a cigarette, but thought it might be impolitic. The water, swirling just under his crotch, was already freezing cold; he had no wish for the elemental to freeze his balls as a disciplinary gesture. Judging by the ruthlessness she'd shown Chas, she just might do it, too.

The King Underneath is only hurrying what mankind has already begun. His purposes are hidden to me; I know only that they are dire. He must be overcome, the poisons contained, and the slaves

he's brought from the upper world, of late, must be returned. They will only make him stronger—and help him in undermining your world and poisoning mine.

"But see here, old girl—you said my enemies were trying to lure me to this place too! That means I'm going to my own doom, down there! They'll be waiting to drop a ton of rock on me or worse!"

They thought to bring you by the barrow tunnel. But you will enter by a way they do not know—perhaps undetected. You have five days and nights! And now, I bid you, be about your quest—

"Five days isn't half enough—!"

Five days is what you have—or your friend is consigned, irretrievably, to the doom I have declared to you! For on the sixth day, the King's plans will be fulfilled.

"But who *is* this bastard? Don't seem to recollect the name."

He it is who rules in the palace which men call Phosphor, in the realm of the Sunless. Once he was mortal like you; he found other means to keep the feeble flame of his life burning. Magic was his making and his undoing both. So much my spies have informed me—it is for John Constantine to learn the rest, and to bring our mutual enemies into the place of woe and despair!

"Christ on a bike, that's easy for you to—"

Do not breathe the name of the Anointed interloper in this place!

Her voice thundered from the ceiling, and a stalactite loosed and fell to crash into ice close beside Chas.

"The Anointed . . . ? Oh! Sorry. Right, if I'm to go about this underground quest, I'd best be off."

At that, Constantine felt a lifting pressure under his feet, and had to scramble to keep his footing as he looked down to see a pillar of ice forming under him, rising up and carrying him with it, lifting him toward the ceiling. Right toward the down-spiking stalactites. He crouched down. "Here, I said I was sorry!"

But the column stopped rising when his feet were even with the top of the waterfall. A bridge of ice fashioned itself to arch out from the passage above the waterfall to the frosty column. Constantine looked down at poor, frozen Chas a last time, and shook his head. "See what I can do, mate. No promises." The elemental's icy body had vanished—but then he saw her face, like a reflection in the pool, watching him.

He made a facetious genuflection toward her, then walked carefully—very carefully—along the bridge of ice to the watery passage above the waterfall. Here a tunnel angled gently upward—but another, above the water level and to the right, went sharply downward. An orb of blue light hovered over the mouth of the right-turning down-tunnel, and he knew this was his route. He stepped into it and found half-shattered, crudely carved steps, descending downward, into a spiraling blackness . . .

And he just kept on going, spiraling down, waiting for it to end. It never seemed to.

4

A DARKNESS THAT CAN BE FELT

Old Duff had waited a considerable time for Constantine and Chas to come back. When he'd drunk the last of the ale and pissed some of it out against a rear fender of the cab—meditating on the absence of his companions as he did so—it came clear to him that magic had taken them away, and that he was not intended to go with them. He supposed the sorcerer MacCrawley, who had cursed the village into the ground, encysting it in the pit of the Sunless, had sent some furious water elemental to carry Constantine to his doom.

But then again, he thought, as the rain clouds broke up and the sun shafted down, *there may be other players in the game.*

"I cannot believe it's all up, no I can't," he muttered. "There's sommat for me to do yet, there is."

That's when the voices warned him that the soldiers were coming, the authorities perhaps deciding to check on the mysterious London cab that had done such a screechingly quick U-turn at their roadblock.

Old Duff hurried across the road, slid down the embankment to the culvert, and walked upstream to the cover of the woods. He mistrusted soldiers and rozzers—they had always ended up thumping him in his Navy days, and later setting about him in pubs and dragging him to jail in the streets.

He had no difficulty eluding the loud, clumsy men in uniforms—this was his turf, and he knew it like the back of his hand. But he was surprised when Constantine's tracks by the stream led to a hill, and a crevice in the side of that hill. Long had a spring run from the hill here, but the opening? Never in his time. The crevice fairly oozed magic—the magic of nature, from the mind of the world.

"Constantine?" he called, approaching it.

But the crevice shuddered, then it rumbled within itself—and then the stone closed over the opening like a garage door coming down. The way was blocked.

He shook his head ferociously and declared, "There's a part for me yet! I will not forget Tonsell-by-the-Stream, village of my youth, which I protected these many years. I have failed you—and I will make it up, or die in the trying!"

But first he had to cross the fields to the inn at Quinbury, where a man might get a drink.

⋆⇒◉⇐⋆

"It's obvious where we are," said Garth, tugging his coat more closely about him in the subterranean chill. His face flickered in the guttering of the candles

Skupper was using to improve on the thin blue light given off by the phosphorescent roof of the great cavern. "We're in Hell. Or on the edge of it—purgatory, like. I reckon they'll come for us here, and take us to be judged, soon enough." He looked up through the ragged gap in the ceiling of the pub, to the almost mist-shrouded ceiling of natural stone arching over the village.

"That's all shite, Granddad," said Bosky, coming into the pub's half-fallen main room. "Hell is hot—it's cold here." He had on a sweater under his hoody and it showed at the bottom; his hood was up.

"What are you doing here, boy?" Skupper demanded, tucking his cold fingers in his armpits.

"Are you going to call the coppers, Skupper, and say I'm breaking the law, coming in the pub?" Bosky asked, shaking his head and picking up the fallen dartboard from the rubble, setting it thoughtfully up against a broken section of wall. "I've heard of being 'above the law'—but we're a good thousand feet or more *beneath* the law here. You think you risk getting a fine down here, do you?"

"Tell you what the risk is," said Geoff, coming after Bosky, picking up a dart from the rubble. "That the bloody ceiling'll fall in on this pub."

Much of the village had come through the lowering remarkably intact. It was as if the town had been lowered carefully, by something, or someone, who had a use for it—or its inhabitants.

It was true that St. Leonard's church was leaning badly, and a couple of brick buildings, standing alone near the edge of town, had crumbled. Old Mrs.

Galway was buried under the bricks of her house, all
but her feet, making Bosky think of the witch in that
Oz movie. They'd dug her out, working in the eerie
blue light from the distant ceiling, but found her
dead. No one thought there was much point in trying CPR. Why revive her—so she could face this
apocalyptic horror, a slow death of starvation or
worse? There were rumors of worse, in the twenty-
four hours since the village had sunk into the crust
of the Earth . . .

"It's strange," Bosky said, looking up through the
hole in the ceiling. "I mean—it's all strange. But one
thing is—there's stalactites on that cave ceiling up
there. Them things take thousands of years to grow. I
saw it on the telly. But that ceiling's only been up
there a day."

"Devil's magic doesn't follow natural laws," said
Garth. "When we came down, I saw that roof come
from the side, like, pushed from someplace else. And
by what? By devil's magic."

Geoff threw the dart at the board; it struck, wob-
bled, and fell off. "Bugger. Yeah—so it's like Bosky
says—what difference does anything make now?"

"Right, boy, what difference indeed," said Skupper,
surprising Bosky. "Here, have a drink."

He poured out two glasses of whiskey and Bosky
and Geoff drank them off before Garth could stop
them. But Bosky wasn't glad he'd drunk it—the
whiskey burned in his empty belly, and he felt only
dizzy, not jolly.

"Ha ha," said Butterworth, returning from the WC.
He pronounced each *ha* as a clear, separate syllable.

He added a couple more as he picked his way over the rubble. "Ha ha. The boy looks like he swallowed something he's not used to! That'll teach you to try to be a man before you're—"

"Here, Butterworth!" Skupper said, scowling at him. "I told you not to use that bog! It's not connected to a sewer anymore! Find an empty house!"

"There's some empty houses at the darker end of the village," said Annie Weathers, her face looking haunted in the candlelight as she came in from the street, stepping through a hole in a wall. "For three more of us have been taken." A prim woman, with her hair still in the same blond helmet shape it had been in before the earth had swallowed up her home, and wearing the same long blue coat, only a little muddy at the bottom edges. Her thin face—too thin for that mollusk of hair—was smudged by tears, however. Her eyes were unfocused; her mouth slack, her fingers trembling at her sides. She had never in thirty years been seen in the village without her purse, until now.

"Here," Butterworth said, taking her arm, leading her to one of the intact booths. "Have a seat, Mrs. I'll get you a brandy."

"Why thank you," Annie said when the brandy was brought to her. "I'm afraid I . . . I have not yet . . . not yet quite reconciled myself to my . . . to my fate. Perhaps—perhaps I don't understand what we've done to . . . to deserve this."

" 'Tain't fair, right enough," said Butterworth, sitting across from her, looking out through the crack in the ceiling at the fluorescent stalactites poised like a mouth full of teeth over the village. "But the Lord works in mysterious ways—so mysterious, even the Vicar's down here with us! And our Vicar Tombridge is well known to be a good man, and no hypocrite. Spoke to him in his vicarage, not an hour ago. He was trying to make a cup of tea by piling up pieces of wood on his stove, talking to himself. 'One makes sacrifices,' he says, 'and this is one's reward—some detestable outer circle of Gehenna,' he says. I don't know what he means by sacrifices, exactly, but I heard Mrs. Galway offered herself to him, and he turned her down."

"Here, don't be speaking of ladies like that!" said Garth. "True or not!"

"The woman's dead now," Butterworth said, shrugging. "And it doesn't matter anyhow. I mean, are you saying I'll be punished somehow for speaking ill? Eh? We're in Hell. What more punishment *can* happen?"

Even as he said this, the gray hand of a grippler was reaching unseen through the crooked frame of the back door, stretching toward Geoff, who stood behind the others. No one saw the gray hand stretching its way into the room. Another hand, on a long, long arm, came through the door just behind the first and a little higher, moving more like a tentacle than a limb . . .

"I reckon we could take up weapons," Bosky said. "My da left a rifle. Mum's got it locked up, but I could get it. Could be them things can be killed."

Garth shook his head from side to side, in the motion of a bell tolling mournfully. "You cannot kill demons, boy. Only God can do that. 'Specially, in Hell, where they're strongest."

"I don't believe this is Hell," Bosky said. "I've read up some on Hell, and there's a lot of descriptions of it, some one way and some another, but none like this. This is more like . . . like a big kidnapping, something like that . . . using magic maybe."

Even as he spoke the word *kidnapping,* the four-fingered hands clamped tightly around Geoff's mouth and throat, and began dragging him backwards—but as Butterworth was laughing derisively at Bosky's remark, the sound of Geoff's struggling went unheard.

"Big kidnapping! Who kidnaps people by dropping them underground!"

"That's the question," Bosky said, mostly to himself. "Who?"

"Maybe they're already digging up there—the authorities, I mean," Butterworth suggested. "Trying to dig us out."

"What, under millions of tons of rock?" Skupper snorted. He had been a military engineer at one time in his life. "Not bloody likely. They're writing us off and trying to figure out how to explain it so no one blames them."

Garth nodded. "You're right, Skupper."

"I am? This calls for another glass of whiskey," said Skupper, his voice slurring. He was just sober enough to stand up and pour a drink without pitching on his face, but no more.

He turned to get a bottle and then gasped, pointed at Geoff being dragged out the back door. Geoff was flailing his arms, his eyes wild with desperation.

Garth and Bosky ran to try to yank Geoff free, but the inexorable pull of the long, slender gray arms seemed unstoppable, all powerful. Bosky and Garth held stubbornly on to Geoff's legs, and were dragged out the door with him.

Outside—outside the ruins of the pub, but still within the great cavern—they saw that Geoff was being pulled upward, straight into the air . . . his screams muffled by another hand, clamped over his mouth.

The two arms lifting him up seemed at least a hundred yards long, perhaps longer. They extended to become mere convergent lines in the distance overhead, reaching clear to the distant cavern ceiling, where they joined with a blob of gray that could only be dimly made out, perched on a dark shelf within an enormous crack. Garth let go, cursing himself, and a moment later Bosky lost his grip too, and fell seven feet to the weedy turf in the open space behind the pub, landing on his back, the air knocked from him when he struck, still clutching one of Geoff's sneakers in his right hand.

Wheezing for air, Bosky stared up at Geoff's frantically waving legs. His best friend receding into the misty blue air overhead . . . drawn up and up, dwindling with distance, until at last he was pulled into the crack, to vanish with the gray blob into the shadows.

Bosky watched for a long time, hoping for some other sight of Geoff. But nothing moved up there.

"Bugger this," Bosky said in a low voice when he'd gotten his wind back. He stood up and fixed Garth

with a hard look. "That hole up there goes somewhere, Granddad. And some have disappeared into
other holes, lower down, near the edge of town. I'm
going to get a gun from that cabinet, and I'm going to
go in one of them holes. There must be a connection,
a tunnel system to the ones up above. I'm going to
climb up and see what they've done with Geoff. I've
had enough."

Garth swallowed and licked his lips—but said
nothing.

Bosky shrugged and turned, stalking off toward
his house. Garth watched his grandson go. Bosky's
father, Garth's son-in-law Pauly, hadn't been a bad
sort, except for the drinking binges. Driving drunk
one night he'd crashed into the river in flood season
and drowned. Ill-luck for the boy, who'd loved his father, and Bosky hadn't been right since. But now, at
last, he was showing some character. Something that
ought to be encouraged—in Hell or not. So Garth
sighed and turned to Skupper and Butterworth, gaping from the doorway. "Well, gentlemen: I'm an old
man after all. What difference does it make if I die a
day or two sooner? May God bless and keep you."

He started off to find Bosky, wondering if he had
any provisions left to take along with them.

Skupper and Butterworth stared after Garth. Then
they went silently back to the bar.

⊷═◈═⊶

Constantine woke up in darkness, profound darkness, on what felt like stone. He couldn't remember

having fallen onto it, not exactly. There had been that endlessly spiraling descent, feeling his way along—and then he'd run out of steps. And out of floor. He'd pitched into a hole. A moment of free fall and then—it was as if he'd been swatted like a fly. He'd supposed himself killed.

No such luck. Only knocked out for a bit.

He sat up, bones aching but intact, and got to his hands and knees, looking around for some source of light and finding none. Pitch black. The bottom of the chute was rough, stony, cold, and bone dry; the air smelled of mushrooms and, faintly, of decaying flesh. A chorus of unintelligible whispering was heard from not far away. Now and then, the dripping of water; the occasional low groan, and a sound that might have been something big and soft being dragged across a floor.

Constantine had no other impressions, because he couldn't see a damn thing. The words *stygian* and *inky* came to his mind and they seemed inadequate. It was darkness without relief.

There was another quality to the blackness too— it seemed to have a palpable weight of its own, a fulsome presence that pressed against him. He remembered a line from the Bible, Exodus 10:21, *Then the Lord said to Moses, "Stretch out your hand toward Heaven, that there may be darkness over the land of Egypt, a darkness that can be felt."*

Constantine got carefully to his feet, waiting for his eyes to adjust, to give him some faint sense of the extent and shape of his surroundings. It never happened. He reached up above him, feeling about—and his hand came into contact with a damp stone ceiling a few feet over his head. To the right and left he felt nothing. "Lady!" he hissed into the darkness, hoping that the dripping water might put him in contact with her. "What happened to the light you gave me earlier?"

Something in the darkness sniggered at that.

"He thinks he wants to see! Oh but he don't, he don't!"

Did he hear that with his ears or his mind—or his imagination? Constantine wasn't sure.

"Lady!"

No reply.

He thought of a spell of illumination that might work here. He yearned to try it out—he felt unspeakably vulnerable in this blackness. Something could be sniffing at him, opening its great toothy mouth for him right now, and he'd never know till it closed its jaws.

And if the spell didn't work, there was always his cigarette lighter, though he was reluctant to use its fuel up. How, after all, would he light his cigarettes if he ran his lighter fuel down?

Some instinct warned him against creating light, magically or any other way, just now. If there were dangerous creatures about him in the darkness, they might be as unaware of him as he was of them. A light would only attract them.

But without a light he might blunder into a pit, or into that toothy maw . . .

Just wait, he told himself. *Hold off.*

So he moved slowly ahead—he hoped it was

ahead—with his arms outstretched, feeling his way
with his feet.

Fuck me, this could take weeks. I've only got five days.

Still he tiptoed slowly forward, feeling his way.
The ground seemed more or less flat, though now
and then something brittle crunched underfoot.

A dozen yards on he ran into someone else feeling
their way along. Their fingertips touching his.

Constantine recoiled, swearing, "Fucking hell . . . !"

"Here, who's that?" said a voice, accompanied by
foul breath, close at hand. "I don't know that voice. I
thought I knew every voice in the deep dark."

The voice had an odd accent Constantine had
never heard before. Almost British but not quite. "My
name's John," he said. "Who's that?"

"Arfur, you can call me," said the voice. A man's
voice, cracked, aged, laborious. "The Brits called me
that."

Constantine took a step back from the smell—a
stench of decay and never-washed feet and mold and
feces. "How long have you been here?" Constantine
asked, wondering how he could get some kind of directions to the Palace of Phosphor without revealing
himself to be an intruder. Whoever he was talking to,
in the pitch blackness, might be a sentry of some
kind—or prepared to call one. It was best he enter
the realm of the Sunless unnoticed by its lord if he
could, especially considering that MacCrawley was
involved. And it made sense that anyone with the
title "Gloomlord" was someone best approached circumspectly. A title like that, Constantine reflected,
wasn't exactly a declaration of welcome on the mat.

"Me?" Arfur seemed baffled by Constantine's question. "How long . . . Why . . . I'm not at all certain, but . . . well, what year is it, friend?"

Constantine told him.

There was a long silence. Then the stranger jeered, "You lie! I came here in the year 1829! I could not have lived so long! Unless . . . but no! I eat, I sleep, I work—I am no ghost!"

"But then the Gloomlord is said to be a long-lived bloke, eh?" Constantine prompted. "If he can live so long . . ."

"His Majesty is no mere mortal man!" There was a touch of reverence in the cracked voice. Then bitter laughter. "And of course it is our toil that gives him his immortality. But one day, one fine day we shall be given our freedom, and wealth beyond imagining!"

"One fine day," Constantine agreed. Thinking: In which century? The twenty-fourth?

"Why do you tell this lie about the years?" Arfur asked piteously. "It is hard enough here, finding our way about by smell, by the threads, and the clacksmacks. Doing the bidding of the gripplers. Hard enough, hard enough."

"Sorry, mate. Didn't mean to upset you. When was the last time you beheld the Gloomlord, Arfur?"

"Beheld him? How should I behold him? Never saw him even when we passed by the palace. They locked us in here and we've never been out since. No, never do they let us out of the lower galleries. It will take a good long time, I should suppose, to adjust to the light of the upper world when the time comes. But perhaps the King will use his magic so that we do not suffer. Now then, when did you say you got here?"

"Well, in fact—I'm a newcomer," Constantine admitted.

"What! When did you come past the palace?"

"Oh, not so very long ago," Constantine said, improvising and aware that someone else was drawing near; snuffling sounds were heard, clickings and crunchings and gruntings and nasty giggles and a wave of awful odors. "Promises were made, as you know, and I'm eager to get to work!"

"That's the attitude! We often get whiners down here. I don't mind telling you they're like as not to become grist for the mill, eh! One has to put one's shoulder to the wheel or one falls under it!"

"More or less that way on the surface," Constantine remarked, mostly to himself. "Your Gloomlord's a right old Tory . . . a bloody neocon . . ."

"But ho, they bring us our meal! You're in luck! You may eat before you serve the wheels! Here, my friend, put out your hand!"

Constantine put out his hand and encountered another hand, covering a large fired-clay bowl of what he supposed to be food, mildly warm. He was hungry and patted at it with his fingers, wondering if he dared eat any. But the hand was in the way . . .

Then he realized that the hand over the bowl wasn't in the way, it was *in* the bowl, severed at the wrist. He could feel the bone-ends protruding from the stump. Constantine drew back his own hand in revolted haste.

"Should be nice and fresh," Arfur was saying. "He's

just come from the surface. He was supposed to work at the wheels with the rest of us, but he would whine and run mad! Still, I'm glad he did, in a way—I was so very hungry! And you and I share the hands!" As he spoke, Constantine could hear him crunching and slurping at his own meal. Sucking flesh from fingers. "We will have more help here, and soon," Arfur went on, the words mushy with the meat in his mouth. "No doubt they are still being sorted. Go on, eat up, don't be shy! You won't get better grub any time soon! Think of it as sausages. 'Bony sausages,' we call them!"

"Where do you come from?" Constantine asked, to change the subject. "I mean, you know—originally."

"Me? Why . . . I . . ." There was a meditative chewing sound. "Oh it's so long since I thought of it . . . I almost forgot . . . but of course it's Boston I'm from."

"In America?"

"Where else? A Boston bean, the other sailors called me, when I was pressed into the Royal Navy. Stepped off an American merchant ship in Portsmouth, got myself drunk, punched a bailiff in the beezer, and they condemned me to be pressed. Some had steam engines on their ships—perhaps you've seen them, they're all the thing in the shipyards—but we had none, and a storm smashed us on a lee shore. We all found ourselves clawing for a hold in the sea cave, glad to be able to breathe. The rising tide trapped us and we went more deeply into the cave and there was nowhere to go but down. We soon encountered the gripplers—and then the King's soldiers. They brought us before the palace . . . Oh, what a glorious sight! The King Underneath, the one you call the Gloomlord, declared us trespassers, but said we might work off our crime and receive a great reward. Some, of course, were eaten—but there are a few left from that crew . . . See here, are you going to eat that?"

"Ah, no, I ate just before I . . . signed on. I was just wondering if you had any notion when you'll be . . ." He broke off, feeling a hand on his ankle. This one was still attached to an arm, for it was feeling its way up his leg. Constantine jerked away from the probing touch. "Here! Is that you clutching at me, Arfur! We'll have less of that!"

"No, 'tisn't me. Lord but this whiner had a tender palm . . . No, 'twasn't me; there are those here who look for fresher meat. Give him a swift kick and he'll sheer off."

Constantine kicked out, but two more hands clamped on to his legs, others his arms, and he felt a long tongue rasping at his right ankle, and another— reeking sickeningly—on his neck, and someone muttering foully, "I wants to suck out his eyeballs. Do but hold him and I'll suck out his eyeballs while he yet lives . . . that's the delicacy, the texture, the fresh warm softness of them . . ."

Constantine began to shout a spell of illumination—but a big horny hand clamped over his mouth, gagging him. A long rough tongue lapped at his eyes . . .

"Avast, there, let my friend go!" shouted Arfur. "If anyone's to eat him it's me, and I've not decided!"

There was a scrabbling, a struggle in the darkness,

and Constantine felt his right hand set free. He reached into his inner coat pocket, fumbled out his lighter, terrified he would drop it, opened it with a practiced flip of his thumb, flicked it alight—

Their screams at the sudden light were piteous, like small girls with their skirts afire. His captors released him and backed hastily away.

Constantine saw a dozen figures in a ragged ring around him. They were only roughly in the shape of men, though he could see that they'd once been human, for within the scabrous gray-green growths of fungus coating them were bits of uncovered human flesh; here a nose, there an ear, there a partial chin, a few threadbare rag ends of clothing. For the most part they were covered with the growth, like barnacles on the hull of a ship but rougher, more uniform. They looked almost like figures of stone. Many had one eye covered by the growth. Their remaining eyes peered at him, blinking, half blinded.

The nearest, probably Arfur, still had a human finger stuck in the corner of his mouth which he worked at like a child slowly chewing up a long piece of candy. There were wooden bowls on the floor here and there, with ragged bits of a person in them, along with what looked like sections of mushrooms. In one of the bowls was the partly gnawed head of what might've been a teenage boy with ash-blond hair.

"It's well you can't see yourselves," Constantine said. "The Gloomlord has betrayed you gits! And if you've got any humanity left in you, you'll take your revenge on him! Just look at you!"

As he spoke he lifted the cigarette lighter's flame to see beyond them. The low ceiling soon ended, opening up in a vast chamber. He caught a dim glimpse of a farther wall on which were stone wheels, each with a handle, and at which other crusted unfortunates toiled, monotonously cranking the wheels to provide the motion that turned a disk up above, itself connected to a mechanism he couldn't make out. Much was obscured by the intervening guidance strings stretched weblike across the cavern.

And many hands—gray-black, four-fingered, on long, long arms—were snaking toward him across the floor. Coming with a multiple slithering, the hands were on arms that seemed to go on and on, reaching to big gray blobs in recesses along the walls . . .

"The gripplers is coming to see to him!" one of the scabrous figures declared gleefully. "He'll soon change his tune! He'll dance a new jig for us!"

Constantine was fairly sure that once those four-fingered hands had good grip on him he'd be done for. He tried to think of a quick-and-dirty spell to deal with this peculiar situation but none came to him.

Still the hands reached for him—closer now—

He had a thought. These men were sailors. He had no rum, but . . .

"Who wants tobacco?" Constantine asked casually, plucking a cigarette from his pocket and lighting it.

"Oh my sweet Lord—is that tobacco?" cried Arfur, peeking through the fingers covering his eye.

"It is!" Constantine shouted. "If those things crawling on the floor grab me . . ." He was backing away from the gray hands—the gripplers, he supposed—but even in the dark he sensed they were gaining on him. ". . . I'll chew the tobacco up and swallow it! But if you want it—and if you don't make a snatch for it—and if you protect me—"

And he blew a seductive plume of smoke toward Arfur.

Arfur made an anguished bugling sound and then pounded toward him, his eyes squinted against the light. The other encrusted men were hanging back, still afraid of the light and the gripplers who were almost upon him. "Put out the light and I'll carry you!" Arfur shouted.

Constantine switched off the lighter, and darkness fell like a guillotine blade. He felt himself swept up in powerful, crust-covered arms. "I'll carry you to the resting repository! The gripplers will have to come out of their crannies to find you there and there'll be just time for a smoke! Oh it seems ages since I've had a smoke."

"It *is*, mate!" Constantine assured him, as—in pitch darkness—Arfur leaped skillfully about, holding Constantine above the gripplers, their finger-centered senses seeking him on the floor. Using his heightened sensitivity to the gripplers' presence, Arfur slipped past the grasping hands, running up between the arms . . .

To where? Constantine wondered. There was no telling where this grotesque was carrying him.

Constantine focused his attention on the psychic field emanating from his own body, compressed its energy, and then extended its receptivity . . .

He obtained a sort of psychic bat's-eye-view of their surroundings, then—an unsteady, monochromatic image derived from sheer soul-prescience. He glimpsed a row of tunnels in the wall beside the wheels where the damned of this outer darkness toiled.

Between the tunnels were big irregular cracks where the gripplers' arms retracted to become part of the main body, which were little more than leathery, hairless blobs. The gripplers' arms literally grew out of, and shrank into, the big shapeless bodies, stretching out or sucking back in like polyps from an amoeba. There was something like a face on the blob, too, a wide lipless, drooling mouth, stretching much of the width of the body, and the suggestion of nostrils—but no eyes.

Then the image faded; Constantine couldn't hold it for long, especially down here, so far from the places he drew on for power, so close to the energies sustaining those who would destroy him.

Suddenly they came into a more enclosed space; the air here was moist and close. A tunnel of some kind.

"Here we are!" Arfur said, putting Constantine down. "Now for that baccy!"

"Certainly," Constantine said. But instead of handing over the cigarette he took a long step back. "How far back does this tunnel go?"

Even as he spoke he could hear the gripplers slithering toward him across the floor, searching, sniffing him out . . .

"This is the resting repository, friend," Arfur said.

"It only goes back a hundred paces. There is no outlet. There is no way out of this region at all, once you're in!"

No way out. Bugger. Had the Lady of Waters been playing with him, putting him here? Was she taking some kind of revenge on him for his avoidance of paying his debt by consigning him to this pitch-black nightmare forever? But she was an elemental—demons and fairies were known to be deceptive, flagrant liars in fact, but not elementals. There must be a way out, and up to the Gloomlord's palace.

"Now as for that smoke," Arfur prompted.

"Yes I have it here for you. You say there's no way out, but there's a place where food comes in, and new people. If something can come in that way, something can go out that way. As for me, Arfur, I didn't tell you the full truth about how I came in. I dropped from a hole in the ceiling. Where else do people come in?"

"So that's why you came from that quarter—I was puzzling on it. That's where we shove the old bones and feces. New food and workers are lowered down the great shaft, but straight and sheer and black the shaft is, and no way up! And the gripplers, they unload whatever comes down. They're always there, there's no way to get past them even if there was a way up it! Well—there's one spot maybe, where you might come to the shaft. I used to work on it, before I despaired . . . but no way to get to the lifting chain from there . . ."

"And where would that spot be?"

"Beyond the wheels, to starboard as you leave the

tunnel. It sounds . . ." He broke off, listening. "Sounds as if the gripplers have missed us, for the nonce—they have moved past the mouth of the tunnel. But they will be back in moments! There isn't much time—and the little cigar is going out!"

Constantine felt Arfur shambling toward him and he held out the cigarette, butt first. "Here, take it, mate—though I'm sorry to get you started again after all these centuries. Somehow they've muddled your sense of time, Arfur, and kept you alive—maybe with that, ah, growth on your skin . . ."

Arfur was sucking at the cigarette. The cherry of the butt glowed in the darkness. He coughed, and then said, "Strange and wonderful tobacco. How the taste of baccy takes me back." He sighed. "That growth on the skin, as you call it, that's the protective coating that gives us life. We would not survive the harsh conditions here without it, they tell us. It comes from the gripplers. They suck a man into their maw and spew upon him, and the spew takes root, a fungal thing that enters itself into the deeps of your—but hark, now, stranger! The gripplers are here! Oh how I pray they don't know it was I—"

"I've found another smoke in my coat, Arfur! Lift me up and carry me out and it's yours!" Constantine whispered.

"But they're . . . they're going to . . ."

Constantine decided some outpouring of power was needed to give them an edge, a momentary out. He turned his attention inward, conducted certain ambient psychic energies—*prana,* thinly available here—that could be converted into light. He extended his hand, visualized certain runic symbols, muttered a name of power, then loudly spoke the words:

"Ignis Ico, Ilaturs!"

A ball of red light formed over Constantine's upturned palm and he saw the long gray arms of the gripplers—six of them—snaking toward his ankles from the mouth of the "repository." The light flared up more brightly as he pulsed energy into it and the hands drew back like startled snakes, uncertain, confused by the burst of warmth and luminosity. The flare of light brought the tunnel around them into view: the walls dripping with slime, the floor unspeakably filthy, edges thick with toadstools.

"You need to have a word with an interior decorator, mate!" Constantine said.

Eyes protected from the light by his fingers, Arfur whispered, "Drive the gripplers back and I'll show you a place you might escape from them . . . but only for a time. Hurry—they are returning!"

The four-fingered hands were once more snaking nearer . . .

Constantine felt his internal energy weakening. He needed real food, and rest. But he reached into the place within himself, the place shown him by the Blue Sheikh, which connected to the source of the All. "Cover your eyes, Arfur!"

Letting the fine vibrations flow into him, Constantine conducted them along both arms this time, facing his palms together, and called out,

"Ignis Ico, Ilaturs—multus plus plurinum!"

And the fading glow surged up, redoubled,

quadrupled, so that it pulsed mightily between his cupped hands, like a bursting firework.

The gripplers flinched well back once more, fingers trembling.

"Come on, Arfur!" Constantine shouted. "Let's scarper!" They rushed out the entrance of the "resting repository" and into the open space of the greater cavern.

"This way!" Arfur called.

Constantine had to let the fireball diminish. He felt too weak to extend his prescience, so he simply took out his lighter. He flicked it alight and made out Arfur ahead of him, stumping hurriedly along.

Arfur led the way past dozens of crusty once-men, stolidly cranking wheels and murmuring to themselves of their forgotten lives, and shrinking back from the sudden alien glare of the lighter as Constantine passed by.

Arfur stopped at a vertical, slightly curving crack in the wall, wider at the bottom, a crevice big enough for some large creature to wedge into. "Once a grippler was laired here, but it was called away to bring more 'volunteers' down. Here, you can see the wall inside the crack is rough enough to climb, and it opens at the top . . ." Arfur began to climb, showing the way.

Constantine closed the lighter. The circle of light vanished and, trying to remember the route he'd glimpsed, Constantine felt the wall inside the crack, and climbed in darkness—slipping only once, but never quite falling—until they emerged through a hole into another space entirely, about forty feet up.

It was warmer here, uneasy with a background radiation of strange energies, and loud with the chugging sound of unseen machines working eternally away in the darkness. It was just as black as the cavern and tunnel below.

"Arfur? You there?" He knew he was there, actually; he could smell him.

"Yes. You'll feel a round stone structure here on your right. It contains the turning axle of the great machine. You follow it along, and there's another crack— I could feel cold air blowing from it, and so found it, long ago, and by feel alone I widened it myself, using a broken piece of iron I found. It leads into the great shaft from above. But a cable's length below us is the floor, where the gripplers pick up our goods: a fine basket of bats, with guano for relish, yesterday. There also the gripplers take the new recruits to be coated. The walls are sheer, and rise many hundreds of feet. There is no hold, no way up . . ."

And yet, Constantine mused, taking a few cautious steps through the darkness—he was feeling his way along the curved stone wall Arfur had mentioned—*something's lowering things to the bottom, and if that whatsit can lower things then it can bloody well raise them up too.*

"Look here, Arfur," Constantine began. "Suppose we work together to get out of here. I might find a cure for that coating of yours."

"Do you think it possible? But to defy the King Underneath . . ."

"What has cooperation got you? Now if we were to—"

But he was interrupted by Arfur's shriek as several gripplers, feeling their way up the hole they'd crawled through, fastened themselves around Arfur's legs. "They've got me! Help me!"

Constantine stumbled back through the darkness, caught Arfur's crust-covered fingers flailing about, and tried to pull him back.

"Use your power, friend, use your light!" Arfur begged. "Please, in the name of God, they'll punish me; they'll pull me apart and feed me to the others!"

Constantine reached down inside him but in the sudden urgency of the moment—and after the psychic exertion he'd already made—he couldn't make the contact. Still, he tried, shouting,

"Ignis Ico, Ilaturs!"

But it was no use just saying the words, you had to have the right inner state to go with them. The light didn't come. He felt himself skidding along the floor as he tried to drag Arfur back by main strength—and suddenly lost his hold on Arfur's fingers. "Arfur! Where are you!"

There was no reply, only a tussling sound, followed by a gurgling, a crackling, a ripping . . .

Arfur screamed, and . . . the scream was abruptly cut off.

Constantine listened, but only heard the sound of something, several things, being dragged away . . . and another sound. A furtive slithering. The gripplers coming back up the hole to look for him.

He backed away and thumped into the curved wall. He turned and felt his way hastily along it. He felt a movement of cooler air, and up ahead saw a faint, faint light defining a roughly diamond-shaped crack in the farther wall. In the upper world the light would probably not have been visible, but here, where there was no other light at all, it could just be made out. He hurried to it and climbed partway through the break in the wall, then lowered himself and hung by his hands in the shaft, holding his breath . . .

Constantine hung heavily in darkness, as quietly as possible. The light was from far up the shaft. He could hear machinery clunking, grinding; felt the whisper of rising air lifting the hair on the back of his neck. He waited, dangling in a void, his arms aching.

The gripplers came. He could hear the fingers snuffling inquisitively around in the chamber he'd just left—he could picture them clearly, in his mind's eye, four-fingered hands, like something on toads, tip-tapping their way along the floor, bloodhounds with their smellers in their fingertips, picking up his scent . . .

His arms throbbed; he felt like his shoulders were slowly, slowly dislocating.

He could hear them coming closer now, tippity-tap, slither, tippity-tap, slither, closer and closer, looking to grab his wrists, perhaps to fling him down the shaft to their fellows, where the other gripplers would pull him apart or, maybe worse, impregnate his skin with fungi that would send their roots worming into his flesh, his veins, and finally into his brain . . .

Tippity-tap, slither, tippity . . . tap . . . tap . . .

They were moving off. He'd managed to dangle

lower than the upper edge of the floor and, as he'd hoped, they'd missed him.

Constantine waited, listening. Slither, scrape . . . then nothing.

They were gone.

But still he hung by his hands, wanting to scream with the pain in his arms, his fingers . . . till at last he had to pull himself up, or drop.

Grinding his teeth with the effort, cursing his bad wind from smoking, he pulled himself up inch by inch, caught the edge of the wall with an elbow, and dragged himself back through the aperture. Then he lay for a time on the floor, panting softly in the darkness.

Now what? he thought.

Behind him, there came a sound. The creak of a pulley . . .

5

YOU'RE AT HOME IN THE PIT, AFTER ALL

"It's not so very much to ask, Vicar," Bosky insisted. "All I'm asking is that you baptize my bullets!" He lifted up the 30.06 hunting rifle his father had left him and shook it emphatically at the vicar. "I've got two boxes of bullets in my coat pocket."

The vicar was sitting on a chair in the darkest corner of the room, his head bowed, lank dirty-blond hair drooping over his pale, long-nosed face. Bosky supposed he was praying, but after a moment it was clear he was quietly sobbing.

The sitting room of the vicar's cottage was dimly lit, everything bathed in the dull blue light of the cavern that had swallowed the village. Inky shadows pooling around the furniture, their shapes defined in ghostly blue, and a man weeping in the corner.

"It's no use, Boswell," Vicar Tombridge said, using Bosky's real first name (Bosky's mother, an English teacher, had done her thesis on James Boswell while she was pregnant). "Baptisms are no good in Hell, nor blessings of any sort."

"Bloody . . ." Bosky choked off the epithet. "Not you too, Vicar! You ever hear of anyone going to Hell the way we came here? You see any flames?"

"But the demons—I have seen those! Their grasping hands! They got my neighbor, Mr. Prakesh! There was no harm in him, poor man . . . The hands of Satan will come for me soon, for I'm the true sinner here! Boswell, listen to me—run from thoughts of lust! Perhaps God will give you a second chance and let you out of here, you innocent child!"

Innocent? Run from lust? Not likely on either score. Bosky thought about Marianne LaSalle, the exchange student he'd shagged in the churchyard of St. Leonard's. Good times. They'd been stoned, and forgot the condom. What a relief when she said she'd gotten her period.

The vicar was babbling on, "Men in the sickness of their souls taking advantage of artless young girls . . ."

Marianne had been two years older than him, nineteen, and the whole thing had been her idea. Not that he'd resisted. He'd been sorry to see her return to Paris.

"You cannot hope to throw down the powers of darkness, boy, with a bullet dipped in holy water. Come here, sit by me and we'll pray together for forgiveness, for release from this circle of Hades."

Bosky's granddad Garth came to stand in the doorway then, listening.

"I intend to get out of this death trap, Vicar," Bosky said, "and not with prayer! We can find our way back

up, through the caves round about here. But first
we've got to shoot the things you call demons! Maybe
they're demons, but that don't mean they're like
demons in Hell. Maybe you can kill the buggers. Me
and me bruvs, we saw some magical-like . . . *things,*
stuck in the ground, out on the edge of town. Marking
off the boundary, like. D'you get it? Someone's done
this to us! If it was God who sent us down here, he
wouldn't need to use magical gimmicks! He'd wave
his hand and down we'd go!"

Tombridge only groaned. "Don't deceive yourself!"
But Bosky waited stubbornly, looking steadily at him,
arms crossed, and at last Tombridge gave a long sigh
of resignation. "If you want to go into the chapel, it's
open. There's a baptistery with blessed water in it
still. Fortunately Becky Withers was away for the day
with her husband and baby when we were taken. I
baptized the child and they went from the chapel to
see her mother in Plymouth, so perhaps she was
spared. But the rest of us . . . are damned."

"Probably wasting your time, boy," said Garth,
coming in. "But I'll waste mine too, if you like." He
raised a flashlight. "Even brought us an electric
torch. And in my pocket, a little food—what hasn't
spoiled. Sausages and cheese and bread gone all
cardboard. Come on."

They left the vicar to his weeping and went outside,
both of them glancing up at the distant, misty-murky
ceiling, looking for movement, for the drooping hands
of the demons that had taken Geoff away, Geoff and
quite a number of others. Bosky saw nothing up there
just now. He looked back at the cracked street and

caught a movement across the way, a woman's face in the window of a low redbrick house. Bosky raised a hand in greeting to her, instinctively trying to be encouraging, but she only darted back, pulling the curtain.

"They're all so scared," Bosky said.

"Can't blame them," his granddad said. "Most of them think they're already dead, and judgment's soon to come. And if they're not dead, then what is all this? I'm not yet sure this ain't a dream myself."

"I'm dead certain it ain't a dream, Granddad," Bosky said. "It's a miracle, in a way—an evil one. But it ain't no dream and it ain't Hell. Not yet."

They went into the chapel and found the baptismal. There was a little more color here, in a sickly sort of way, coming from the stained-glass windows, and a green-blue sheen fell over the stone baptismal: a basin carved with baby angels, set on a low dais to one side of the altar.

Bosky set the rifle aside, took out the box of bullets, and opened it.

And then sat back on his haunches. "This is stupid. I don't know what I was thinking . . . It ain't going to bloody work . . ."

"I doubt it works, too, lad," Garth said. "But who knows? Why not try?"

Bosky sensed Granddad was just trying to keep him going with a little harmless encouragement. He shook his head.

But then he rocked back on his heels as the baptismal began to seethe, its waters boiling, sending up a quivering light. A majestic woman's voice, emanating from the font itself, said,

Approach, bring your weapons hither . . .

"Stone me!" Bosky blurted. "Granddad—did you hear that too?"

"I did! And look!" He moved cautiously closer to the baptismal, pointing to the woman's face appearing in the water, like a reflection—when there was no woman there to be reflected. She was a beautiful woman, made of light and ice and bubbling water, manifesting even as the waters quieted . . .

"An angel!" Bosky breathed, impressed.

An angel? The woman's face seemed obscurely amused. **Yes, if you like. The ancients knew me by another name. But I have always given my blessings to those who properly acknowledged me.**

The woman's voice resonated in Bosky's mind in English, and yet he seemed to hear the words echoing indistinctly in other languages, languages he had never heard before but somehow recognized.

"*I* acknowledge you, Missus," Bosky said, "and I'll acknowledge you whenever you like, if you'll help us! You don't seem like no demon, and it's demons who're keeping us here, and culling us out like fat sheep to become mutton—and we've got no wish to be mutton! Anything you can do, it'd be brill!"

Then approach, child, and take the arrows of metal in your hand . . . and lower your hand here, into my bosom . . .

Arrows? Bosky reckoned she meant the bullets. He poured a handful of rifle bullets from the little cardboard box into his palm, came closer to the baptismal and, after a moment's hesitation—afraid she was going to do something wickedly witchy to him when he touched the water—he lowered his hand, bullets and all, into the water.

The font began once more to seethe, and he thought he felt something vibrating between the bullets.

Enough. It is done. The other arrows now . . .

When all the bullets were bathed, and when, as an afterthought, Garth had dipped his pocketknife in the shimmering water, Bosky turned to the baptismal and said, "Lady, are you a saint? The vicar'd be pleased was I to tell him your name! You the Madonna, then? The Virgin Mary?"

He thought for a moment that the beautiful face in the font rolled her eyes. **No, child. I am the queen of all waters. Call me the Lady of Waters. Know that I am here to help you—for your enemy is mine. My power is limited in the depths of his realm, but I can strike at his minions through you, and through the other one I've sent to help you. Look for the man with the sad eyes, the bitter mouth, the long coat, in the dark places, where the Palace of Phosphor shines like dark deeds in the eyes of the Reckoner.**

The water seethed once more and then settled, all at once, as if oil had been poured on it. The baptismal was empty of anything but water and the hint of a perfume, a scent both rank and sweet, a smell of slow green rivers, algaed ponds, brine, and water lilies.

"Well now, could be something will come of all this after all," said Bosky's granddad, leading the way out into the cracked and buckled street. They started toward the nearest edge of town and they were nearly there when Bosky's mother caught up to them.

"Uh-oh," Garth said. "Better let me handle this, lad. Ah, Maureen, my darling-dear, just you wait at home, the boy and I are off; we're going hunting! We will need meat, you know!"

She came puffing up, red-faced from running; a compact little woman, but shapely, with flashing green eyes, wavy shoulder-length auburn hair, a spray of freckles. Her mother, Garth's beloved Aileen, had been Irish: a strange, dreamy woman, afflicted with the second sight, who'd seen her own death a year in advance. "Oh I'm not to run in these shoes and you're making me do it, Da!" Maureen cried. "And you're not to lie to me any longer! Hunting! The vicar told me what you're about, when I'd shaken him enough to get him to stop his blubbering! Hunting demons!"

"That's hunting too, innit, Maureen?" Garth suggested feebly.

"Mum, we're going after Geoff! Those things have taken him and I've had enough of sitting here, waiting for them to squeeze us and see who's right for the meat table!"

"What? You don't know that's what happens to people they take!" She looked nervously at the ceiling, swiping a damp strand of hair out of her eyes. "Oh Da, is all this real?"

Garth shrugged. "I reckon it's real if death is real. I buried more than one who died in the great shaking when we came down."

"Mum, an angel has helped us. She's put a blessing on our weapons!"

"A what?" She looked at him closely.

"A lady who appeared in the baptismal font—she said she was the Lady of Waters!"

"Did she . . ." Her voice matched the softness, the distance in her eyes. "The Lady of Waters?"

Bosky expected her to tell him he was mad, ask if he'd been smoking greens. But she just gave a brisk nod and hugged him, kissing him on the cheek. She drew back and looked at him, smoothing his hair, and said, "The Lady of Waters was better known to people once, and she's always about somewhere. I've heard her singing at times, down by the river. Well then— I'm coming with you and Da too. Anything to keep busy . . . to do something about this."

"No, Mum, I want to think of you being back here, safe—or safer, any gate. Right? Listen, there is something you can do. I was passing the house where those Pakis live—"

"I've told you, you're not to speak of people like that, Boswell!"

"Right, well, they're from *Paki*-stan ain't they? Anyway, the father's gone, the woman has six kids about her, she's half out of her mind—you could talk to her, help her keep the kids busy. See to the other children in town."

She crossed her arms on her chest and looked at him curiously, her head cocked to one side, and a slow smile climbed her full lips. "I don't know when last I heard you speak so much sense before. When things were hard, your father would always rally just like that." Her eyes filled with tears and she bit her lip, glancing at Garth.

Bosky knew what she was thinking: . . . *rally just like that and put the bottle down.*

But he hadn't put it down for good and it had got him in the end anyway. He shrugged. "I just know, Mum, I have to find out what this is about. And maybe . . ."

He turned and looked at the dark wall, pocked with mist-shrouded caves, at the edge of town.

Maybe, if I live long enough, I'll have an adventure.

"Right," Maureen said. She kissed Garth on the cheek, squeezed Bosky's shoulder just once, and turned decisively away, walking slowly back up the street, toward the house where the Pakistani family lived. Bosky watched her go for a few long moments, wondering if he'd ever see her again. "Granddad . . . What did she mean, she's heard the Lady of Waters talking? Is she . . . Is all this too much for her?"

"Oh no, if your mum said she heard the Lady, then she did, right enough. Your mum's own mother was fey, some say."

"Fey? What's that? Like gay? You're saying me Mum's a lesbian?"

"Christ, no. It means they have the sight. And those who're fey got the sight from the world of faerie. From the invisible ones—the fairies, the spirits of the elements, all those. Long ago some intermarried with mortals, they say, and your grandmother, I've always thought, got some of that blood, and passed it on to your mum."

"Fairies! Go on with you, Granddad!"

"Are you going to sneer in that disrespectful way, after what we saw in the chapel?"

Bosky remembered the lady in the font. And all that had happened to the village. And his mother had always had her odd moments, when she seemed to be listening to things other people couldn't hear. "All right, then, me mum's fey. Right: I'm off. If you're coming, come on."

"One thing first, boy."

"What's that?"

"Load the rifle."

Bosky swallowed, then nodded, took out some bullets and loaded the gun.

Then he shouldered his rifle once more, and he and his granddad headed for the darkness at the edge of town.

✦═◈═✦

Sitting in deep darkness, unseen enemies somewhere near at hand, Constantine found himself having to smother laughter. It was the laughter of a man on the teetering edge of madness, certainly, and it would come pealing out of him shrill and giddy if he didn't muffle it, and might get him torn to pieces.

Well here you are, mate, he thought. *You let yourself sink into self-pity, and you followed the path of least resistance, letting an old man con you and a stream of water bully you, and you found your way to where you were heading all along: the pit. You're at home in the pit, after all. What could be better, what could be more perfectly designed? It's the very realization of your viewpoint on life. You were in an internal pit and you found an external one to wallow in. Brilliant!*

He heard the creaking of the pulley, out of his reach in the deep shaft to one side of him, and he thought: *Probably can't get to it. Starve to death here just out of reach of a way out. Your own private dark little crypt thousands of feet underground, the energies of the Hidden World humming in the stone. You chose your own world—your dingy little corner of the Hidden World, John. Truth is, you've always been here. Everything till now was a dream—maybe someone else's. Maybe you were someone's nightmare, mate. And now they've woken up, and you're back down in your hole underneath old Britain, where nightmares go to wait till they're called again.*

He barked a laugh at that, and then clapped his hand over his mouth.

Quiet, you fool. Sod your solipsistic little fantasy— Chas's life's at stake. Maybe a lot more. But Chas is enough—he stood by you a dozen times and more. Find your way out of this fugue, this hole, or she'll make him suffer for eternity. Endlessly drowning.

Christ I want a smoke. But light one and they'll see the light and come crawling to pull you into wiggling pieces.

Come on, John. Either throw yourself headfirst down that shaft or pull yourself together, you tosser.

Constantine sat up on the stone floor, straightening his back and arranging himself in the posture of meditation. He contained his attention, turned it inward, and became aware of his breathing, the beating of his heart, the weight of his body; the present moment, to the sensations of his inner world.

The self-lacerating anger sprang into relief inside

him. He saw it as a thing, like a cobra in a basket, swaying, hissing . . . venomous.

A moment before, he'd *been* that cobra. Seeing it, sensing it, he was outside it; he no longer was the cobra, was no longer identified with the anger. He sustained his state of inner concentration for a while, feeling his energy drain out of anger, out of meaningless tension, back into his inner reservoir of *prana*. When it had built up enough, he extended the field of his psychic attention outward, into the shaft nearby.

Prescience returned an image to him: a double length of chain hung there, swaying slightly. It began to move, one of the chains clinking and rising, the other descending, as something was lowered into the shaft.

On a platform attached to one of the chains was a bundled figure—a human being, a male, hands tied behind him. Someone young, Constantine thought. He was still a bit above.

"Hey, you on the platform!" Constantine called out, in a carrying whisper. "If you get to the bottom of that shaft you'll be done for! Push on the chain, get it swinging toward me!"

"Who the bleedin'—?" A boyish voice.

"Just shut up and do it, you git! Quick! Rock the thing back and forth!" But then what? Constantine moved to the edge of the shaft, felt along the rough edge of the diamond-shaped hole in the wall, and found a spur of stone sticking out, partway down. That might do . . .

The youth was swinging the platform near now, and he was almost level with the hole in the wall.

Constantine was losing his prescient image of him, but he could hear the chain's swishing, clinking near, and in the faint light from above he could make out a shape swinging against the darker background of the shaft. Holding on to the stone edge of the hole in the wall, Constantine leaned out and swiped his arm through the air. His fingers slapped into the thick chain links, and he grabbed and pulled the chain toward him, grimacing with pain from the weight. "You can just see me, kid! Jump for the floor here, to my right!"

The kid jumped, stumbled, and started to fall back into the shaft. Bracing, Constantine let go of the chain and pulled the youth close. The boy got his footing as the chain swung like a pendulum across the shaft, then back toward them. Constantine once more grabbed it, and this time he pulled with all his might, drawing it closer, and, grunting, managed to wind it around the spur of stone on the broken edge of the hole. The chain continued to lower, rattling around the spur and back down the shaft. "Turn around, boy, let me get at your bonds."

The teen mutely did as he was told and Constantine found what felt like copper wires twisted around his slender wrists. A few experimental twists . . .

"Oh, you're pinching! The other way!"

"Stop whingeing, boy!" Constantine twisted the wire the other way and got it loose.

"Right, now we've got to figure out how to get up this thing."

"Who *are* you?"

"My name's John."

"Well I'm Geoff, but 'my name's John' doesn't explain much—"

"Just help me pull in the platform. It's going back up."

"I don't want to go back up! There's *things* up there!"

"There's worse down here! Come on!"

Constantine and Geoff pulled the little platform close and when it started back up again they climbed onto it, swinging out into the open shaft, holding on to the chain, nearly losing their grip but clinging desperately. It swung sickeningly back and forth, clacking on the walls of the shaft, and then steadied, beginning to carry them slowly upward.

"You don't get it," Geoff said. "There's things going to be waiting up there. When we get there, they'll do something bad to us—something real bad."

"Right. But maybe when you get high enough there's some other place to get off. The gripplers unload it at the bottom and we're some distance above them. The others won't be looking for visitors from below."

The platform was cranked up a long, inestimable way, before the light began to increase, and it grew only slightly, with a thin ray of blue-white sharing a hole in the shaft's ceiling with the chains. There was just room for the platform to fit through the hole . . .

"Look!" the boy said, pointing. There was a rusty, old, wrought-iron maintenance catwalk running across the shaft close below the ceiling. They jumped onto it, Geoff first. It creaked but held, and they crept across to a shelf along the edge on the left side, under a great slowly turning gear of rusty iron.

"Feel like a bloody mouse in a grandfather clock," Constantine muttered, lighting a Silk Cut and sitting under the big, slowly grinding gear. He needed a breather. He sat there, looking at Geoff and smoking, waiting for his heart to stop its pounding. Geoff had a mousy face, so it seemed to Constantine—or maybe it was the clock effect. He was about sixteen, and wore wire-rim glasses and the sloppy, oversized clothes teenagers affected now. Geoff sat beside him and put his hand out for a cigarette. "You're too bloody young to smoke." But Constantine lit another and gave it to him. This boy and he had saved each other's lives after all, so it wouldn't do to be poncey now. "Don't be asking for a fag every two minutes. Or even every two hours." His eyes adjusted and he could see that the iron teeth of the gear overhead interlocked with a larger gear half hidden in the shadows above. "A great bloody clock—or maybe a silent movie. *Metropolis*. Still, it's a relief to have a little light. I was giving myself a headache, seeing things without me eyes."

"How'd you see without your eyes? Like—psychically? I was wondering how you'd seen me."

"Yeah," Constantine said, shrugging. "That's more or less it."

"So you're some kind of psychic magician, then?"

"That's the dead best definition I've heard of me in a while. It beats 'sodding bastard'—what I usually get. The gripplers pull you out of that village Old Duff told me about, did they?"

"Yeah, they—oy, you know Old Duff! He's trying to get help for us?"

"I'm afraid I'm all the cavalry you can count on, mate. And I've come without so much as a horse."

"I'm sorry I made fun of Old Duff," Geoff said, tapping his cigarette ash off onto the stone. "He tried to warn us."

"The old geezer practically begs to be made fun of. Some may doubt it could be true, but I believe he drinks more than me."

"We shouldn't stay here. They'll figure it out soon enough."

Constantine nodded and got up. "Whoever does maintenance on this machinery will be along in time. That gear's been greased not long ago, right enough. Come on, mate."

They followed the shelf around a big column that stood parallel to the shaft they'd come up. The column creaked and rumbled with the turning of the gigantic hidden axle inside it. It was rotated, Constantine figured, by the crusted half-men, like the late Arfur, turning cranks in the eternally dark chamber far below. As they came around to the far side of the column from the down-shaft, the light grew, and Constantine thought he smelled something he'd given up hope of smelling again any time soon: food cooking. His stomach rumbled in response.

"You smell that?" Geoff whispered.

"Aye. Careful now—" They went on tiptoes, padding around the column—it was perhaps twenty yards in diameter—to an open space beyond. They peered around the curve of the column to see a gigantic man using a big silvery ladle to stir a four-foot-high cooking pot set into a glowing recess in the floor. As he stirred he rumbled a tune to himself, singing in some gutteral language Constantine had never heard.

"Stone me—look at the size of him!" Geoff whispered excitedly. "Must be close to eight feet high!" He was all of that, and barrel-chested and wide-shouldered too.

The stranger had a star-shaped mane of hair and beard; his hair stuck out in three distinct gray-white spikes above and to the sides of his head; his beard was double-spiked below. It was the shape of a pentagram perhaps, or even a flower, but this, Constantine thought, was one ugly blossom. The great round face was blackened with soot, creased like old saddle leather, the nose stubby, the cheeks pitted, the small flinty eyes set deep in the sockets of the heavy-browed skull, his mouth a wide slash showing teeth worn to nubs. His hands were also blackened, and he wore a long tattered sleeveless robe, dark with grime. The biceps on his exposed arms were as big around as Constantine's head. The boots on his shovel-sized feet were tied-up wrappings of what might be human skin.

But what caught Constantine's notice was the silvery, adamantine chain, with links big as his hand, crisscrossing the man's chest and then running to a hole in the stone wall behind him.

Reassured that the enormous man was on a short leash, Constantine stepped into view. "That the usual human flesh stew that's so popular round here, squire?"

he asked. He wasn't going to sink that low. No, never. Well . . . Not this side of two weeks in a lifeboat.

The big man looked up at him, slightly startled, but with steady eyes that seemed to brim with experience, an experience stretching back ages.

"It is not human flesh!" The giant seemed insulted. "You are not gripplers, nor Administrators—you have the look of escaped food for the mushroom men!" the big man rumbled. He had a curious accent to his English—clearly not his first language—perhaps tinged with something like Danish inflections. "As for the stew, I am boiling some very fine plump cave rats, and my own garden mushrooms, and very nutritious they are too. Occasionally we have a fine fat sheep down here, brought from the surface, when the gripplers do their task as they should. But they are sluggish creatures, without much enterprise, and they have been remiss, so cave rats will have to do today. So you are hungry, are you? Then step forward and eat. Here is the ladle."

He laid the ladle across the pot, which was about four feet high, and stepped back.

Constantine looked closely at the chain and decided that it only just reached the pot; if he was careful he could get close enough to eat without getting in reach. He edged close to the pot. He had to get sustenance in him—he could only draw so much energy for living from the psychic world. And physical energy was the raw material of magical energy.

He stopped a stride before the pot, hesitated a long moment, then leaned forward, grabbed the ladle—

The giant was on him with remarkable speed for his size, his big hands closing around Constantine's neck, lifting him off his feet. The chained giant smelled of primeval sweat and musk. "Ha!" said the big man triumphantly. "The chain on me extends from the hole in the wall a good long ways so I can do the maintenance here—it's on a spindle, you see. Now let us find out what comes out when I squeeze your neck hard enough . . ."

His windpipe all but shut, Constantine barely managed to squeak out, "About them chains, squire—like to have them off? I know a spell for that! I can help you, friend; I can set you free!"

The big man—the *inordinately* big man—stared into Constantine's eyes, and then let go of his neck, letting him fall to the floor. The giant gazed balefully down at him.

"My name," the giant rumbled, "is Balf Corunsiggert Stonecracker of the Icy Black Unseen River Which Seeks the North Sea."

Constantine, getting up and gasping for breath, nodded. "If it's all the same to you, squire, I'll call you Balf."

"What is your name?"

Constantine hesitated. His reputation wasn't sparkling-immaculate in every corner of the magical world, and this was clearly a magical being. But looking into Balf's eyes he decided dishonesty would be a lethal mistake. "My name's John, squire—John Constantine."

"John Constantine? The one who's both young and old? The one who was once the beloved of N'Hept and remains the enemy of Nergal?"

"The same, mate."

"I have heard the stone spirits speak of you. Some speak with disdain, some with amusement, some with admiration. But they did not speak of your truthfulness. Do not move. I will examine your verity, yes?"

With that, Balf reached into a pocket of his robe, took out two large irregular chunks of crystalline stone. He took one stone in each hand and clapped them, fairly hard but not bone-crackingly, against the sides of Constantine's head.

Constantine yelped. "Oy! No more of that, mate, please!"

The stones were humming, ringing, resonating like tuning forks from their contact with Constantine's skull—his skull was doing its own ringing, just then—and Balf lifted them to his pointed, tufted ears and listened, first to one stone, and then the other.

"Ummmm . . . it sounds as if . . . you are not false. You may be able to release me from the chains, and it seems you are willing to do so. And you are not a servant of my enemies. Very well . . . Have some stew."

6

THAT'S WHAT I CALL ALTERNATIVE ENERGY, EH?

Bosky and Garth had been climbing up through the warren of caves for an hour and a half before they came to a cross-tunnel that led to an opening high up, looking out onto the great cavern that had swallowed up the village of Tonsell-on-the-Stream. It was all there below them, the whole village except Smithson Manor, though some of the village buildings were crumpled; a few of the taller structures were tilted, making Bosky think of that tower in Pisa.

Their ledge was still a good hundred yards below the ceiling of the cavern. Bosky squinted up at the overarching stone that had taken the place of the sky, trying to see into the crack in the cavern ceiling, a black crevice zigzagging between the glowing blue stalactites. He could just glimpse cave openings up there, and a gray shape that seemed to quiver, gelatin-like, as he watched, before settling back again.

Isn't very likely Geoff is alive, he thought. *But I'd want someone to look for me, even if I was likely dead. If nobody looks for you when you've gone missing, what are you?*

He looked back down at the village. A mist hung over the rooftops and strangely large birds flapped around the crooked steeple of St. Leonard's. One of them alit on the top of it and folded its wings.

Birds? Would birds have come down with the village? Not bloody likely. Then what were those things? "You see those things, Granddad? What do you make of them?"

"They look like vultures, but bigger. Like condors. But . . . those aren't feathers on them, exactly. Look like flying people to me—except for the lower half of 'em."

"They weren't around the village before we set out, Granddad. Someone brought us here for their own reasons. They got to be watching us. Maybe when we left the village, our going was noticed, yeah? And those buggers were sent to keep the others from leaving!"

The old man nodded. "You could well be right, Bosky."

They stepped closer to the edge of the precipice and the movement attracted the attention of one of the flyers soaring near the ceiling. It started toward them, weaving its way between several phosphorescent stalactites. Bosky stared in fascination as it approached. It was an old woman with wings, he thought at first—but that was only partly right. As it came nearer, its featherless, leathery wings beating

with the rhythm of a raptor on the hunt, he saw that
while its taut gray-black upper body was like a lean
old woman's, its legs were like those of an eagle, but
bigger, with scales instead of feathers, and the lipless
mouth in its cruelly-human face—its eyes were without whites, black as coal—was baring snaggly fangs;
its talons were larger than a big man's hands, talons
getting closer and closer, opening—

"Bosky!" Granddad Garth yelled, shoving him
aside.

The creature screeched in furious frustration,
talons raking the air where Bosky had stood a moment before as it arced away, having to push off
from the face of the cliff. It did an aerial somersault,
turned, and came back at them, while Bosky was
still getting up, bringing his rifle to bear. Before his
fatal accident his father had taken him shooting at a
range, seven or eight times, and he'd gotten fairly
competent with a rifle. It was already loaded, and as
the creature dived at them with a blood-icing
scream—its wings outspread, its arms clutching in
front of it, its legs forward, talons slashing—Bosky
flipped off the safety with his thumb and fired almost point-blank, the butt recoiling painfully into
his shoulder.

The flyer's scream this time spoke of pain, as the
bullet caught it between its flattened breasts, shat-
tering its sternum, smashing up to emerge, jetting
gore, from the back of its neck. The impact of the
bullet knocked it back from the ledge and it plum-
meted, falling end over end to the stony ground at
the base of the cliff outside the village.

"Good shot, Bosky!"

"Ow, I forgot what a kick this thing has—Oh, shite, here come the other ones!"

A flock of the creatures was now screaming and flapping toward them, spreading out to make it harder to hit them. "Come on, Boswell—back in the tunnel! We'll bottleneck the bitches!"

They backed into the cave, reluctant to turn their backs on the ledge, and moments later the creatures began to land out there, their talons clicking on the stone, hissing to one another, one of them calling screechingly out:

Paradido Anthropinos!

Bosky reloaded the bolt-action rifle, popped it to his shoulder, braced himself, and fired at the two creatures who were starting one after the other into the tunnel; they could only come one at a time because of their wingspread. Two of them, just thirty feet away, went down with a single bullet, flapping in their death throes, and the others scattered from the ledge, intimidated, at least for now. Gunsmoke made Bosky and Garth cough and they backed up, rifle at ready. The vulturish creatures could be glimpsed at the end of the tunnel, like something seen in the objective of a telescope, circling and diving past the ledge, but no more tried to enter.

"That's holding them for a while," Granddad said, as they started back down the tunnel. "Vicious brutes."

"What the hell were they?"

"Some kind of harpy, I expect. I've seen them in old books. Magical creatures. I doubt an ordinary weapon would do them harm. You did well to get the Lady of Waters to bless them bullets."

A short distance past the tunnel crossroads, deeper into the stone that enclosed their village's cavern, the tunnel widened out to a roughly square-edged chamber of granite which rose vertically into blackness, broken here and there with horizontal shafts of dull blue light. A stone stairway zigzagged up the farther wall. Around the base of the stairway were piles of loose rock that looked freshly chipped away. The rough stone steps that were cut into the wall seemed of recent manufacture.

"This stairway, Granddad—it looks like it was cut recently."

"Could be that they'd prepared the big cave for Tonsell. They cut some steps in for their own use because they knew we'd be coming down. Look, there's another door, over there, with steps going down—to where I wonder?"

"I don't know. I'm going up. That's where they took Geoff."

Granddad sighed but assented and they began to climb. A good long climb, and Bosky was sweating, his legs aching, and Granddad was wheezing, but at last they came to a landing that followed the edges of the shaft, going to a tunnel on the far side that Bosky estimated was about level with the crack Geoff had been pulled into.

They went cautiously along the wall, afraid to look down, and entered the tunnel. The sound of trickling water drew them—a thin underground spring ran through a fissure in the wall, to one side. Here they sat down and ate a quick meal of the supplies Garth had brought, washing it down with the spring water, which tasted heavily of minerals. Garth began to doze, sitting up and nodding, before they'd quite finished, and Bosky had to shake him. "Come on, Granddad, wake up—we've got to find out what became of Geoff."

"Right, I was just closing my eyes for a mo'. We're off."

They traveled onward through the tunnel, the walls dimly lit by the same phosphorescence that provided illumination everywhere in this underground realm. A quarter mile of winding tunnel on, and then Bosky, out ahead, came back with a finger to his lips for quiet, and led his granddad back up the tunnel to where it met the crack in the ceiling over the village.

Up ahead, great bulky gray things humped along in the shadows.

⤖⊙⟞⊶

"You know, cave rat's not half bad, stewed," Constantine remarked, putting down his bowl and wiping his mouth.

He and Geoff were sitting against a stone wall near a litter of iron tools, wooden blocks, chunks of stone, wedges of some shiny unidentified metal that Balf used in his toil, and stone jugs of grease for oiling cogs. Still festooned in chains, Balf hunkered near the cauldron, which sat in a basin of crystal in the floor, the crystal glowing from an unknown energy source, providing heat and most of the light. In a stone recess across from them was a bed of moss and sand covered with tanned skins. A few more urns stood beside the bed.

"You got anything to drink back there, mate?" Constantine asked.

"Only water," Balf said.

"Oh. Well. I'll have some of that . . . later." Constantine studied the chains crisscrossing Balf's body, constraining him to the adamantine leash of the King Underneath. "Those chains are enchanted, are they?"

"I would break them easily, were they not. The metals of the earth are like clay to me; I am a son of the earth spirits, the last of my kind, so far as I know."

"Are you now. You wouldn't be one of the Azki-Hak?"

"I am! Perhaps the only one still living."

"There may be others. I have heard stories . . . They're often mistaken for 'abominable snowmen' and such."

"What are Azki-Hak?" Geoff asked, picking suspiciously at his stew.

"According to Scofield's *Grimoire of the Underlands,* they're bred from earth elementals and Neanderthals. In old times, they called them trolls."

Geoff's head snapped up, and his eyes widened. "What?" He looked at Balf, who was close enough to easily reach him. "He's a . . . ?" And Geoff shrank back against the wall.

Balf sighed and shook his head. "Many are the wicked stories told about my people. Calumnies they are, and lies! For the most part."

Constantine smiled. "For the most part?"

"There were a few . . . rogues," Balf admitted. "An Azki-Hak—what you call a troll—would suffer from a toothache and run mad, now and again, slay a few dozen humans. Or he foolishly drank the human's vinous brew—such drinks corrupt his soul!—and he became violent under its influence. He may also fall under the malign authority of a demon, whereupon he may indulge in the eating of human flesh and the occasional destruction of some unimportant small town . . . here and there."

"Quite understandable, when you consider the circumstances, really," Constantine allowed.

"Myself, I am enslaved by a malevolent human—if human he still is—but I have done no evil I was not compelled to do. To roam free in the caves of the great mother, that is all a true Azki-Hak wants."

"Then it looks like trolls have gotten a bad rap, squire," Constantine said. "Got any writing materials?"

"For the freeing spell?" asked Balf, suddenly eager.

"I hope so, squire; these surroundings ain't the best for me magic. I'm more of a tatty hotel room or abandoned junkyard sort of magician. But maybe this one'll work, because the spirits I'll summon are from the dark places of the world, and those're right handy to us here."

"Good!" Balf said. "I have something that may serve!"

He went to his rubble pile and fished out a large fragment of mineral chalk. Constantine used the chalk to draw a magic circle around Balf, and then wrote the words *ADSERTORIS LIBERTAS* over and over around the circle. He asked, rather hesitantly, for a few drops of Balf's blood but the troll was happy to comply. Balf put his own wrist in his mouth and bit down hard with one of his remaining fangs— blood spurted, trickled heavily from his lips. He grabbed one of Constantine's hands and spat a mouthful of blood into his palm.

"Ah," Constantine said, grimacing. "Thanks."

Geoff watched skeptically as Constantine dripped the blood into the center of the circle around Balf's feet, muttering certain words of power as he did so. Then he laid his hands on the chains and shouted, *"Adsertoris! Libertas!"*

The chains vibrated . . . and then hung limp, not visibly different than before.

"Didn't work, did it, mate!" Geoff said. "These things never do. Superstition, really."

"That right, Geoff?" said Constantine, stepping out of the circle. "Then how'd you and your little township end up down here, eh?"

"Well . . ."

"And what kind of creature snatched you up? You think them things are natural?"

"Oh well, if you want to be technical . . ."

The troll, meanwhile, was straining at his chains, holding a length of it in his two beefy hands, growling to himself.

And then the chain snapped with a *crack*. "Ha!" roared Balf. "It worked—the spell of protection is lifted!" A few moments more and he was entirely free. There were marks on his skin where the chain had abraded and scarred him over the years. "You see

what they have done to me! Five centuries and more
have I endured these chains! I will make them pay for
that delay in my plans!"

"Five centuries!" Geoff exclaimed. "How old are
you?"

Balf shrugged, a movement like the quaking of
hills over centuries. "The mother has circled the
great shining god that men call Sol three thousand
times and seven, since I came into the world!"

"The shining god that men call . . . You mean the
sun? Three thousand . . . You're more than three
thousand years old!"

"Why that appalled look on your face, boy—you
make me feel old! Others of my kind have lived far
longer. I am but a stripling. We can live twelve thousand revolutions of Sol and more!" He kicked happily
at the discarded chains, flinging them clankingly
away. "And now I will more truly live! And I will take
revenge on the King of this place!"

"I'm on a mission to bring the bastard down meself," Constantine said, lighting a cigarette. "But best
we approach the job circumspectly, like." He blew a
thoughtful plume of smoke at the ceiling. "He's got
the gripplers, and he must have another gang of bul-
lies too . . ."

"He has a small army of men!" Balf asserted. "They
are pale, strange, inbred men, but they can fight! He
keeps them in fighting shape by pitting their legions
one against another in his coliseum! And the harpies!
He found them dozing in the crypts beneath the
sunken city your people call Atlantis, deep underneath the sea. He woke them, enslaved them to his

will, and brought them by cave-ways to this place! A hundred of them serve him!"

"Harpies," Geoff muttered, wryly. "Trolls. I'm going to have a word with my biology teacher when I get back. He never mentioned those species."

"Where'd the King get this army, then?" Constantine asked.

Balf scratched at his groin thoughtfully. "Iain Culley, the one some call the Gloomlord, found his way here through some magical means; it is said he used the power of a great elemental to bring him to the Underlands. Above, he was thought a heretic, and believed they'd burn him if he stayed. Here he found a people to overpower: an old Roman settlement, sunk down in a great upheaval of the mother's skin long, long ago. There were survivors of that quaking in this corner of the Underland, whom we call the Fallen Romans. These he enslaved with his magic, and his control over the harpies and the gripplers. He designed his palace to be like those he saw somewhere in the surface world, and he made the Fallen Romans build it."

"And he makes you keep his machine in good repair?"

"He did—there were others too, but they are dead now. They lost heart and refused to eat. I am the only surviving Azki in this place."

"You talk about revenge," Geoff put in, "But it sounds risky, mate. I mean, you're big, but if he has an army . . ."

"Enough men could destroy me, it's true," Balf admitted grudgingly. "Two or three score might suc-

ceed in destroying me. A score of harpies might be
enough to kill me, perhaps. Fewer if they catch me
napping."

"What's this machinery all about, Balf?" Geoff
asked, pointing at the curved wall behind them. It
rumbled endlessly with the torquing of the enormous axle rising from the deep darkness below.

"Why, that is the power that drives the engines of
the Palace of Phosphor, and the metropolis the King
Underneath calls Danque. But more importantly, it
provides the energies which are drawn into the loom
of life with which the King reanimates himself upon
awakening each day—for the King has arranged a se-
quence of day and night in his realm. Without this re-
animation, human mortality will return to him and
quickly. Immortality which is stolen, and neither natural nor earned, comes at great cost. The cost is great
power and the suffering of thousands, all for the life
of one man. I have brooded over this for centuries."

"What do they use to power the machine down
below?" Geoff asked.

"They use *you,* Geoff," Constantine said. "Or they
would have. They use hapless blokes like you. If I
hadn't pulled you out of there, they'd have fed you to
a grippler, then put you to work. If you'd shirked, or
complained, you'd have become food."

"Fed me to a grippler—and then put me to work?
Makes no sense."

"You don't want to know, mate. The grippler
doesn't eat you, it works some kind of mold into you,
to change you into a meat machine, like, that turns
the wheels, works for centuries, and loses all track of

time . . . stops caring about anything but his next meal. If he's not the next meal himself, that is."

"But they're deep underground; you'd think they could use geothermal energy, you know, instead of turning bloody wheels for chris'sakes . . ."

"I do not know this gee-oh-ther-mall," Balf said, "but the power of the machine must come from human beings, subjected to suffering, complying mindlessly. This is the alchemy of King Culley; it is part of the magic. The formula requires the slow wasting of human souls, and this gives satisfaction to the demons who eke out the force by which the Gloomlord lives. The power draws on the strength of lightning—"

"It's electrical?" Geoff asked.

"If that is what lightning is, then yes. But that is not enough. It must be fused with the sacrifice of the mindless, toiling in darkness."

"That's what I call alternative energy, eh?" Constantine commented. He drew deeply on his cigarette, so it burned quickly to the butt, and stubbed it out on the floor, adding musingly, "The sacrifice of the mindless, toiling in the darkness. Really is like our own economy back 'ome." Scratching his stubbly cheek, Constantine turned to Balf. "You hear something about the King Underneath having a plan to poison the ocean?"

"The ocean? We are far from there. I know nothing of such a plan. But I have not been away from the machine for many years. They tell me nothing."

"John," Geoff said, "we should be off, shouldn't we? Won't the gripplers come looking for us?"

"Right enough they will, boy. But there are things we need to find out. Balf, old sport, who *is* this Gloomlord geezer exactly? I mean, originally. You said his name was Culley?"

"Iain Culley—a man who was born back more than four hundred turns around Sol. He was a student long ago, of another mortal named Fludd . . . this is all I know, though he became an alchemist, and a magician, who fled to the Underlands to escape the persecution of his fellows, and used his power to make himself mighty."

"Flood, you say . . . Hang on—*Fludd?* Not Robert Fludd? The Renaissance alchemist?"

"This word, Renn-ay-sonz I have not heard, but perhaps this Fludd is the same man."

"Blimey—that opens some doors."

"John!" Geoff said urgently. "We'd best hurry out of here!"

"Right. Balf, old chap, what else can you show me of this great huge machine of yours?"

"Much! Come with me . . . We must ascend."

Geoff looked at him with renewed interest. "Ascend? As in *to the surface?* As in get the hell out of these bloody caves?"

"I cannot take you there, not yet. Our ascent will only be to the next level of this machine. This way! Ten paces and around this corner, a passage opens!"

⤛═◎═⤜

"Granddad, they're pulling someone else up from the village!"

"So they are, Boswell. Oh, God forgive them—it's the vicar!"

They watched in horror as Tombridge, dangling by an ankle a hundred feet below the crack in the ceiling, was pulled up from the village, alternating between wailing and hysterically praying as he came.

Bosky and Garth were flattened on a crag at one end of the crack in the ceiling of the huge cavern that had swallowed up the village. They had crawled up to the crag to where they could see but still be out of sight of the demonic creatures that undulated humpingly along like gigantic, gray, eyeless sea-elephants farther along the shelves, at the top of the zigzagging crevice. One of them was unnervingly close, on a shelf of rock about a hundred feet away. It was occupied just now in sending its long sinuous feelers, with four-fingered hands on the ends, into holes in the rock behind it.

The grippler—as the stranger at the barrow had called them—lifted the vicar to its wide, oozing slash of a mouth.

"Oh my sweet lord, it's going to eat him!" Garth gasped.

Vicar Tombridge did indeed vanish into the big lipless maw of the grippler and it seemed to chew. Bosky had to look away, stomach lurching. Should he try to shoot the thing? But surely it was too late to save the vicar now, and he wasn't such a good shot he could be sure of hitting even so big a thing as the blob-like demon from here. And a gunshot would alert the creatures to him and Granddad. Already he was worried, seeing the harpies circling back and forth between their crack and the village. If one of them should notice Bosky and his granddad up here, they'd attack—and with the tentacular demons to worry about, too, the odds didn't seem good.

"Cor and blimey, it's letting him out!" Garth said, jabbing Bosky with an elbow.

It was true—the grippler was pulling the vicar out like a man pulling a bone from his mouth, only in this case the meat hadn't been stripped away, only the vicar's clothing, which the beast seemed to chew thoughtfully, like chewing tobacco, as the still-living Tombridge was set onto a path above the crack nearby. He stood there, swaying, covered with a gray slime. Then he began walking listlessly toward the edge, apparently planning to throw himself off. But that's when one of the harpies flew up and snatched him from the rock, carrying him with its talons on his upper arms toward a tunnel at the other side of the cavern.

"You see that, Granddad? The harpy's taking him to the tunnel, over there! There's a ledge like the one where we got in the fight with them!"

"And . . . and what do you reckon that means, Bosky?" Garth asked, worriedly.

"Just that we've got to go there!"

Garth sighed. "I was afraid you'd say that."

"That's where they must have taken Geoff! And look, there's places to clamber along over the shelves with those blobby devils on them! We can pass above them and get to the far side of the crack! Then we'll look for a passage to wherever Geoff is . . ."

"Bosky, my dear lad, has it not occurred to you that your friend is certainly dead?"

"The vicar's still alive, ain't he? You could see him kicking as that harpy bitch carried him off. Maybe they're basting them to eat later, I don't know. But I've got to find out!"

Garth allowed himself only one more weary sigh. "Very well. But let's us be quiet as ever we can be."

They got up, Bosky being careful not to knock the rifle against stone, afraid of the sound it would make. They traversed the irregular path above the shelves at the bottom of the crack, edging carefully along, fearful that they might dislodge a pebble onto one of the demons. They were partly hidden by the mist that clung up here and by the dimness within the crack, set back from the cavern's phosphorescent illumination.

Toiling carefully along, having to climb as much as walk, it seemed to take forever; but at last they had gotten nearly to the tunnel at the other side of the ceiling over the cavern, and were within fifteen paces of entering it . . .

. . . when Bosky felt an inexorable grip fasten around his ankle. He looked back to reproach Granddad, who he supposed was trying to help him climb and was holding him back more than helping. Only it wasn't Granddad grabbing his ankle, it was the gray hand of a grippler, its long, long arm stretching back to the humped body on the shelf below. It pulled Bosky off his feet, hard onto his belly, the stone knocking the rifle from his grip. It clattered, rolled, and stuck between two boulders nearby.

Granddad was fishing in his pocket, cursing himself in a mutter, "Goddamn you, Garth, you old fool, find it!"

"Granddad! Get the rifle!" But by the time Garth climbed down to the rifle it would be too late. The demon was dragging him faster now—soon he would fall off the crag and onto the shelf, to be sucked into the grippler's drooling mouth. He held on to a boulder, tried to pull free from the grippler, and for a full second he managed to hold on, and the arm quivered, as if frustrated. Then it gave a heave and Bosky was pulled loose from his hold, his palms scraping on the stone.

"Granddad!"

Garth was there, crouching on a flat rock beside the grippler's arm, opening the pocketknife he'd brought along, the blade the Lady of Waters had blessed, even as another hand from the same grippler was rising like the head of a sea serpent to poise over him, fingers opening like the serpent's jaws . . .

"Granddad look out, it's right over you!" Bosky yelled as he was dragged closer to the edge of the precipice.

Garth was sawing at the arm now, and the blade, shimmering with enchantment, was cutting through it, releasing the mercury-like ooze that passed for the grippler's blood.

Then the arm parted with a twang and Bosky jumped up, kicking the loosening hand away, and climbed hastily to the rifle. It took about thirty seconds to reach it and when he pulled it from the crevice and turned he saw Garth straining against the grippler's other hand, trying to cut at the arm, but the thing's wrist was behind his neck and he couldn't quite reach it.

"Bosky . . . run!" Garth rasped. "Just run!"

Bosky fitted the rifle butt into the hollow of his shoulder, aimed down at the grippler's body, and fired. The bullet went home, and the gelatinous creature contracted away from the wound, wriggling and twitching, hissing to itself, as Bosky cocked the rifle and fired again.

"Let go!" he shouted. "Or you'll get a third one!"

It seemed to understand the threat in his voice if not the words and it let go of Granddad's neck. Garth fell forward over a rock, wheezing for air.

The injured grippler was compressing, squeezing within itself, getting smaller and smaller, oozing a blue smoke from its wounds . . . before exploding like a fungal pod, leaving only tatters and two long, limp arms.

But the other gripplers were aware of them now, stretching their feelers out toward Bosky and Garth, and the harpies were beating their wings at the air, climbing to get at them, screaming as they came.

"Come on, boy!" Garth rasped.

Bosky chambered another round and fired from about thirty feet away at a harpy. The bullet caught the harpy in the breast and it shrieked hideously, its eyes revealing, for a split second, the terrible knowledge of its approaching death, and Bosky felt a regret, reflecting that he was killing a creature that was older than civilization, a creature from the times of ancient heroes—a being which, perhaps, had laid eyes on the likes of Jason and Ulysses. For Bosky now believed those men had existed. He was ready to believe a great many things he'd scoffed at before.

The harpy tumbled away and Bosky turned and followed Garth up onto the thin, wending path. A few steps more and they jumped down onto a flat ledge that led to the opening of a tunnel into the wall of the greater cavern. They dashed inside, with another grippler's fingers probing at the stone where they'd stood moments before.

⋆⋅◦═◦⋅⋆

"My hair's standing on end," Geoff said.

"No need to be scared," Constantine said. Adding lightly, "Except, of course, of almost every bloody thing down here."

"I'm not scared; it's literally standing on end."

Constantine realized his hair was standing up too, even more than usual. "I see what you mean, Geoff; my hair's all at attention as well. You're looking like a bloody 1980s rock star, your hair like that."

They were feeling the powerful electrical field given off by the arcs of lightning between the curiously warped electrodes, five of them, just where the points of a pentagram would be—a pentagram three hundred feet in diameter—around the gigantic central column of the torquing shaft that emerged into the chamber from far below. Eventually the same axle connected, far below, to the cranks that were turned by the crankers like the late Arfur, trapped forever in the bottommost chamber of the Sunless Realm.

Geoff, Balf, and Constantine—Balf looming over both of them—stood on a leather-covered iron balcony high up on a wall overlooking the "alchemical transfusion chamber," as Balf called it: a bubble-shaped separate cavern above Balf's domicile. The silver-coated struts that ran to the electrodes from the central shaft whipped around and around, turning between each crackling, eye-searing discharge of purple lightning. Crackle, roar—and then the five struts, like vanes on an umbrella, would spin each to the next electrode. Crackle, roar—spin. The whole construction was about two hundred fifty feet high and one hundred fifty across. Now and then Constantine seemed to glimpse big lumbering spectral figures in the darkness between the electrodes.

"There's power in the air here, Balf," Constantine observed. "If this is the source of the King's power, why don't we just pop in there and, I don't know, fling a wrench in the works? We could have this whole expedition over, bob's your uncle, in no time and I'm out of this hell hole and looking for a likely pub."

"You do not see the guardian demons? The Il-Sorgs are there. Look close, when the lightning flashes, and you may glimpse them."

"Oh. Them? The big chaps with the tusks? They don't look so tough; you could take them."

"I'm afraid I could not, as you say, 'take them.'"

Constantine looked closer. Then he nodded. Difficult to make out what they looked like—creatures thirty feet high, made of some astral material; they were bipeds, with great up-curving tusks, resembling the guardian demons seen on temples in the Far East. It was hard to get an astrotaxological fix on them, for they flickered in and out of visibility and

for the most part weren't visible at all. But that
didn't mean they weren't dangerous.

"Right. They look like what my American friends
would call major assholes. But isn't there a way to
get past the bastards?"

"This machine provides the kind the energy that
sustains him, and gives him magical vitality, but the
source of his sorcerous control over the kingdom is
said to be elsewhere. In a certain chamber in the
palace, locked away, there resides a powerful being,
trapped, whose magic the King uses to give him
power over the gripplers and the harpies. Were that
being released, the Il-Sorg would be released in turn,
and the machine could be stopped. With the machine
stopped, the King's power would diminish, his vitality
draining . . . and his minions would scatter."

Constantine snorted in disgust. "Never simple, is
it? Just once I'd like to shoot some bastard in the
head or throw one fucking switch and get it all over
with. Well let's do this right. A botch job won't do.
And MacCrawley's involved somehow; got to get him
out of the way. Right. Here's the plan, then, Balf, if
you're of a mind to trust me . . ."

They spoke for a good ten minutes, and then Balf
escorted Geoff and Constantine to a staircase that
angled upward along the wall of a great high-
ceilinged gallery. Balf led the way, taking three steps
for each one of theirs, waiting patiently on the topmost landing—he had learned patience over half a
millennium—till they at last arrived, puffing, at a
height Constantine estimated to be some three hundred yards above the floor. Here stood two towering

doors, each made of bands of iron framing blocks of black stone. The portal was about eighty feet high, the doors weighing countless tons, their stone panels figured with threatening images of harpies, trolls, and skull-faced soldiers, above which was emblazoned the head of a cadaverous man wearing a five-pointed crown.

"It is well I am here," Balf said. "For you would never be able to open these doors alone."

Balf reached into a pocket of his robe, took out the crystals he had used earlier, and tapped them on the door in carefully selected spots. The crystals vibrated, and a fulsome clicking came responsively from within the metal portals. "It is done: they are unlocked. I will push them open and retreat below. You know how to call me." So saying, he passed Constantine two of the crystals, which the magician put in his trench coat pocket.

Balf set himself and slowly heaved the great doors open. Then he hastily retreated down the stairs.

The doors continued to swing inward after he'd already gone, creaking vastly as they went, with a sound like a god tearing a moon of metal into pieces . . .

Constantine and Geoff walked through the door, into a hallway every bit as high and wide as the enormous doors. It seemed empty at first, and their footsteps echoed. Peculiar perfumes—incenses from some forgotten Atlantean temple—wafted to them from the darkness at the end of the hallway. The walls were carved with figures blurred by erosion from the trickling water running over them into gutters along the edges of the floor. Were the figures etched on the walls demons, gods, or men? The distinctions had merged over time.

"John?" Geoff asked, his voice hushed. "You sure about this? I'm no magician; don't really know what I'm about here. Wouldn't want to get in your way."

"Going to need you, boy," Constantine said, lighting a cigarette. "Not sure how yet. But I know I'll need your help. Remember, you're my apprentice."

"Right. Your apprentice. I'm fucked, aren't I?"

"Probably."

That's when the doors at the end of the hallway swung open and the skull-faced soldiers swarmed through and charged.

7

IT'S LATE GOTHIC, OF COURSE!

"I really think we should take our time and reconsider this, MacCrawley," Smithson said, nervously gazing at the tunnel entrance in the barrow.

It was a gray, drizzly morning, but birds were chirping and insects buzzing in the woods around the clearing containing the mossy old barrow, and it felt almost cheerful out, in comparison to the hungry obscurity of the tunnel waiting for them.

"Don't let it spook you," MacCrawley said, his voice a study in mockery. "It's just another tunnel. Why, you've been in deeper ones when you've taken the Underground—oh, I forgot, you never have taken the Underground, M'Lord. It's limos for you; a point of pride, yes? Well. I assure you it's just a tunnel. You won't encounter any peasants in it. Other things perhaps, but you who have gone through *several* initiatic trials of the Servants of Transfiguration could not possibly be afraid of a tunnel to Hell."

Smithson whirled, looking at him with the eyes of a frightened deer. "To *Hell?* You're joking!"

"No, I'm using poetic license. It isn't actually Hell. Oh, Hell exists, but it is not 'under' the earth. It is forever at right angles to us, like paradise; it is in another realm of whereness. No, this is merely 'hellish.' But it is nothing that a Great Initiate like yourself would be afraid of, surely!"

And with that he handed Smithson the electric torch and made an "after you!" gesture.

"You don't mean I'm to go first, MacCrawley?"

"I assumed you would want to! You are of the high blood, as you have often reminded me! That makes you a *leader!*"

At last this mockery was too much for Smithson. He switched the torch on to see if it was operating and plunged into the tunnel.

Chuckling, MacCrawley ducked his head and went in after him.

They descended in a winding, looping, down-angled tunnel, dirt sometimes pattering down from the roof, making Smithson jump, which usually resulted in his knocking his head on the low stony ceiling. It seemed to Smithson they descended for more than an hour, and it got colder as they went so that he regretted not bringing an overcoat. As they descended, Smithson found himself thinking of the gold he had transferred to MacCrawley and how he might conceivably get it back. Perhaps he might persuade the King Underneath to seize MacCrawley on some pretext. Surely royalty would understand royalty . . .

Still they descended.

At last they came to a flight of steps carved from naked rock, bringing them into a large dusty room, which was pierced by a cross-tunnel.

"You can switch off your light here," MacCrawley said.

Smithson was loathe to do so, but he switched it off and found there was still a soft bluish illumination coming from short glowing stalactites on the curved ceiling of the tunnel. Then he stepped hastily back as a grasping gray-black hand on a long, stretching arm, more like a tentacle to Smithson than like the limb implied by the hand, reached toward him, fingers wriggling as it sought his throat.

"MacCrawley!" Smithson squeaked.

"Leave this to me!" MacCrawley commanded, stepping between him and the hand. "I've come better prepared this time!" He drew an amulet from his pocket and dangled it before the four-fingered hand. On the amulet was an opal, carved in the image of a kingly figure with a five-pointed crown. The exploring, predatory hand stopped moving, drawing back an inch. Then it stretched out its fingers and seemed to sniff at the amulet without quite touching it. The hand then made a gesture that Smithson took to be a kind of *salaam* and withdrew, like a worm contracting into an apple, to vanish into the left-hand passage.

Smithson swallowed and slowly exhaled the breath he hadn't been aware he'd been holding.

"This way," MacCrawley said, leading him to the right.

They trekked another twenty yards before Smith-son asked, "The King Underneath has been . . . been informed that he will have, ah, visiting royalty?"

"He has. Through this door . . ."

They passed through a crumbling wooden door, the old iron hinges sagging, and entered a cavern big-ger than any he'd ever seen before.

Smithson gasped, gazing at the Palace of Phos-phor, an intricate Gothic structure glowing with an inner light, and set atop a ziggurat-like formation to his right; on the stony ground below it was a collec-tion of buildings that made him think of one of the old Roman settlements unearthed by archaeolo-gists—another Pompeii. "To think that all this was beneath our very feet all the time that we . . ."

His voice trailed off as the gaunt, pale, red-eyed, hairless troops emerged from the streets nearest the palace, running up a ramp to their overlook.

"We must run, MacCrawley—those men—!"

"They are the Fallen Romans! Do not move! Stand where you are! To run would be disastrous!"

The soldiers rushed up to surround them, their skull-like faces unfathomable—but certainly not friendly.

MacCrawley held up the amulet. "Some of you may know me from my previous visit!" he said. Then he spoke to them in another language, some bas-tardization of Latin, Smithson thought. He caught the word *socialis,* which he remembered to mean *allies.* Their leader, an almost spectral figure, tall and thin in a black leather cuirass, a curved sword in his bony hand, nodded in response to MacCrawley's speech

and gestured for them to walk ahead of the escort—
or perhaps ahead of their captors—and they started
for the palace.

And Smithson thought: *Oh God, what have I got
myself into?*

⋆⊷◉⊶⋆

Maureen was a little sadder every time she went
into the garden behind the little house she'd shared
with Bosky. Her roses and irises and the little poplar
tree, bluish in the glow from the phosphorescent
ceiling of the cavern, were bowed, shriveling, crisp-
ing away. Perhaps some of the grass was still living,
but nothing would live much longer in the garden,
not without sun, without water. What water they had
in the village was being hoarded. The town store
had already been looted of food and bottled water;
luckily she'd had some water put away before the
"big fall." A shadow passed over her and she looked
up to see a harpy—surely those were harpies?—
flapping about a hundred feet overhead, glancing
fiercely down at her, moving on. Others circled
higher up . . . terrifying creatures. They stopped anyone who tried to leave the village; Bosky and Garth
had gotten out just in time. She wondered if they
were still alive.

But she knew they were. She would feel it, if they
were dead. She'd always had the ability to know
something of those important to her, even when
they were off somewhere, apart. She hadn't been
terribly surprised to see the harpies; something in

her, some buried, cellular memory, seemed to recognize them.

Some of the men were drinking the last of the liquor in the pub; they were fools, for alcohol only made people dehydrated, made them want more water. She lived only a block from the pub and she could hear the noise of their carousing—the carousing of despair—even at this distance. Someone threw a bottle through a window with a tinkling crash.

How soon before one of those drunks came after her? She'd already had to block the front doors and windows of her cottage at night with furniture and boards. Someone had tried to break in twice the night before. She'd called out to them, demanded to know who they were, and two male voices only giggled in response, but at last they went away.

The village was falling apart physically and socially, which was understandable. Someone was taken every day, sometimes two or three, taken to an unknown fate. When they'd all watched the vicar lifted into that crack in the sky, the heart had gone out of them. No one was safe.

She sighed, and tried to envision Bosky and Garth, to get some sense of where they were, what was happening to them. She closed her eyes and turned her attention to her heart, and caught a flickering image of Bosky moving down a tunnel, rifle in hand . . .

Then a thumping sound from above, a reek, and a wave of palpable hatred made Maureen lift her head and look—just in time to see a harpy diving at her.

She turned and ran for the house, and got three steps and then shrieked in pain as the talons closed around her upper arms, one of them piercing the flesh of the muscle above her right breast. The thumping sound—the beating of the harpy's wings— redoubled its rhythm, and the garden began to recede underneath her. In moments she was looking down at the roof of her cottage, then at the street and the shocked face of Mr. Gardiner, a pensioner who lived across the way from her, the pipe dropping from his gaping mouth as he saw her carried away.

She screamed and struggled, despite the pain. It would be better to fall to her death than die in some filthy nest; she pictured the harpies tearing her apart, feeding her alive to little harpies, like an eagle feeding its young, and she struck at the harpy's scaly legs, to no effect.

Up, up, the jerky ascent was accompanied by the rhythm of the harpy's beating wings, until they were nearly to a ledge jutting from a hole in the cliff-wall of the cavern enclosing the village. Pale men—were those men?—in black armor, blades and spears and crossbows in their hands, came out on the ledge and stood out of the way, awaiting her. Their faces . . .

She screamed once more—and fainted.

⊷═◯═⊷

Constantine looked out the barred window of the prison cell at the town of Danque below. They were in a malodorous circular room in a columnar tower, with a pile of rags in the corner offering the only bedding, a wooden bucket their only plumbing.

"Not quite the Tower of London," Constantine said,

glancing around while lighting a cigarette with a practiced flick of one hand.

"Give us a brown, John!" Geoff said, staring at the cigarette.

"You can have this one when I've smoked it down halfway," Constantine said. "Got to conserve."

"This cavern's sort of like the one the village is in," Geoff remarked, peering out the window. "Except even bigger. Shite, who knew all this was down here."

"That bastard MacCrawley knew," Constantine muttered. "Or found out. Question is, why didn't *I* know? My job is to know those things. Didn't take Scofield seriously enough . . ."

"Your job? You've got a job?" Geoff asked dubiously.

"If it's not my job it's my . . . responsibility, like. 'Course, I've heard about the Underlands, but I always thought it was like that Hollow Earth mythology. Didn't look any closer at the literature. My oversight."

"This ain't the center of the Earth. But it's close enough for me," Geoff said. "Come on, give me a smoke."

Constantine handed him the cigarette. "You shouldn't smoke. I shouldn't've started up again myself."

"I thought we had a plan, John. I don't recall you mentioning being locked up."

"I expected to be incarcerated, or under guard, for a while. But I've got a call in, so to speak, to the King—and I think he'll see me. I've got to convince him I'm the magician who can renew his body for good." He glanced at the locked door—he suspected someone was listening—then winked at Geoff as he added, "And of *course* I can."

Geoff nodded and put his finger beside his nose. "But . . ." He lowered his voice to a whisper. "They know me from the village. How will they think . . . realize . . . I'm your apprentice?"

"*You* remember, I sent you into the village and there was a bit of a misunderstanding, they didn't realize you didn't belong there?"

"John," Geoff said, his voice an even softer whisper, "what about that spell that . . ." He mimed opening a lock with a key.

"If we have to."

"Might be too late if we wait for—"

"Hey—apprentice?"

"Yes, uh—master?"

"Do me a very large favor, and shut your pie-hole."

Geoff shrugged, straightened his specs, and blew smoke out the window, watching it drift out over the capitol of the Underlands. Their tower actually rose from the corner of a fortress wall that enclosed the Palace of Phosphor. It was the palace that drew the eye. It was an almost perfectly preserved palace from at least half a millennium in the past; peaked roofs topped with serrated spikes of iron stretched achingly up toward the ceiling of the vast cavern, as if the palace wanted to push its towers beyond the ceiling and penetrate to the upper world. The outer walls were decorated with flamboyant traceries, the windows with intricate designs in leaded glass. The whole, interconnected by walls decorated with ornate figures in iron, pulsed faintly from an inner light.

"You recognize the architecture?" Geoff asked.

Constantine shrugged. His hand moving with a will of its own, he took out his pack of cigarettes, started to take a cigarette out, and stopped himself. He looked at it wistfully and put it back in his inside coat pocket.

"It's Late Gothic, of course," Geoff observed airily. "The Perpendicular style. You see the fan vault, there? It's like the Rayonnant thing you see in Gloucester Cathedral—they insert tracery panels into the vault—"

"*Hang* on," Constantine exclaimed. "Where's all this coming from? You making it up?"

"I'm going to study architecture, once I'm in college. Been reading up. The history of buildings is dead fascinating."

Constantine cleared his throat. "You mean, as a hobby. When you've"—he tilted his head toward the door—"finished your apprenticeship with me."

"Oh. Yeah. After that."

Constantine looked out the window again, studying a gargoyle on the eave of a building, and was startled to see it spread its wings and fly off. "Not a gargoyle—a harpy!"

Geoff stared at the harpy as it flapped over the rooftops. "I'd be gobsmacked by that sight." He shook his head and exhaled a long slow breath. "Except nothing surprises me now."

"Then stand by to take that back, mate," Constantine said. "There's always another rabid rabbit in the hat."

"The city down there," Geoff remarked, "beyond

the palace walls—totally different architectural style, like something from Pompeii. Looks older, too. That must be what Balf was—*ow!*"

Constantine had jabbed him to keep him quiet. He mouthed, *Don't mention Balf you git!*

They heard the tramp of boots outside the door then, and a key turning in a protesting lock. The Captain of the Fallen Romans stood in the doorway, crossbow in hand. His distinctive winged helmet—the ornaments on the sides shaped like bat-wings— seemed to denote rank. Several other soldiers waited behind him in the narrow landing, short-swords in hand.

"You gents here to have a cuppa with us?" Constantine asked, with mock congeniality. "We're a little short on tea. Also on water, fire, pots, cups, and crumpets. But I'll see what I can do."

"*Adesdum!*" the Captain commanded, in a high-pitched, petulant voice.

Constantine had a fair command of Latin, something a reader of ancient books on magic needs, and understood the Captain as saying, "Come here!"

"Could be this is the audience with his nibs, apprentice," Constantine said in an aside to Geoff, with a sharp look to remind him of the role he was to play. "Come along, then."

They went onto the landing, and were escorted down through the turret on a spiral stone staircase and out to a rampart built right up against the outer walls of the palace complex. The embrasures enclosing the ramparts were edged by iron spikes, some of them decorated with moldering human heads. Geoff stopped in his tracks and stared at one.

"Oh shite!"

"Better keep moving," Constantine whispered, as a sword-wielding guard jabbed him warningly from behind, not quite hard enough to get through his coat.

"That—I *think*"—he stared transfixed at the head, a middle-aged man from the surface—"I think that's my history teacher, from school!"

Constantine grimaced. "Could be. They might've decided to make a few public examples of some who didn't do whatever they've brought the villagers down here to do. Come on, or we'll join him up there—and watch what you say."

"Confuto!" the guard commanded angrily. *"Hoc agere!"* Silence, continue onward!

Geoff swallowed, letting Constantine pull him along by the elbow and they continued down the open-air walkway. From here they could see people moving through the distant settlement below, even a few children. Most of them seemed paper-white, like the guards, but a few darker individuals stood out from the rest. *Genetic aberrations or the result of kidnappings from the surface?* Constantine wondered.

He glanced back at the guards, and looked more closely at their faces. They were fleshed; the skull effect came from the dead-white skin, the extremely upturned noses which were little more than holes in their faces, the lipless mouths, the sunken eyes. A form of albinism, and some inbreeding problem.

They were both outdoors and indoors: on the top of a wall, outside the buildings, but within the cavern.

Hundreds of yards overhead was the blue-glowing ceiling, like the one over the village, though this cavern was even bigger. As Constantine watched, it grew darker, the light source increasingly obscured by a gathering of dark clouds covering the ceiling. The swift movement of the clouds and their unnatural thickness suggested magic at work.

"It's getting darker," Geoff observed, a catch in his voice revealing his growing fear.

"I reckon the King Beneath, as Scofield called him, likes a day and night cycle to try and keep a sense of time," Constantine theorized. "He's got a spell going to make those clouds gather this time of day. It'd be just sunset up above."

As the cavern grew darker, the palace's own inner glow, barely visible before, now pulsed eerily into prominence, making it seem to shine with the potency of the King Underneath. It would have a powerful psychological effect on his subjects, Constantine supposed, living literally in its shadow.

They reached the end of the wall and were herded down a staircase to a courtyard. There were horses here, tethered to iron rings in the walls of wood-and-stone barracks—white, eyeless horses with enormous legs, short backs, and tusks like those of boars.

"Them horses have got no eyes!" Geoff blurted.

Constantine looked at him, suspecting the boy had been through too much and was about to panic. He squeezed Geoff's elbow hard. "Keep your wits about you, Geoff," he whispered, "and we'll get you out of this to the upper world, I promise you!"

The boy nodded, chewing his lower lip, and Constantine silently asked himself: *Should you be making promises you can't keep to people who matter?*

They entered the great central building of the palace through a side door and found themselves in a low hall that seemed in a sad state of decay. There were Gothic and early-Renaissance decorations on the wall, often framing murals showing alchemical signs, representations of alchemical vessels, and runic invocations to power. But most of these were difficult to see, streaked with mildew, peeling away. The occasional article of furniture was leaning, skewed, splintery. The light came from the walls themselves, and in some passages from strips in the floor, intermittently pulsing crystalline panels. Since they pulsed at different rates, enough were illuminated at any given moment that the light never completely failed, but the effect was of a sputtering power source. The palace's air smelled of incense, mold, cooked meat and, faintly, of rot.

Up ahead two sagging doors, flanked by sullen, bored skull-faced guards leaning on their pikes, opened onto the throne room. The prisoners were hustled into the throne room, where a clutch of other prisoners waited—watched by a lazing circle of guards—in the center of the throne room's polished black-marble floor. The two thrones on a dais at one end of the glittering high-ceilinged room were empty. It appeared they awaited the pleasure of the King. The general impression given out by the room was of a gigantic music-box, tackily ornate, with gems studding the columns along the walls; golden trac-

eries on the walls set off panels painted with fantastic
images of a kingly figure wearing a five-pointed
crown, standing with his foot on the neck of a troll—
resembling Balf but fiercer-looking—like St. George
about to slay the dragon.

Constantine turned his attention to the other prisoners, one of whom was glowering angrily at him.
Two of the prisoners seemed to be ragged, pallid
men from the settlement below the palace, presum-
ably miscreants who'd transgressed some local law;
the other two were captives from the surface, if captives they were. One of them was MacCrawley, the
source of the baleful glower. The other, Constantine
didn't know—a tweedy, balding little man whose expression alternated between muted terror and an attempt at magisterial snootiness.

But as they were chivvied to stand with the other
prisoners, Geoff identified the stranger with a whisper. "That's Lord Smithson, from the manor by the
village! Owns more than half of Tonsell!"

"His property value has gone *down,* then," Constantine observed dryly. Adding more loudly, for
MacCrawley's benefit—for Constantine's old enemy
was standing just a few steps away— "Lovely room,
in a kitschy kind of way, to be held prisoner in, eh
MacCrawley?"

"Bah! Go the devil, Constantine! For good this
time! I'm no prisoner here. I have been summoned to
an audience with His Majesty! King Culley and I are
old friends!"

"I had 'an audience' with a copper, not long ago,"
Constantine said. "Had to spend the night in the

drunk tank. Threw up my supper. Thought of you about then, mate, as I was looking at the upchuck. And here you are! Funny old world, innit?"

"Maneo captivus!" the Captain of the guards ordered them. Wait here, prisoners!

And the darkness thickened in the chilly realm of the Gloomlord.

8

THE NIGHT HAS A THOUSAND EYES

The sickly, pretty lady with the blond, elaborately coiffed hair had been at work over Maureen for several minutes, cleaning the wound over her breast, washing and bandaging it, humming to herself all the while, before Maureen really came to herself on the silk cushions of the gloomy but lavish room.

"Oh . . . where am I?" Maureen asked, feeling quite unreal. The air smelled of incense and the light seemed to pulse, to mute, to intensify and then, after a few moments, to go dull again.

"Here, put on this little dress, hon," said the woman, helping Maureen to sit up. She handed Maureen a dress of blue silk, with a plunging neckline but an ankle-length skirt. "You're in the queen's quarters. I'm the queen, by the way. Queen Megan. I'm, like, nursing you back to health so you can be hella grateful to me and be my servant and my friend and my lady in waiting and, y'know, all that! I asked the King to have a maidservant selected for me from that village they brought down, and you're it, I guess."

"You—you sound like you have an . . . American accent . . ." Maureen said, rubbing her head, still feeling dizzy. But she put on the dress, wincing with pain when she slipped her arms into the sleeves. She had sense enough to know she was lucky to be alive, and if she wanted to stay that way she'd better do what she could to make her new "employers" happy.

"America! Don't mention America; the King *totally* doesn't like it! He doesn't like people to talk about the upper world, even though he's, like, always obsessing about it himself, the old hypocrite. But yeah I'm . . . from there. I was, anyhow, a few years ago. I don't fucking know how long, it's hard to keep track of time here. No calendars, and the only holiday is *Gratitude to the King Day,* which is whenever he says it is." She looked wistfully at the barred windows, through which could be seen the cloudy ceiling of the cavern and little else. "I wish . . ." She shrugged. "No use thinking about it. He brought me here and it's been kinda tight in some ways. Well, sort of. But what good is it being a queen if nobody knows I'm one but these ugly nerds down here? I mean, if I was married to a King up above, I'd be all up in a photo spread in *People* magazine and they'd interview me in *Cosmo* and shit, and Paris and Britney would've come to the wedding . . ." She sighed.

She was a tall, slender, long-necked woman, perhaps late twenties, with dull, red-rimmed blue eyes and a slightly weak chin, though she was for the most part conventionally pretty. Her hair looked a bit brittle to Maureen, and her fingernails were badly chewed up, and her hands trembled. She coughed, seeming obscurely unwell. She wore a long blue chiffon dress with a train, the hems curling up with age, the collar sewn with threads of gold.

"Do you feel okay, um, Your Majesty?" Maureen asked.

The queen's lips trembled as if she might burst into tears, but her expression became stoically wooden when a man stumped into the room, a stooped old man, shorter than the queen, with a long pale face, shoulder-length white hair, a wisp of white beard, and hooded rheumy eyes. He wore a black doublet and stood regarding them with his head tilted to one side, as if he were looking out of only one eye; he leaned on a cane that seemed made from human bones, its handle a skeletal hand folded into a fist. Draped over his shoulders was a purple robe; on his head was a five-pointed crown of gold, its points tipped in opals.

"My Lord," said Megan, standing to curtsy for the King.

Maureen gaped for a moment, then remembered to curtsy. "Your Majesty."

"At least her manners are fitting," said the old man, sniffing, his voice creaky. His accent was peculiar, utterly foreign and yet somehow innately British. "You may keep her as a servant, for the remainder . . . for as long as you like, my darling, if she behaves herself," the King continued. "I have come to tell you, my queen, that we are needed in the throne room."

"Very well, My Lord and King," said Megan, her voice as wooden as her expression.

He turned and stumped away. One of the guards followed.

Megan went to the door and closed it. "I suppose you'd better help me put my tiara on. It's there behind you on that table. It's kind of a pain in the ass. There are some pins . . ."

Moving stiffly, Maureen got the tiara—little more than a circlet of gold, with a few diamonds woven into it—and pinned it on Megan's head with some rusty old pins of iron. Some of the queen's hair crumbled away at the pressure.

"Queen Megan, it must be hard for you to have such an elderly husband. I don't mean to be rude, but you're so young . . ."

"Oh yeah, I know but"—Megan shrugged wearily, straightening the little tiara as she looked at her reflection in a girandole of polished silver—"he'll be young again in the morning. He's got a machine he goes into; it does something, makes him young again, but it only lasts the day. When it starts to get late, about when it would be dark up above, he's getting really hella old. In the morning he's a young man again, but in the afternoon he's, like, middle-aged, and in the evening he's getting pretty damn old all over. By eleven or so he'd be dead except he gets his rejuvenation charge. Then he falls asleep. It sort of works on him overnight and then in the morning he's all young again—for a while." She smiled wryly. "I kind of like him in the mornings. He's more upbeat, all full of plans, and of course we have sex, which is okay sometimes, only he does it in a funny way; he never kisses and he plays weird little games with it." She patted at her hair again and frowned when some of it came away on her fingers.

"Your hair, Your Majesty," Maureen said tentatively, "it's like you're not getting enough vitamins . . ."

"I'm so totally *not* getting enough vitamins! I *told* them that! I need vitamin D, I need sunshine, I need a more balanced diet, not just meat and mushrooms and those weird little moss things and those—I don't know what it is and I don't want to know. Just like . . ."

"Just like what, Your Majesty?"

"You can call me Megan when we're alone. Oh, just like I don't want to know when the end is coming—when he's going to . . ."

"Going to what, Megan?

"He has a new queen pretty often. I mean—sometimes, from what I can find out, he keeps them for as much as, like, ten years. One, I heard, he kept for seventeen. It's only been a few years for me, but he's already bored. And the one before me . . . I guess he got rid of her after a few months. She was pretty bitchy or something. She tried to pull some shit on him."

"He gets rid of them? You mean—a divorce?" But she knew that was not what Megan meant.

Megan shook her head. "I don't know exactly what he does with them . . . I don't think I want to know that, either. I just know he doesn't let them go. And they disappear."

"Oh God! Don't you think about escaping?"

"I heard about one who tried. But the gripplers caught her. He fed her alive to the crankers. They eat human flesh."

"Fed her alive to . . . what are crankers?"

"Oh he puts a lot of his prisoners down below to crank his machine. They live in some sort of really nasty-ass pits down below. They get changed into things by . . . Gawd, I don't know how they do it. But that's where Queen Loreen went."

Maureen felt a hand clutch at her heart. Bosky could be down in that pit. He might've been captured by now. Anything could've happened. She couldn't feel him, not exactly; she thought he was alive, but in a place like this life could be worse than death.

The queen wiped tears away and added resignedly, "Oh, come on . . . let me fix your hair a little, and then we have to go. And don't talk to me all familiar and stuff out there; we have to be, y'know, really formal and, like, regal—and all that kinda shit."

⊷═◦═⊷

"What do you reckon they're doing, Granddad?" Bosky asked, as they crept out to the ledge overlooking the smoky, foul-smelling cavern.

"I'm buggered if I know," Garth muttered hoarsely, surprising Bosky. He rarely used such language around his grandson.

This was a much smaller cavern than the one the village was in; it was about the size of a high school gymnasium but with a higher ceiling, its floor mostly taken up by a stack of rusted oil barrels and a sump, a big hole filled with multicolored fluid, bubbling and surging with glutinous muck, all mixing together, of ugly brown and shiny black and vitreous green. Men worked on the tables of stone to either side, watched by soldiers in black and silver armor, their faces pale as paper, and overseen by a man in a black hood.

Bosky squinted through the caustic murk for a while, then decided that none of the people below could be Geoff. One of them could well be the vicar. There were others he was sure were from the village. This was part of why the village had been brought down, he supposed. Some kind of urgent project. And the village of Tonsell was the closest surface town to this cavern.

About forty feet above the sump was a crane of iron, with silvery cables running through it to two dangling hooks holding up a big cauldron of stone banded with iron.

Granddad opened his mouth to say something and then broke up into a spasm of choking, spurred by the fumes from below. He squirmed back, shaking his head, gesturing for Bosky to come away from the ledge.

Bosky drew back from the ledge and they returned to the tunnels, Bosky carrying the rifle. Without it they'd never have gotten this far—they'd barely gotten into the tunnels ahead of the gripplers. Only now they didn't know where to go.

Bosky found himself thinking of Finn. They hadn't tried to go in that barrow tunnel after Finn, the way he was going to find Geoff now. Of course, him and

Geoff had been closer, but still, Finn was his bruv, and he'd given up on him . . . and let the gripplers take him. Partly it was that MacCrawley geezer. Looking into his eyes had turned Bosky's spine to jelly, that one.

Maybe Finn would be wherever Geoff was. Or maybe they were both dead, and already cold . . .

"The light's growing up ahead, Bosky!" Granddad said, his voice raspy. He stuck his electric torch in his coat pocket. "I think there's a big cave out there . . . maybe the same one we come from, maybe another . . ." He paused to cough. "Be very careful now, Boswell."

"You okay, Granddad?"

"Got a lungful of them fumes back there, and they did me no good. I'm an old man, and tired. Maybe we'll look for a place to rest a while . . ."

Then they emerged onto another stony balcony, looking down over a gigantic cave. The ceiling of the cavern was dark with smoke or clouds of some kind, and most of the light came from the walled-in palace, a complicated structure glimmering with intricate ornament, fanged with towers, watched over by gargoyles. There was a strange little town beneath the hill of stone the palace was built on, with square flat roofs, twisty streets, a maze of clay and wood and stone, very old, with scarcely a wall uncracked. Fires burned here and there in the little town; dark figures moved around the fires. At first they saw no harpies, but then he saw that what had seemed gargoyles were harpies roosting on the battlements of the Gothic castle, their wings folded.

"Get an eyeful of this place, Granddad!" Bosky exclaimed.

"Strangely dark, compared to the one they had the village in," Granddad remarked. "I didn't see the stairs here at first, in all the shadow."

"Stairs?" What he'd thought was a balcony was in fact a cupola-like landing topping a flight of stairs down to the town. "Oh yeah." But he didn't suggest descending them.

"I don't know as we should go any farther, Bosky," Granddad said. "It's all too big to search through. And look there—soldiers on those walls at the palace. Like the ones in that cavern with the . . ." He paused to cough. ". . . with that bubblin' pit. And I tell you the truth, I'm not sure we're doing the right thing, boy."

"We're going to find Geoff and the other people who were taken. I thought I saw the vicar in that chamber with all the bad smells. And other people from Tonsell. Maybe we can rescue him!"

"But what about your mum? I think we should be looking for a way *up!* Someone had to be going up there, to set this thing up. We should be looking for a way up, so we can get your mom out that way!"

Bosky thought about it. Probably Garth was exhausted, and feeling sick, and wanting to get back to someplace more familiar. But he was right too. There must be a way up to the surface. He looked up at the thick swirl of clouds near the ceiling of the cavern; stalactites glimmered through the clouds, dimmed but still glinting, like thousands of eyes in the night. It was not an encouraging sight.

"Okay, Granddad, we'll go back to the village, and find our way back up. Come on—"

He broke off, gasping at the sight of the skull-faced soldiers rushing from the tunnel mouth, weapons raised, faces contorted. They shouted something in a language he didn't understand. He whipped the rifle around to point at the soldiers, who came to a stop, for a moment unsure of themselves as they stared at the unfamiliar weapon. There was already a bullet chambered, and Bosky pulled the trigger.

The rifle didn't fire. He looked at it and saw it was loaded, the safety was off, it should fire—he felt something slam into his chest then, knocking the wind from him, and he went over backwards onto the stone, gasping and in pain. The soldier who had hit him with the butt of his pike was standing over him, aiming the point down at him. Then Granddad was rushing at the soldier, swinging his electric torch like a club, shouting,

"Back off, you!"

The soldier turned the pike's spear point to Garth and caught him just under the sternum. The old man yelled in anguish and staggered back, clutching at his belly. Blood seeping out between his fingers, he turned to look down at Bosky. "Boswell . . . you were always the . . ." He didn't manage to say it, but the sad twitch of a smile on his mouth said it somehow. And then he pitched over backwards, off the landing, falling from sight.

"Granddad! No!" Rifle still clutched in his hands, Bosky scrambled back from the encircling soldiers, got to his feet, and looked over the cupola's edge—

and saw Granddad's body far below, sprawled life-less on the rocks. Afire with rage, he turned and swung the rifle at the skull-faces, shouting, "Sod the lot of you ugly bastards!"

The nearest soldier blocked the rifle blow with his pike, while another stepped in and swung a short-sword at Bosky's head.

This is it, Bosky thought, seeing the sword slash down at him, his sense of time protracted so he could watch it come. *Now I'll see my da again, and Granddad.*

But the soldier had turned the sword so it struck him with the flat of the blade, hard on the side of the head. Bosky staggered, and then his knees buckled. He was out cold before he hit the stone floor.

⊷⊙⊶

"John!" Geoff whispered. "That woman with the queen, she's the mum of my mate Bosky!"

"Is she? What's her name?"

"Maureen, I think."

"Seems to be a lady in waiting now. By the way, have I told you lately to belt it up? The less said the better."

The King was a very old man who was dressed in kingly raiment that, to Constantine's eye, could've come from a costume shop's catalog. Leading a short procession to the thrones, he came stumping along with his bony cane, his wife just behind him, Maureen behind the queen, holding the queen's train, her lips parted, eyes darting around; a fright-

ened woman, Constantine supposed, but holding up
bravely in the circumstances.

Other people had showed up to gather under the
gaudy columns, talking and tittering, some of them
sitting on palanquins carried in by slaves. Constantine took them to be the courtiers, as decadent-
looking a bunch as he'd ever seen, and he'd been to
California. They wore a mélange of robes, kimonos,
sashes, Arabic robes, everything of some form of
satin or shiny silk, woven with strands of precious
metals, the collars lined with gems. Many of the
women had their breasts exposed, the nipples encir-
cled by gemstones glued onto the skin, some of them
with the gems in concentric circles covering the entire breast. Some of the courtiers were of the pale,
skullish variety; these typically wore what were
clearly artificial noses of intricately etched silver, affixed over their own stubby snouts; others repre-
sented a variety of races from the surface world,
though when he looked close Constantine made out
a good many deformities: one eye strikingly smaller
than the other; some were missing chins, or had
extra fingers, or were wanting fingers; others had
grotesque overbites. A few of them were superficially
attractive, but who knew what deformity of inbreeding was hidden under their clothing?

This garish, repellent crew, some two hundred of
them, laughed and tittered at the prisoners. A skullish man with a false nose, his face painted black,
licked his lips and blew kisses at Geoff between puffs
on a hookah that he carried under his arm like a bag-
pipe. Many of them were smoking some peculiar sub-

stance; Constantine didn't recognize the smell but it had a mushroomy quality.

"Well at least the higher classes here are more or less the same as the aristocracy on the surface," Constantine muttered to Geoff.

"The nobs up above don't look as bad as this lot."

"Not on the outside. You ever read *The Picture of Dorian Gray*? Maybe this is where the upper class keeps its souls hidden."

Geoff visibly shuddered.

The King and queen were in their thrones now, and Maureen was sitting on a cushion behind the queen's throne. Constantine found himself looking at her; he was drawn to her, somehow. Their eyes met. He smiled—and winked. She returned him the flutter of a smile but wrung her hands on her lap. She was probably worried about her son as much as herself.

You've got enough people to take care of, Constantine told himself. *You were smarter when you were the only one you worried about. Now it's Chas and this Geoff. Don't add a woman you don't even know.*

But he knew he already had.

"Bring the guests forward . . . and the prisoners, too," the King said.

The whole lot in the center of the room were chivvied forward, so it was still difficult to tell who was guest and who was prisoner, which was perhaps an omen, an insight into this kingdom, and MacCrawley went down on one knee before the throne, intoning, "Great King Culley, as arranged, I bring the man who offered up the little community of slaves recently added to your retinue, in exchange for your miraculous favor . . . as *discussed.*" He added an odd emphasis to this last word.

"That pig," Geoff hissed. "Lord Smithson was in on it!"

"Geoff," Constantine growled, "I'm getting tired of . . . Oh, sod it." And he turned and gave Geoff a hard slap to the side of his face. "Silence, apprentice!"

Geoff looked at him with outraged astonishment.

"Who is this?" the King asked, his attention drawn to Constantine by the slap, as Constantine intended. "Perhaps they are the magician and his apprentice who have asked for an audience?"

Constantine raised his eyebrows as if impressed. "Your Majesty is perceptive."

"Magician?" MacCrawley snarled contemptuously. "Him? Nothing could be further from the truth! A charlatan, merely, that one!"

"Your Majesty!" Constantine said, just managing to sidestep past the guards and stepping forward to give his courtliest bow. "Allow me to introduce myself . . ."

One of the soldiers raised his sword to strike Constantine down for advancing, but held back when the King raised a commanding hand. "Let him be, I will hear him! There is something about him that promises amusement! And I weary, at this hour. I am desperate for amusement!"

The courtiers giggled and sniggered at that, some of them caressing their crotches and muttering to themselves.

"First," the King said, "I should like to know how

you found your way here unescorted, and what your purpose was in coming."

"A very good question, Your Majesty," MacCrawley said, looking coldly at Constantine.

"Ah yes," said Constantine, relieved that the King had not heard about his escape from the crankers at the bottom of the shaft. But he had to come up with some explanation for his presence and he wondered which lie to tell. He cleared his throat, and settled on one. "Why, I came by an old tunnel, from above—one used by the druids, I believe. I followed a guiding sprite—some call them Will-o'-the-Wisp. Traditionally, they lead the traveler wrongly, but of course enslaved to my will, the creature led me aright, her glow providing me with light on the way down. A little-known tunnel; I will show it to your advisers, when Your Majesty likes. As for explaining my purpose here, I had heard of Your Majesty from Scofield's grimoires. I came to see if your realm was still as marvelous as described, and if I could be of use."

"Oh what a crock," MacCrawley scoffed. "Your Majesty—"

"Great King!" Constantine interrupted, inclining his head respectfully, as he stepped closer, jostling MacCrawley to cover up the thump of the fist-sized crystal he dropped into MacCrawley's greatcoat pocket. "I am here to serve you, O King! It would be bullsh—ah, disingenuous to say that I don't expect something in return. Your kingdom abounds in riches and there is great knowledge here to be gained. In return, I—"

"Don't trust this rotter, Your Majesty!" MacCrawley said, pointing an accusatory finger at Constantine. "This is John Constantine! He destroyed the good works of the Servants of Transfiguration, a brotherhood that has brought you the new slaves you now enjoy!"

Constantine looked at him pityingly. "Rotter? You're such a prat, MacCrawley. I've come here to serve His Majesty and to entertain him however I might!"

Smithson looked at Constantine skeptically. "He does look a bit shabby, this man. Like someone who'd try to ask one for a shilling outside a pub." But everyone ignored Smithson. He noticed their indifference to him and scowled.

"So you're a magician, Constantine, eh?" the King asked, his voice quivering with some secret amusement. "Why not impress me with your ability? Give me a simple demonstration of your power—nothing overwhelming, merely something . . . impressive."

"Very well, Your Majesty."

But what? It was gloomy in here. The spell of illumination might be impressive without making anyone feel threatened. Constantine gathered his inner power, his *prana,* focused it through the lens of his attention, sent the energy down through his upraised hand, muttered the appropriate word of power and then cried out, *"Ignis Ico, Ilaturs—multus plus plurinum!"*

And nothing happened. No light burst forth.

He looked in puzzlement at his hand. He'd found enough power in himself; it should have worked . . .

Then he became aware that the courtiers were

laughing uproariously, and the King was wiping away tears of hilarity. MacCrawley was merely sneering at him. "You idjit," he said. "The King is amusing himself at your expense. No magic will work in the palace or in the cavern. Except for the King's."

"Heh heh, yes yes yes," the King said, still chuckling. "I'm afraid I played a little joke upon you, John Constantine. There is no magic in this cavern but mine. Once you step through the great doors, your magic will not work. And indeed, did you not notice that none of my men carry firearms? We are well aware of firearms, but I promise you, no firearm will work here, either. I instituted that enchantment so that should the men from the surface come, they would have no more power here than my own people—less! For the armies of the surface dwellers use no swords, no crossbows, eh?"

"You are indeed a powerful magician, Your Majesty," Constantine said, and he meant it. He was impressed by Culley's magical achievements. But then again, he reflected, Iain Culley had had many centuries to develop his ability, his knowledge. Still, there were vulnerabilities in this man and overconfidence was just one of them. His cyclical senescence was another. And Balf had mentioned a core, a vulnerable center to his magical power, beyond the machine driven by the crankers . . .

"You pretend to be impressed," King Culley remarked, eyeing Constantine shrewdly. "Perhaps you are impressed—or perhaps not. Just so that you respect my power, and so that you do not try anything foolish, while you are my guest, I will demonstrate it a little further for you. Bring the prisoners forward, and loose their bonds!"

Surly, scarred men who looked around with unconcealed hatred at the sniggering courtiers, the two prisoners were brought forward, released from their chains. The King nodded at the Captain, who gave each of the prisoners a sword. The two men were within six paces of the King Underneath.

"You two tried to escape the work that was set for you!" the King said, in the tone a judge uses right before levying a hefty fine. "But I am willing to give you a chance at greatness! You hate me—I can see it in your eyes." He stood up, leaning on his cane. "Come then and kill me. Succeed, and you may go free! I hereby declare it!" And saying this, the King went very still. Constantine knew what that meant; an inner process was taking place within the sorcerer.

The two men rushed toward the King—who simply raised a hand, sending twin bolts of purple lightning which struck the men before they took two steps. Both were flung backwards, somersaulting, arse over elbow, to land in burning, charred heaps of bubbling flesh, cracked bone, their eyes cooked out of their skulls. Twitching but quite dead.

The King yawned theatrically and the courtiers burst into dutiful applause, many of them laughing gleefully and shouting "Bravo!"

Constantine bowed, thinking, *If he's that powerful when he's in his aging state, what about when he's been rejuvenated? A dangerous man.* It had not escaped him that the King's thunderbolts had been the same kind of energy he'd seen crackling from the rotating vanes in the chamber below. He derived them somehow from the same energy source.

"But I have one weakness," the King said, sitting back on the throne with a sigh, "and it is no use denying it, since you can see it for yourself. The temporality of my rejuvenation. And you claim, Constantine, you want to be of use—can you help me overcome that problem?"

"I believe I can, Your Majesty," Constantine said.

Smithson opened his mouth to say something but MacCrawley shook his head at him and turned to the King. "Constantine lies, Your Majesty! I have promised you the full resources of the Servants of Transfiguration to solve the problem! If this man, with his feeble ability, could do anything about aging, he'd have rejuvenated *himself!*"

Constantine chuckled disdainfully, pretending that shot hadn't gone home. "And if this old prat here could help you, Your Majesty, he'd have done it by now. And certainly I cannot pretend to be a patch on your sorcerer's robe, O King." He put on his best high-magic diction: "But a new perspective can sometimes solve a problem that years of analysis have failed to discover. And it could be my recent research in the outer world, in rejuvenation, has given me the edge, here."

"Oh? You've found out something new about rejuvenation?" the King asked, leaning forward, interested.

"Your Majesty, this con artist—" MacCrawley began.

"Silence!" the King shouted, and then gave himself over to a coughing fit, brought on by the shouting.

The queen—an odd little blond, who looked like she might've come from the upper world not so long ago—patted him on the back till it had abated.

"Thank you, my dear. And by the by, what do you think of this new magician? Should I have him skinned alive and fed to the crankers? Hm? Or perhaps put him at work on one of my special"—he glanced at MacCrawley, and a look of closed cunning came into his face—"projects?"

Watching the King, Constantine suspected that MacCrawley didn't know about the sea-poisoning project. Which would make sense; the Servants of Transfiguration would want Britain intact for their own exploitation."

"Oh, I think he's kinda cute," the queen said, looking vacuously at Constantine. "I think you should give him a shot, I mean, like, it's all good. What the hell. Um—My Lord and King."

"What the 'hell' indeed," the King said, gesturing to a steward, who brought him a glass of something that might've been wine. He drank deeply, then went on, "What a curious expression that is. Perhaps one might more forcefully say, 'What particular hell.' For there are so many; more than six billion, I believe. And yet we are reluctant to give up our little hells . . ." He spoke bitterly, wiping his mouth with a shaking hand marked with age spots. Then he looked hard at Constantine. "I can see the gift in you, and you used the right incantation for that failed spell of yours, just now. It seems you are indeed a magus. Here then is my decision: the two magicians—or *consultants,* since I am the only magician in this realm—

will come with me to look at my rejuvenation device. And offer their contrasting advice. I will choose. But if either one tries to confound or mislead me, I will kill him quite horribly, with the help of my faithful courtiers. Welcome to the Palace of Phosphor, in the realm of the Sunless."

There was a tittering, giggling cheer at this, from the courtiers, and the hair stood up on Constantine's neck.

9

THE ONLY WAY TO PRESERVE BEAUTY
IS TO KILL IT WITH ICE

Bosky was sorry he'd woken up. He'd been dreaming of walking with his father down a country lane on a spring day . . . Perhaps more a memory than a dream . . . A sunny day, his father putting his hand on his shoulder . . .

And then he woke to find himself chained to a wall in a dimly lit chamber far underground, and his head was throbbing with pain, and it was cold and his granddad was dead and his mother might well be dead and he was disarmed and would either be enslaved or dead himself soon.

Would've been better to stay unconscious, forever.

He took a deep breath, groaned at the pain it brought, and sat up, looking around. Glowing stalactites illuminated a natural cavern that had been given double duty as a dungeon; it was about the size of a barn, with a number of men chained up in it, the chains affixed to the drippy stone walls, and a man in a black hood was staring through a barred window in the locked door. Staring at him.

Bosky looked at the other men, most of them deep in the sleep of exhaustion. A curious chemical smell rose from them, like paint remover. There were several dozen of them, some of them the pale skull-faced men, but many others clearly from the village, almost in a vegetative state. And very sickly, half-covered in gray scales. There'd been a lot of people in that little Roman-looking town in the big cavern. Why weren't there more of them here? Maybe because the work being done in that cave with the bubbling pit was killing the workers; the King didn't want to use his own subjects for it. One of the men in chains was sitting up, muttering to himself. A naked man with dirty, lank hair, his body covered with gray scabs, a glum face. "Vicar?" Bosky called. "Vicar Tombridge?"

Tombridge looked over at him. "Who's that?" he asked, barely interested.

"It's Bosky. You remember; I came to have my bullets blessed. The most amazin' thing happened in your chapel, an angel sort of woman, who said she was the Lady of Waters, appeared in the baptismal—"

"A demon," said the vicar dismissively. "Just another demonic trick, another guise."

Bosky didn't think so but decided it was useless to argue. "I reckon they're going to put me on your work crew; I saw you in that other cave. What have they got you doing?"

"Why, the demons have us reenacting our sins on Earth. We were poisoning the world, all of us, with

our solvents and our motor cars and our coal burning, and now they punish us for it here. And who,
pray tell, is the King of this place but Satan, I ask
you, eh?"

"I'm not so sure of that, mate. I think whoever did
this has some kind of magical hack going on, but he's
human, I'd bet my bollocks on it."

"Liar! You're a demon yourself, disguised as
someone I knew! Tormenting me with false hope! I
won't have it, demon. You can report back to Satan
and tell him that Tombridge will do his time in Hell
but won't play along with any games; he will wait for
the last day in which the Lord will find those who
have truly repented, and lift them up, lift them out
of the darkness!"

"Oh Christ, Vicar, give it a rest," Bosky said, rubbing his temples. "Oh fuck me, that hurts."

Suddenly aware of someone looming over him,
Bosky looked up to see that the hooded man had
come to peer at him more closely; only the lower half
of his brown-bearded face was visible in the shadow
of his hood. The man grunted to himself, and said,
"Stand up, boy!" in a low, gruff voice.

Bosky got painfully to his feet, stretched to the
limits of his chains. "Who're you, guv?"

"Never you mind that," said the man, clearly an
Englishman, looking Bosky up and down. "Here, let's
have this down."

He reached out and tugged at Bosky's pants, beside his right hip.

Bosky sucked in his breath and swung a fist clum-
sily at the man. "Sod off you old perv!"

The man caught his swinging arm by the wrist and held it effortlessly as with his other hand he jerked Bosky's pants partway down, enough to show the birthmark on his hip. "Aye, there it is. That mark, boy." He stared at the red birthmark for a moment; it was a four-pointed star, the top and bottom points much longer than the horizontal ones. He let go of Bosky. "Who's your mother, then?"

"My mother? What about my mother?"

"I said who is she? Or do you want to stay chained up in here?"

"Well, her name is Maureen."

"Ho, wait, you don't mean Maureen of Irish parentage, about forty-one or so—who was married to a man who went by Pauly?"

"He was me da!"

"Stone me!" the man muttered. "But then it makes sense. I heard you were the one who'd killed a grippler. Is it so?"

"I shot one a couple times. And some of those harpies things."

"And did your bullets destroy a harpy?"

"They did. The Lady of Waters . . ." He broke off, wondering if he should be telling this man anything else. The stranger was working for the enemy, clearly, so he was the enemy himself.

"So that's who did it? An elemental infused it with her emanation, did she? The Lady, you say; perhaps the queen of water elementals, then. Well now. And you thought she'd do that for just anyone? No. It's because you're of the blood, boy. That's how she was able to appear to you so easily."

"My granddad . . ." His voice caught in his throat. He seemed to see, once more, Granddad, stabbed in the middle, falling off the balcony. His broken body far below.

"He said something about . . . fairies. My mother having fairy blood."

"Your granddad. I heard that an old man was killed with you. That who you mean?"

"Yes. He wasn't just some old man, he was me granddad. And he gave his life for me."

"Oh aye, he wasn't just some old man, he was my half brother!"

"What? On your bike! Maybe the vicar's right, there're liars about."

"I'm not lying to you." He drew back the hood of his robe, showing a haggard face that looked vaguely familiar. The eyes were much like Granddad's. "I have a different last name from your granddad's. Scofield, you see. And as he was a Christian he wouldn't speak to me—or of me, I suppose—after I took up what he called 'the black arts.'"

"Didn't mention you that I remember. Here, you're saying this mark on my hip means I'm . . ."

"You're of the blood. Related to what you call fairies. The mark only shows after seven generations. It means you've got a special connection to certain spirits of the Hidden World. Like the Lady of Waters. So that's why I was drawn to you. I cannot do ritual magic in this realm. But psychic ability is possible here, and I saw you in my mind's eye, in this place. And no wonder; look there—!" He nodded toward a man who was licking water, dripping down from a crack in the wall. "You see that? Water. *Her* water. Her power is weak here, but she can watch, and listen, where water flows. She sent you here because she knew I'd be here, likely. Hence the 'magic bullets.'" He scratched in his beard, and went musingly on, "And if the Lady is aware of what's going on, despite the King's efforts at concealing it, then maybe . . . just *maybe* . . . there's hope after all."

"Ha, you hear that?" Tombridge cawed, his chains rattling in the gloom. "They taunt you with hope! Don't heed them, Boswell!"

"So she named you Boswell?" the man in the black robe said, amused. "I'm not surprised."

"You say you're my uncle?" Bosky asked, dubious. For all he knew, the vicar could be right. "How'd you end up down here?"

"Yes, I'm your uncle Philo. Philo Scofield. How I got here is of no importance; suffice it to say I was too inquisitive. The King has a short way with intruders and if not for my knowledge of alchemy, I'd have provided entertainment on my last day . . . or worse. Well. Let me see if I can do something for you; the King will want to use you differently than toting barrels about. Which will mean, perhaps, that you can stay with me at the palace. Better than here, any gate."

"And suppose I don't want to be used by the King?"

"Do you want to die in chains? Or slinging toxins?"

Bosky didn't want that, no. And he supposed he might play along for a while, await his moment. It was a chance, when he'd had none before. "But are you part of the reason the village was brought down below? Your magic?"

"Not mine. That was Smithson and MacCrawley's doing. All I am is a slave of King Culley's now." He glanced at the door to see if anyone was listening. "You noticed that your gun didn't work in that cavern. Nor will it here. Both firearms and most enchantments will fail within a certain distance of the Palace of Phosphor. He has powerful spells in place to suppress them. And my power is all but gone too, in his realm. Below the palace, magic still works, and above it. And *his* magic works, here. In this place we are still within the ring of his enchantment. He extended it to the village up above, with fetish markers made by that villain MacCrawley. One hundred feet from here, farther outward from the palace, his spell of suppression ends and my own ability to do magic would return."

"Well then, if you don't want to be a slave, why not leave here and go there?"

Scofield touched a sort of silver choker around his neck, just above the collarbone. "You see this collar? He knows where I am at all times because I wear it. It cannot be removed, not here. If I try to leave the area, the King will know and send an Il-Sorg after me, to bring me back. They are beings you cannot argue with, are the Il-Sorg. And the King's punishment will be terrible."

"What's he got you doing, then, if you can't do magic?"

"I can supervise magical operations if they're the King's doing—alchemical operations, in this case.

The creation of the Universal Solvent, which is what all these men are here for. He doesn't want to use his own people; it kills them too fast. No need to foment a rebellion, after all. As for the Solvent, it's too much to explain, boy, and it might be best you never knew."

"You have a key for the lock on this chain?"

"No. I will have to get permission to bring you out. Wait patiently, Boswell, till I return."

"Oh well, I don't know about that," Bosky said, sarcastically, rattling his chains as Scofield put up his hood and walked away. "I mean, I thought I'd go for a bloody *walk* while I waited."

Scofield ignored him, and the guards let him out, clanging the door shut behind him.

⭐══◉══⭐

"Come this way, gentlemen," said King Culley, unnecessarily. Now that the steel doors behind the thrones were locked behind them, there was nowhere to go but down this corridor, carved out of one gigantic piece of black volcanic glass. MacCrawley, Smithson, Geoff, and Constantine were escorted by silent, pallid, black-armored soldiers—six behind and two between them and the King. The light, and a little warmth, was provided by a strip of glowing crystals centered in the arched ceiling. The King, more decrepit as the hour passed, was carried in a litter by two linebacker-sized, beefily muscular, nude men who'd had their genitals clipped away. Metal tubes strapped to their legs, running to leather pouches, acting as urethra;

their identical babyesque faces had big brown bovine eyes. They were perpetually drugged, men become beasts of burden.

Thirty yards and they reached the end of the glassy corridor, stopped by a door of iron. Climbing from his litter, the King opened the door with a key on a chain about his neck. The guards pushed the door open, he returned to the litter, and they passed through into an almost identical corridor, but on the left were shelves and shelves of books, and several comfortable chairs to read them in. "Perhaps you have been wondering about my command of contemporary English," said the King. "I have books brought down by my agents on the surface, books of science, of all topics, and I study the language. My wives also give me some fresh command of dialect, though my current queen is regrettably vulgar at times. One reason I brought the village down to the Sunless Realm is to have a wider selection of women to choose from, should something . . . happen to my queen. My agents above are rather arbitrary in their choices. And, of course, there are certain other tasks for which I need the surface dwellers of the village— tasks unsuitable for my loyal subjects."

"What tasks are those, Your Majesty?" MacCrawley asked.

"One of those duties is to become food for my crankers; we have lately been running short. As for the other task"—he looked suspiciously at MacCrawley—"it is nothing you need to concern yourself with."

Looking into the smoky volcanic glass on the

right, Constantine thought to see dark shapes moving about in it, silhouettes of figures he remembered from his visits to Hell. It was as if it were a kind of aquarium of dark spirits. Was it his imagination? The shapes were just ambiguous enough that he couldn't be sure they weren't tricks of the light. One of them, though, seemed to pause in its restless movement, the silhouette of its head turning to watch him go by, as if in recognition . . .

And he thought he heard a voice whisper in his mind. *Constantine . . . Some day . . . You will be ours.*

They reached another door, this one a slab of granite, covered with hoarfrost, and Constantine buttoned up his coat, for the door emitted waves of cold air. The King stepped off the litter, removed the chain from around his neck, found a keyhole where none was easily seen, and unlocked the door. He then restored the chain to its hiding place. Strange that he didn't keep it in his hand for the consecutive doors, Constantine reflected. He was almost maniacally protective of that key.

The stone slab made a grinding sound as it swung aside. Their breaths pluming in the cold, they entered another corridor, but in this one, the right-hand wall was of glass. *Was* that glass? No, it was ice. A transparent sheet of ice, of such quality that it only faintly distorted what lay behind. And on the other side of the ice window were some three-score women, standing and sitting, motionless. Queenly, splendidly clothed women, they were of various types, none of them very old, and none noticeably unattractive. They were all quite obviously dead, but their looks were mostly intact, since they were frozen solid.

"What do you think of my little collection?" the King asked. "The only way to preserve beauty is to kill it with ice. They become tiresome sulking and flouncing about the palace, and I weary of them . . . and now they serve me forever, as decorations, trophies if you like." He reminded Constantine of a man who had once proudly shown him his beer stein collection.

The former queens, all dressed in splendid period costume from the last four hundred years, had iced over in various postures. Some were sewing, others were in lascivious postures on chairs or rugs, another was gazing rapturously out a false, painted window at a false painted landscape; others seemed to be gossiping, or doing one another's hair. One erstwhile queen was blowing a kiss to the King; he went to stand in just the right spot to receive the kiss and he blew one back. The occasional icicle seemed arranged like jewelry on them; indeed, as Constantine looked closer he saw that they all wore crowns made of inverted icicles.

"Oh my God," Smithson muttered, aghast at the tableau.

"What did you say?" the King asked, giving Smithson a sharp look.

"What? Oh, I was just stunned by . . . by the beauty of the . . . the spectacle. Your Majesty."

"Most women," Constantine said, "would freeze over anyway if you were to let the cold from their hearts spread out to their bodies."

MacCrawley sniffed. "For once you've uttered a truism."

But Constantine didn't believe it. He had said it in order to please the King and Culley's expression told him he'd succeeded.

The King Underneath spoke for some minutes about the contrasting qualities of each queen, and how they'd come to be regarded as "tiresome" and "tableau fodder." At last he concluded, "There is one other I've preserved differently. She was preserved alive until this morning, in the room we are about to enter. The bitch has managed to end her own life. I had given her a particularly terrible punishment. You see, she had tried to stab me in my bed. Of course, the headboard of my bed is sentient—is a powerful protective being—and it watches over me. It prevented the assassination and woke me. You gentlemen might do well to remember that, along with the display I gave you in the throne room. Come along, and I'll show you the would-be assassin." The King gestured for his bearers to proceed and they started for the next door, this one of oak banded by iron.

"I cannot help but admire Your Majesty's command of the Great Work," Constantine said smoothly. "Perhaps it is not so surprising, as I have heard that you were the student of the great Robert Fludd."

The King raised a hand for a halt and turned to look at Constantine, who casually lit a cigarette, just as if he were not worried that he might be executed in a few moments for saying the wrong thing. "How did you know that, Master Constantine?"

"Scofield, Your Majesty, refers to it in his writings."

"Does he? I didn't know. I shall have to ask him about it."

Constantine was startled to hear that Scofield was alive, and apparently handy. Which meant that Constantine might well be caught out in a lie. For he had read no such thing in Scofield. He had heard it from Balf.

The King looked at the keys in his hand. "Fludd was a great man. A great alchemist; he might have been a great magician."

Constantine decided it wouldn't hurt to show the King Underneath his esoteric erudition. "I've read his *Silentium Post Clamores,* and I slogged through his *Tractatus Theologo-Philosophicus* and his *Utriusque Cosmi Maioris scilicet et Minoris*—his Mosaic interpretation of scripture was a bit old fashioned, I reckon, but his ideas about 'divine light' were dead bril—that is, they were quite powerful. His Trinitarian view of the macrocosmos seems sound to me . . ."

The King sniffed. "Fludd had greatness—he understood the correspondences, inner and outer; the microcosmos and the macrocosmos. But he . . . was too judgmental. Too much the precious little Christian. And underlying that, a right-hand-path hermeticist."

"Indeed," said MacCrawley, eager to show his agreement with the King. "Witness his smarmy obsequity to the Rosicrucians, even writing an apologia for them. The Servants of Transfiguration have repudiated the Rosy Cross."

"Oh yes," the King said, tugging fretfully at his small beard. Some of it crumbled off in his hand, but he didn't seem to notice. "Fludd, you know, claimed some people have more particles of light in them—a Zoroastrian doctrine, indeed, Mr. Constantine—and some, carrying more darkness, worked for darkness without knowing it themselves. He thought a man could attune his perceptions to see in a flash who was working for light and darkness . . ." His voice trailed off and he stared into space for a moment, his lips compressed bitterly.

Constantine suspected that Fludd had used that very perception on Iain Culley. He remembered a line from Bob Dylan: "*You got to serve somebody. It may be the devil, it may be the Lord . . .*"

At last King Culley went on, "In the end, Fludd fell short. Short of . . . the real source of power." He shrugged and turned away, getting out of his litter and stumping on his cane to open the next door. The litter bearers followed like trained dogs.

The final room at the end of the corridor was voluminous, and dominated by a high structure whose central part was spindle-shaped and comprised of metal rings alternating steel, brass, and silver. From the upper part of the structure, over their heads, extended five steel vanes, reaching almost to the walls, each ending in a big cuplike vessel containing a gray growth itself entrapping a human being. The spindle-shaped column rose up from the floor through the middle of the room, crackling with violet and orange energy, a pentagonal plate at its top giving off pulsing rays of red-edged purple light, which struck out along the five vanes to their grisly fixtures. Constantine intuited that this was the continuation of the machine he'd seen below. If he followed its axle down far enough, through level after level, he'd come to the lightless chamber where Arfur and his doomed colleagues had served.

But nothing spun here; the spinning below produced power that was transmitted upward to this cavern, its most intense form passing through five grotesque figures twitching and moaning in iron fixtures, where the points of a pentagram would be . . .

Looking up at them, Constantine felt sick to his stomach.

"Please," one of them rasped. "Please kill me . . ."

10

IT WERE BETTER FOR HIM THAT A MILLSTONE WERE HANGED ABOUT HIS NECK

"Mum!"

"Bosky!"

They were in each other's arms, in the queen's chambers, within two seconds of seeing one another. Scofield watched glumly from the doorway. "We cannot stay long. Someone will wonder why we are here, and it is better that no one knows she is your mother."

Maureen stared at Scofield. "Aren't you—?"

Scofield nodded. "I am. Your brother-in-law, once."

Bosky turned to him and asked, "Why shouldn't the King know she's my mother? You said she's a maid or something for the queen. So she can't be too awfully out of favor or whatever."

"If it's known that you're related, the King will wonder what sort of plot you two might cook up. His paranoia is muscular and keen. Which is one way he's stayed alive for so long."

"Bosky, how did you get here?"

Bosky explained, saving Granddad's death for last. She went to her knees, hearing of Garth's dying; weeping, shaking her head. "He said he'd become a foolish old drunk, said it just last week. And I told him not to say such things. And then he gave his life for you . . . he loved you so, Bosky. And me."

"I know, Mum."

"There's no time for this," Scofield put in. "Now your mother knows you're alive, and that's enough. We may need her help. She will have to get the queen to do something difficult—to take a necklace from the King's neck, while he sleeps. It sounds easy but it's not. He's protected."

The door opened then, and Megan came sweeping in, pouting. "Where's my lady in waiting? My hair's a mess and I'm all, like, *so* not presentable for the orgy tonight . . . Oh, hi Scofield. And who's this?" She goggled at Bosky, looking him over. "He's cute, in a kid kinda way."

"He is to be a servant to the King," Scofield said. "We were paying our respects to the lady, exchanging gossip about the world above."

"Oh, did he come from there too?" She turned to Bosky again. "Hey, I've been meaning to ask Maureen, but maybe you know. I mean, I know you're not American, but do you know who's president of the USA now?"

"Believe it or not," Bosky said, "it's—"

But he broke off when a courtier came sauntering in. A tall, round-shouldered man, with jaundice-yellow skin and black lipstick, gray, glaucous eyes that made Bosky think of oysters in just-opened shells, a beard carefully shaved into a cluster of pointed spikes, like a cactus, and a robe ornately figured in silver, black, and red.

"Lord Spurlick," Megan said dourly, as the newcomer bowed to her. "What's up."

"My Adored Queen . . ." Spurlick managed to make the honorific sound both unctuous and mocking. "Forgive the interruption. We beg that you will approve the decorations for the feast." His eyes strayed to Bosky and he licked his lips.

"Oh yeah okay whatever, just let me fix my hair and . . ." She seemed to remember the appropriate diction. "I will attend to the matter."

He bowed again, and backed out of the room. Megan shut the door. "He is like, so gross. I'm so glad he's a pedophile, the King won't make me have sex with him."

Maureen looked startled. "The King makes you have sex with . . . with other people besides him?"

"Oh sure, when he's in the mood. He calls it 'the royal blessing.' Sometimes I like it, it depends on who it is—hey where's my gold hair clip, the one shaped like a man with a rope around his dick? That's my best one. The King gave it to me when I complained that Lord Pifuss was following me around and stealing my shoes and licking them and just *bothering* me so he had Pifuss hung by his boy-parts at a feast, and gave me the hair clip to, y'know, commemorate it, and shit . . ."

She was poking through a large jewelry box, talking to herself, so Scofield gestured for Maureen and Bosky to come close and whispered, barely audible, *"Not yet. When the time is right, we'll try to enlist her. Beware of Spurlick . . ."*

"What?" Megan said, turning. "Did you say something about Spurlick? I hate that guy. But I guess he's not much worse than some guys I knew in Beverly Hills. That's where I'm from. Did you ever go to Beverly Hills? I miss Rodeo Drive so much."

"No," Maureen said. "I've not been out of the UK."

"My Lady, we will take our leave," said Scofield, bowing to the queen—and giving Maureen a significant look.

Megan turned back to the jewelry box, and Bosky gave his Mom's hand a squeeze and mouthed, *Don't worry.*

He followed Scofield out, thinking bitterly, *What, after all, is there to worry about?*

⋆⇒◎⇐⋆

Leaning on his cane, King Culley was twenty minutes into a pedantic explanation of the principles underlying his device, but Constantine was having difficulty attending. He was distracted by the throb of energy from the machine, by the psychic tension in the air, and by the occasional moan from one of the people trapped above him, invariably begging to be killed. He was trying not to stare at the people trapped in the gray growths overhead—five people in all, faces twitching in perpetual horror, mounted in the cup-shaped fixtures of brass and iron. But his eyes kept straying back to them. Their moans made him look. *"Kill me . . ."*

"What do you call this device, Your Majesty?" Smithson asked. He stared, fascinated, at it; perhaps thinking that he might utilize it himself somehow.

"You may call it the rejuvenation projector. It draws a vast amount of energy; to restore youth is to pay a great price, which must be paid in the bowels of this kingdom, by the crankers, and of course by the subjects you see in the containment vessels."

The faces of the "subjects" were mottled blue and white; their hair had fallen out and was replaced by growths of gray-white fur-like mold. They were up to their necks in an enclosing growth that looked like dirty steel wool. Thicker outgrowths of the carefully bred fungus, like sections of artichoke but of a leather toadstool-like material, kept them immobile. It was more thoroughly restraining than any strait-jacket, the King boasted.

"How, ah, long have they been there?" Constantine asked. As he asked, he noticed another door, just visible in the shadows beyond the spindle-shaped machine dominating the room. Where did that door go?

"How long have they been there, you ask?" The King mulled it over. "I get so forgetful, at this time of day. Perhaps two or three centuries? Yes; they've been alive in there for centuries." He chuckled to himself. "Yes indeed!"

"They're kept alive by the fungus, like the 'crankers' I have heard about?" Constantine asked innocently.

"It's a much more elaborate variation of the fun-

gus I developed for the crankers. It first clamps the
body immovably in place—forever immovably—
then penetrates it with micro-pistules through the
pores of the skin. They force their way in ever more
deeply, and grow up through the veins to all the
organs, even the brain, ultimately penetrating every
cell needing to be restored. Death by aging is prevented—at a great cost, of course, to the individual.
They are fed through tubes in the vessel, which go
directly into their bellies. The fungus feeds on them
at a cellular level through the micro-pistules. More
importantly, psychoactive chemicals are secreted
by the fungus, which keeps the subject in a state
of perpetual dreamlike—or perhaps nightmarish—
passivity. This chemical also serves to increase the
radiance of inner selfhood, which is the key to the
device. You see the purple rays, emitting from
yon pentagonal artifact—I have lapsed into old-
fashioned speech. Let me rather say, emitting from
that pentagonal artifact, the locus of the rejuvenation projector. The rays penetrate the spiritual fields
of the five subjects, and are transfigured within
them. The metal vessel in which the subjects are
contained is far from merely a support; it drains the
transfigured energies, and radiates them downward,
whence they penetrate my person. I must walk anti-
clockwise around the circle, under them, exactly five
times, to receive the emanations. I thereupon feel
weary, and must sleep, but when I awake I am physically restored, once more young. This effect begins
to ebb as the day wears on, as if the day is a micro-
cosm of a man's life. By afternoon I am approaching

middle age, and so on, like the Sphinx's riddle. More exposure does not help the effect; to the contrary. The repeated fiveness you perceive is not accidental; it relates to my personal . . . well, that is information you do not need. Not as yet. And so gentlemen, consider the problem—not the first time for Mr. MacCrawley—and see if you can look for a way of perfecting it, so that the juvenescence becomes either more long-lasting or, ideally, permanent. Now, if you will direct your attention hither, that is, over here . . ."

With the soldiers following closely, the King shufflingly led the group to stand not quite directly under one of the vessels in which the "subject" sagged—a woman, quite obviously dead. "This one died this morning. One of my queens, she had been unusually naughty and so I placed her here, replacing another who'd died due to a feeding accident. But Dierdre here, my divorced queen, has killed herself. A remarkable achievement. Do you know how she killed herself?" He lowered his voice so the other "subjects" wouldn't hear. "It was almost admirably resourceful. She had been here for, oh, a mere twenty years, and went quite mad—well, they all do—and in her madness managed to bite off her tongue and chew a hole in her cheek. You can see it there. A hole so big that, together with the bleeding from the stump of her tongue, she bled to death. We failed to notice it until too late."

"Oh . . ." Geoff muttered, staring at the woman's body, mounted overhead. "Oh that . . . this is fucking sick. This is all . . . just all of it . . ."

Constantine looked at him, the boy swaying in place, looking like he might faint. Overcome by what he was seeing.

The King frowned at the boy. "Your apprentice has a weak stomach. How you can have much hope for him, I don't know. Perhaps you might want to sell him to me. I'll give you a box of gems for the wastrel. We have plenty of those. I could find some better use for him."

Geoff gaped at the King, looking dangerously like he was going to retort. Constantine, inwardly wincing, made himself turn to Geoff and give him another sharp slap across the face. "Boy! Stop gaping at the King so! Now walk around the device and make observations! Forget nothing you see!"

Geoff put a hand to his face, blinking. Then, seeing the look in Constantine's eyes, he nodded. "Yes . . . master." He started around the column of the rejuvenation projector, staring at its base.

Constantine inclined his head apologetically toward the King. "My apologies; young people now have attention deficit problems, Your Majesty. For now, I will retain the boy; I have invested a great deal of time training him."

MacCrawley looked suspiciously at Constantine and then at Geoff, but said nothing.

Clearly, the King needed a new "subject" for his projector to replace the dead woman, and soon. Constantine, aware that he was near powerless here, and very aware of the presence of the guards behind him, thought he ought to try to appear useful, and quickly. He forced himself to look at the whole construction. "I have some thoughts on a redesign, Your Majesty, but I will need a few days to organize them, and perhaps time to observe the rejuvenation projector a little more. It is a work of genius, and thus not simple to understand."

"True, true," the King Underneath conceded magnanimously.

Constantine pointed at the small, locked door in the shadows. A door of brass. "I'm curious as to that other door, on the farther side of the room, sire. Is there more machinery there? Perhaps some equipment I should know about, so that I can help perfect it?"

"Hm? That?" The King seemed suddenly pensive, annoyed. "No, nothing of interest there. Just storage. And now . . ." He clumped on his bony cane over to the central shaft of the rejuvenation projector, opened a panel on its side, and twisted a lever within the panel. The vessel with the dead woman at the end of its vane quivered once, then lowered itself mechanically to the floor, making Constantine think of a seat in a carnival ride lowering for a rider. The King took a vial from a pocket in his robes and approached the fungus enclosing the dead woman, and sprinkled blue fluid from the vial on the fungus. It shuddered and withdrew its gray-black petals, its steel wool interior shrinking back with a sound like tearing paper, and the woman's body slumped, freed. The King muttered in Latin to his litter bearers, who reached in, pulled the corpse free, and dragged it unceremoniously to a corner of the room. "We'll clean that up later," the King remarked. "I don't like to be untidy."

Then he gestured to the skull-faced guards and spoke in Latin. MacCrawley took a quick step away from Lord Smithson, who looked around in blinking uncertainty—which became a horrible certainty as the guards seized him and dragged him to the now-empty vessel where the hungry fungus awaited him.

"No! Your Majesty!" Smithson wailed, his face contorted in naked fear, as he realized who was to replace the dead woman. "Is this how a great sovereign repays those who have given him a gift? Is this how a gracious King shows his hospitality? No no no! Take that useless boy there! I believe I have seen him in the—"

Fortunately, before Geoff could be outed as merely another of the residents of Tonsell-on-the-Stream, Smithson broke off to howl in terror as the guards ripped his clothing away. They stripped him nude, knocking him down with the butts of their weapons when he tried to run or fight back, and then four of them grabbed him and forced him snugly into the open center of the artichoke-like cluster of giant fungus in the containment vessel.

He screamed even more shrilly when the big fungus closed around him, gripping him with implacable firmness, and the wooly probes rustled and climbed up around his neck, beginning to penetrate his pores . . .

"No no no . . . *no!*" Smithson screamed. "MacCrawley! You led me into this! I have done all you asked! I gave him the village, I transferred my gold to you!"

"And you're getting your desserts in return!" Mac-Crawley crowed.

"This cannot be! For God's sake! You may not betray a lodge brother, MacCrawley!"

MacCrawley showed his teeth like a shark; it might've been some form of smile. "Why, I've given you what you bargained for! Immortality! Or as close as possible! You will live for centuries, perhaps even millennia, right there, never dying! You wanted to be a King? Long live the King!"

The King laughed creakily at that. "How I do enjoy a good prank! Especially one that may last a thousand years and more." He shook his head with amusement, still chuckling as he returned the control lever to its former position and the vane lifted up into place with Smithson, who was now whimpering madly, muttering to himself, "Oh I feel them . . . they're so . . . so very dry and crisp and eager, pushing into my . . . into veins, into my heart . . . my brain! But it's like the roots of royalty stretching out, stretching out into the body politic . . . and it tickles from within, tickles most painfully! Oh hee hee hee hee heeeeeeeeee . . . oh hee oh *heeeeeeeee* . . ." And then the mad giggles stopped for a moment and he spoke out in awed tones, each word spoken with a surprising clarity, quoting from the gospel of Luke: *"It were better for him that a millstone were hanged about his neck, and him cast into the sea . . ."* And then he resumed his babbling: "The sea . . . by the beautiful sea, the sea-ee-eee . . . hee-hee-*heeeeee* . . ."

The faint purple rays were now emanating from the pentagon outward to all five of the vessels, and as the King threw another switch, Constantine could see a corresponding glow, more red than purple, shining down from the bottom of the vessels, to pool onto the floor. "And now gentlemen," said King Culley, his voice rusty with age, "please observe closely."

The King walked anti-clockwise around the circular room under the vessels, through one pool of reddish-purple light after another, shuffling along without his cane, arms upraised, muttering certain words of power.

When he'd passed through the final pool of light he called for his litter. His nude littermen carried it to him and the King, looking like he might fall without the litter to lie upon, stretched out on it. To Constantine's relief, they all trooped out of the horrid room, leaving its smell of decay and fungus, its moaning, its burbling, its palpable emanation of misery.

"By the sea, by the sea . . . by the beautiful sea-ee-eeee . . ." Smithson warbled. *"Kill me, kill me, kill me-me-me-me-ee-ee!"*

And then the door clanged shut behind them.

⊷══◎══⊷

They had almost passed through the corridor that led past the chamber of frozen queens when Mac-Crawley, feeling the chill from the ice window, put his hands in his pocket and said, startled, "What the devil?"

And he pulled out the crystal that Constantine had planted when he'd jostled him in the throne room. He stared at it in astonishment. Then he scowled.

Constantine reached into his own coat pocket and closed his fingers on the other crystal. He squeezed it hard with his hand, concentrating his psychic field, sending current down his arm into the stone, all as Balf had instructed him. Ritual magic was not possible here, except the King's, but telepathy was another matter (or more precisely, another energy), and Constantine sent a telepathic message directly to Balf through the troll crystal. He thought Balf's name first, so that his transmission was directed to the stone that Balf held, in a cavern somewhere far below . . .

Balf! Constantine thought, *The time has come! Do it now!*

"What are you doing with that sensing stone, MacCrawley?" the King asked, looking over sleepily from his litter. "That is a troll artifact! What have you to do with troll-stuff here?" He sat up, glowering with suspicion at MacCrawley through his hooded, red-rimmed eyes.

"But someone must have . . . Constantine!" MacCrawley turned to accuse Constantine, but already Balf's voice was emitting loudly from the stone MacCrawley held in his hand. The telepathic impulse, coming through at the receiving end, was translated into spoken words.

"When are we to move against the King, MacCrawley?" came the voice from the crystal.

"So!" The King said, standing. He pointed to MacCrawley. "Take him!"

"Your Majesty—no! It was Constantine!"

The soldiers crowded around the black magician,

and he struggled for a moment before one of them
thrust a crossbow against his temple and grinned.

MacCrawley slumped in their arms, but spoke to
the King with all the dignity he could muster. "My
Lord and King, John Constantine planted the stone
on me! He is the one clearly in league with the trolls!"

"It is not Constantine's name I heard Balf speak
just now, for that was that rascal Balf, if I am not
mistaken. I may be feeble at this time of night, but
my hearing is not gone yet, MacCrawley!" The King
took the crystal from MacCrawley and then pointed
at the door. "Drag him to the work pits! He'll join
the sump slaves until I've decided how best to kill
him! Perhaps he might take someone's place in the
projector; it would please Lord Smithson to have
the company! We shall see! Take the traitor out now!
I don't wish to hear another syllable of his dissem-
bling!"

"Your Majesty—it was Constantine—in the throne
room—he—!" But they had dragged MacCrawley
through the door, and away down the corridor.

"And see that he is well chained! He is not to be
trusted!" the King called after them. "And then get a
deputation out to find that troll! Send fifty men and
kill him if he won't surrender!"

Constantine felt confident they'd never catch
Balf now that he was unchained. He tried to look
more concerned than pleased, but it wasn't easy; he
had succeeded in eliminating an enemy who would
have destroyed him at the first opportunity. And
now he was the only "consultant" the King could
turn to.

The King looked at Constantine with a grim curiosity. "I wonder . . ."

"Your Majesty?"

"Hmph. We shall see. I'll be watching you closely, Constantine. You'd better make yourself useful to me, and soon. Or *you'll* be in the vessel on the other side of Lord Smithson, making yourself useful in another way entirely. For a long, long time."

11

CURIOUS 'TIS, HOW SEDUCTIVE NUMBNESS IS

"You want me to trust *this* geezer?" asked Bosky dubiously, looking at Constantine. Who looked especially shabby, after the tunnels, the pit of the crankers, and Balf's quarters.

"Well," Geoff said, grimacing a little, "it's true he's not exactly . . . the *best* ally. I mean, the only way he could think of to impress the King was to *slap* me, and really *hard* too . . . twice!" The last he said looking at Constantine with narrowed eyes.

"All theatre, my lad," Constantine said airily, shaking a wine bottle to see if anything was left in it. "Had to give it me method acting best, yeah? Bloody hell, this one's empty too . . ."

They were in the servants' quarters, down a granite-walled corridor adjoining the throne room: Bosky, Maureen, Geoff, and Constantine—waiting for Scofield to arrive. There were three cots, a wash basin, two rough wooden cabinets, a glowing crystal in the floor for heat and light, a hole in a corner of the floor for elimination, and little else. Constantine and Geoff had been escorted here to "await the King's pleasure" and found Maureen talking to Bosky.

"There's some kind of wine in that cabinet, I think," Bosky said. "I sniffed it. Didn't want to touch the stuff."

"Where's this Scofield bloke?" Constantine asked, looking in the cabinet. He found a clay-pot bottle of wine that contained a green slurry floating on a liquid which smelled of alcohol and God knew what else. He tasted it and made a face—and tasted some more. Felt a creeping numbness around the edges . . . not unpleasant.

"Went off to talk to the King about me," Bosky said. "Got some kind of permission to bring me round and he wants to prime the pump, he says. Don't think I like the idea. I think we ought to get the bloody hell out of here before the queen wakes up and finds Mum missing. Find a way to the surface."

"Not so easy to do, from what I've seen," Geoff said. "Those gripplers guarding everything. Not to mention those skull-faced bastards and them ugly bitches with the wings. Pardon, Mrs." This last to Bosky's mum, who was sitting on a cot gazing at Bosky with a kind of muted wonder.

The door opened then and in came Lord Spurlick. He introduced himself to Constantine, though his gaze tended to return to Bosky and Geoff. "I saw you, Master Magus, during your audience in the throne room. I honor you for your boldness, and I'm here to inform you that the King has found better quarters for you. Also you and your apprentice are invited—

more properly, commanded—to appear at the feast this morning, when the King arises. You will shortly hear a gong ring to announce the event." He smiled at Geoff, showing teeth intricately carved into gargoyle faces. "Clothes are optional."

"You mean breakfast of some kind?" Constantine asked, ever hopeful.

"There will be a repast. It will be breakfast for the King. For the rest of us it will be the capper of our evening; we time things like that so that we can feast with him when he's young. We sleep for much of his day."

"Right, I'll listen for the gong then, mate."

Spurlick bowed. "Shall I show you to your quarters?"

"Actually, I'd rather stay here. If the King don't approve, I'll move, how's that?"

"You prefer these Spartan surroundings to luxury?"

"It's, you know, a sorcerer thing."

"Is it? The King is not that sort of sorcerer. Very well; I shall see you at the feast."

He lingered but as the atmosphere was not welcoming, he shrugged and said, "You might want to bathe, Master Magus. We're rather sensitive to odor in the confined spaces in which we live." And then he abruptly made his leave.

Maureen looked at Constantine with approval. "Good you'd rather stay here than take their luxury suite, or whatever it is. I'm glad you stayed—I mean, since Geoff vouches for you."

"He saved my life, I got to admit that much," Geoff said.

Constantine was looking at his coat. "Reckon I am a mite grubby, at that."

Maureen took an urn of water from a cabinet. "Why don't you take off that shirt and coat, Mr. Constantine; I can clean them a bit. There's water in this tub . . ."

Constantine looked at her, started to answer, made eye contact—and couldn't quite make his mouth work, at first. There was something about her that arrested his glibness. "I . . . well . . . yeah, that'd . . ."

Geoff looked back and forth between Constantine and Maureen and grinned.

Constantine scowled at him. "What are you grinning about, 'apprentice'?"

⋯⊙⋯

Men were coming to find him, and kill him.

Shivering a little in the rising cloud of mist, Balf the troll heard them coming long before they passed under his hiding place, their torches flickering in the gloom.

He was sequestered on a shelf of rock in the cavern of the Stabbing Falls, overlooking the churning cliff. There was little light here, just trace phosphorescence, but Balf could see well, though things looked blue and red for him, as his troll's eyes had automatically shifted to the specialized vision his kind used in the darkness.

The skull-soldiers of the King Underneath marched double-file along the stony path which followed the stream. This was the Stab River, a little ways farther, it pitched over the falls into the echoing cavern. The water fell a long ways, nigh six hundred feet, to crash into a pool which became a river that eventually, after many pitch-black miles, found its way to a sea cave.

Trolls called this place something that translated to "the cavern of the Stabbing Falls," but Balf wasn't sure why. Because the falls seemed to stab down in the darkness? Or had some significant killing happened here long ago?

His mind ruminated over these questions without concern for the pallid men trooping below, though he knew full well they were searching for him. King Culley would have told them to take him prisoner only if he did not resist. He might well kill thirty or forty of them, he supposed, in pitched combat with a wall at his back, but there were full a hundred down there, bristling with weapons. They couldn't see him in the mist and darkness; they didn't know this little shelf was up here. Behind him it narrowed to a passage just big enough for him to squeeze through, which in turn rose to a chamber above, an old volcanic bubble, which was his current hideout. It was a place so dark that not even his specially evolved eyes could help him; he had to ignite light-crystals so he could see his tools and materials. There he had spent his waking hours, when not hunting blind cave fish and rats to eat, making the tools that he hoped would destroy the King's great machine.

Of course, he might stop the machine temporarily by dislodging some of its smaller gears; he might even jam the great cylinder. But the machine kept a charge for a full course of the Earth's turning, during which time a guard would be set up, and it would be repaired and quickly restarted, giving the King time to be rejuvenated.

Only the section of the machine guarded by the Il-Sorg was vulnerable enough to stop the machine for long.

And then Constantine's plan might, just might, go forward.

Of course, Balf was a troll, who had lived thousands of years, and he knew well that the doings of men were evanescent and conceived without the benefit of real experience. They had a tendency to fall apart. They did not take years to plan things as Balf did. When Constantine came along Balf had just been about to make his move to escape . . .

Well, in ten years or so he'd have done it. Probably.

Now, as the soldiers, finding nothing in the channel leading to the great cavern, turned about and went back to search in exactly the wrong places, Balf put his patience back to work again. He climbed to his hiding place and set to work scraping away at the tools he was modifying for the sabotage, the undermining, of an entire kingdom.

The question was, could the scruffy yellow-haired human, John Constantine, do his part?

Balf doubted it.

⵻

"You'd be John Constantine, then?" asked the man walking up to Constantine on the battlements of the castle. Constantine had been on the ramparts looking out over the cavern, as the clouds over the glowing ceiling began to disperse for "morning." He was wearing an old robe he'd found in a cabinet while his clothes were being washed. He might've passed for a local except for the cigarette in his mouth.

"Who's asking?"

The stranger drew his hood back, showing Constantine a world-weary, bearded face that he supposed must be Scofield's, from the description Bosky had given.

"I am Philo Scofield," the man confirmed. "The boy from the village told me you'd be here. I suppose you're surprised to see me alive."

Constantine nodded. "Well, it's a right old convention of sorcerers down here in these bloody damned Underlands of yours: the King, that bastard Mac-Crawley, and here we two stand, yeah?"

"Yeah."

The two men looked each other over but did not offer to shake hands. Sorcerers don't trust one another that much. A curse could be transferred through a hand clasp, if one knew how, among other things.

Constantine, though, seeing Scofield staring at his cigarette, offered him one. Scofield hesitated.

"Oh take a chance, mate. I'm not going to give you the fucking poison cigarette. I need allies here. Might need my poison cigarette for some other troublesome cove, yeah?"

Scofield nodded and took one; Constantine lit it for him.

"Silk Cut, eh? I appreciate it. Know it's a risk; you may never get another pack." Scofield drew on the smoke, and coughed. "Forgot how rough smoking is on the lungs. But then it's nothing compared to what I breathe in the sump chamber . . ." He glanced around to see if anyone was listening. "We're being watched, but I don't think they're listening."

"Watched? Where?"

"Up there on that tower—you see the harpy? That one's followed me here. There's something else that follows me down below. It watches what I do, but doesn't seem to pick up on what I say . . ."

"What is it that follows you, uh, down below?"

"Flying shadows, I call them. Looks kind of like a bat, except the bat's not there. It's a magical version of those flying-drone things with the cameras they were developing on the surface, when I came down."

"Right. Royal Air Force uses those in the war in Iraq."

"There's a war in bloody Iraq, is there? Why?"

"No good reason anyone can figure out, mate. This thing watches you, inside? How many has he got?"

"The King has only three I know of. He'll put one on you. But I don't think they can hear us. Now listen, he's got me on an alchemical project that's going to destroy all life in Britain."

Constantine coughed on his cigarette smoke at that, amazed at the almost matter-of-fact way Scofield had decreed the imminent doom of his nation. After a short coughing fit, Constantine allowed, "I heard something about it, but I didn't get anything that extreme. How's it work?"

"The Universal Solvent—he's worked up his own version of it. He's been gathering canisters of industrial waste, toxins of all kinds from underground sites around the world. He knows tunnels that connect this land and the other Underlands—"

"Hang on! How much more Underlands are there? I read about some, but I thought it was just one place somewhere."

"Oh, there's a great deal of it; tens of thousands of square miles, at several subterranean sites. It's not the 'hollow Earth,' exactly, it's not that far under the surface. Three other civilizations, there are. You think this one's peculiar? They practice a kind of crossbreeding make you sick to look at it, underneath Mount Shasta over in the States. Then there's one under China where everyone's blind, see their way around with some kind of sonar. Used to be human beings, not so much anymore. Great builders, they are. Used to be five great Underland civilizations, but two of them were destroyed in earthquakes."

"And their sorcerers?"

"Low grade, when they've got them. Specialize in eccentric forays into technology instead. Some of them have planned invasions of the upper world, but they can't live up there so it ain't practical. The King Underneath inverted it—"

"Appropriately enough."

"He plans to bring the upper to the lower. And he wants to invade the rest of the Underlands. But he wants to force thousands of slaves from the upper world into his armies and to build a new underground civilization he's got in mind. So he plans to make Britain and probably France unlivable up there, which will drive a few million survivors down here.

He'll take them by surprise and enslave them. He's going to open up tunnels for them across Britain, and beyond, to draw them in once the poison starts to spread."

"And how's he plan to spread it, then?" Constantine asked, feeling a chill spread out from his spine as Scofield unfolded the plot for him.

"The poisons he's collected will be carried on the Universal Solvent—which has the power to distribute a poison far, far from its source. The toxins will be released into the Stab River, where they'll run off the Stabbing Falls—it's a place deep underground, about ten miles from here. Those tunnels will be sealed off so the poison doesn't come in here, but it won't reach its full destructive capability immediately. It'll spread out through other channels too . . . one of them goes right to the Thames in London! Another goes to the sea. It'll react with the seawater, setting up a chain reaction that'll kill the sea round about Britain! That's *all* life, including plankton, algae, everything—marine photosynthesizers, don't you know. Surface people rely on those kinds of organisms in the sea for the creation of oxygen. There'll be great banks of air with no oxygen all round southern England and London—down here we'll have enough air. The King has farm caverns that produce oxygen."

"The sea'll stop making oxygen round the UK, and the forests won't be enough?"

"Right. But that's not all; once the Underking introduces his toxin, the sea will give off a poisonous miasma."

"Hold on, the sea is awfully fucking big, mate. It's already polluted round Britain, but it's surviving."

"There are vast tracts of dead sea they don't talk about much in the papers. The fish are dying back, the whales and sea lions sickening and heaving themselves on the beaches; that's already going on, thanks to the ordinary pollution out there. It makes the sea animals weak, so they can't fight disease, don't you know. A healthier ocean might survive Culley's poison, but not this one. And d'ya'see, the Solvent will carry the poisons at great speed around much of the UK. *The shortage of oxygen and the poisoned air will drive hundreds of thousands, maybe millions of people underground!* The King will seem to offer them shelter, but what he's got in mind is slavery. Slavery is the source of all his power, d'ya'see."

"And the ones who don't make it underground . . . or to some other safe place . . ."

"They'll die. Who knows how many."

Constantine blew smoke over the crenelated walls and watched it drift toward the crumbling old Roman settlement of Danque down below. Drifting clouds of poison. "You think it could work?"

"The chemistry and the alchemy seem to be there. He's got help from his secondary source of power. Of course you know about the machine. It lights the palace, provides warmth . . . and his rejuvenation."

Constantine snorted. "I saw how he gets his rejuvenation. I've been to Hell, thought I had a thick skin. But this made me sick, it did."

"So that story about you and Hell is true?"

Scofield asked enviously. Hell might be hellish—but it was a big draw to a magician. "You actually went there . . . and came back? How?"

"I didn't go as a condemned spirit. There's no coming back from that, this side of God's intervention. And him and me are scarce talking. I went by another route, you might say. What's this other source of power?"

Scofield hesitated, looking at Constantine with cold, calculating eyes.

"Not sure if you want to trust me to tell me everything you know?" Constantine asked. "Right. Suit yourself. But from what I hear, there's precious little time to waffle about in."

Scofield grunted. "Got to trust someone. All right . . . in a room, beyond the upper room of the rejuvenation projector, is a powerful elemental, trapped. Once the King trapped him, he forced him to help him create the gripplers, and to give him control over the harpies. Within the caverns, the harpies obey the earth elementals. The King used this power to make the Fallen Romans his minions—"

"Fallen Romans? Oh, those noseless, pasty fellows with the pigstickers I've been running into?"

"The very chaps. Once they hated Culley's guts. Now he's gotten them completely under his sway. He's a cult of personality to these gormless idjits. They live to try to get enough service so they can be elevated to the pleasure merry-go-round of his courtiers; a lot of vile wankers, his courtiers."

"That was my impression. Tossers all. But, Scofield—" Constantine had spotted the collar around

Scofield's neck. He'd recognized runes that meant the destruction of anyone who tried to remove it, and the runes kept the wearer contained within a certain distance of its maker. "He's got you enslaved too, then, has he?"

"I saw you looking at the collar," Scofield said bitterly. "Aye. Once I was the best magician in England." He looked narrowly at Constantine as if challenging him to deny it. Constantine shrugged. "But now," Scofield went on, his voice dripping with self-contempt, "I'm but Culley's magical potboy. His assistant he calls it, but in fact his slave."

"Meaning you've helped him develop this . . . this toxic sump he's going to release?"

"It was all his design. But . . ." Scofield sighed and threw his cigarette butt over the balcony's edge; everything about the gesture spoke of disgust. For himself. For the world. "But I've been supervising the work, getting it ready," he admitted.

Constantine flicked away his own cigarette butt, watching the dying ember turn end over end as it fell, a spinning red spark. "It don't bother you, killing millions of people, enslaving thousands more?"

"I'm not so coldhearted as that. Only there's *that room*. The people in the projector vessels, the invasive mold—Culley threatened me with that, and . . ." He chewed his lower lip so hard it began to bleed, ever so slightly. "I should have hung myself first chance, instead of taking the job on. But he had gotten the collar on me, so there was no escape. I talked myself into doing his dirty work by figuring I could find a way to sabotage the process. I couldn't do it right away; he checks on it too closely. Every bloody day. Still, I figured I could bide my time. Or maybe . . ." He lowered his voice so it was all but inaudible. "Or maybe watch for some way to get past his defenses, kill him in his bed, d'ya'see. I put one of his queens up to stealing . . ." He glanced nervously around. "Well. It doesn't matter. She failed. And the worst happened. I had hypnotized her, so she'd forget her encounter with me if she were caught. And she was caught. She . . ." He broke off, closing his eyes. Looking like he was fighting tears now. "God I hate him."

"You know she's dead, don't you?"

"She is? Thank God! I'm glad for her. Often wish I was dead. I know, reeks of self-pity. But having to do this work so I could find a way to stop it. It's maddening. This whole fucking place is maddening."

Constantine scratched his thatchy head and, tense with the imminence of catastrophe, lit another cigarette. "When's he plan to release this poison, then?"

"Why, about forty-eight hours from now."

"Strewth! We've bloody well got to stop him, fast!"

"A cauldron containing the Universal Solvent now hangs over the sump; I've just helped put it there. You might say it's cooking, coming to complete transmutation. It'll be ready in about forty-eight hours. When it's completed its transmutation it'll be poured into what he calls the lower cauldron, the toxin sump. That'll set up a chain reaction that will dissolve the stone walls between the lower cauldron and the river. With the walls down the mixture will then pour freely into the river, and from there into the sea, in a matter of a few hours."

"You have a plan for blocking that sump room up to keep all that muck in there? Diverting the Solvent? You said you hoped to sabotage him and I hope to fuck you thought of *something*, Scofield, considering if you don't want to be remembered by the survivors as one of the worst mass murderers in history. You and Culley'll make Hitler and Stalin look like amateurs, mate."

"There might be a way. But I've got to divert his army; they're fanatically guarding the thing. And his gripplers must be dealt with. If his machine ends, you know, he'll first be weakened and then he'll die. You'd have chaos throughout his kingdom. In all the chaos, we might, we just *might* get away with it. The harpies and the gripplers, though . . ."

"You leave them to me. I've got some thoughts on that, and on that machine of his."

"Constantine!"

He jumped at that, expecting to be seized by the Fallen Romans. But it was Bosky. "You're to come and change clothes and go to the feast," the boy said, trotting up. "The gong rang."

"Well I bloody well didn't hear it and we have no time for feasts."

"You'd better go," Scofield advised him. "You'll be too conspicuous by your absence. Culley will assume you're up to something. We need to think before we act. There's one we can trust—Fallesco, his name is. He'll be in touch with you. He'll be there and he'll act as my go-between . . . Uh-oh."

The harpy who'd been watching them had leaped into the air, was circling close overhead, exuding a rank smell of wet leather, and shrieking something in Latin that Constantine couldn't make out.

"It's telling me to go back to the cave, to get back to work," he said. "The King must have looked through its eyes and sent it the message. Oh, check this boy's hip. And now—" He bowed slightly to Constantine, giving him a significant look, and turned to stride away toward the sump cavern, the harpy flying above, swooping back and forth, chivvying him along.

"What'd he mean?" Constantine asked. "About your hip?"

Bosky groaned. "Oh I suppose . . . wait." He looked around. "Be sure that Spurlick perv's not around. Right. Have a gander." He pulled his waistband down just enough to show the birthmark on his hip.

"Hmmm . . ." Constantine said, looking at the birthmark. "He must figure it's a fairy thing. You've got fairy blood, then."

"That's what my granddad said. It comes from me mum's side of the family, he said." His eyes misted when he thought of Granddad. He cleared his throat and went on, "Though how those little fairy creatures could, you know, manage to shag with a grown woman—"

"Nah, that's all wrong about fairies being small. That's sprites, the small ones. Fairies are the same size as people. They're a kind of people—magically empowered people from another dimension, like. But one that overlaps with ours, you might say. Scary, treacherous bastards, for all their pretty looks and elegant ways, are fairies. That mark must be why you're wandering around free. The King's got something in mind for you. We'd best get you out of here fast."

"You coming to this feast or not?" After a moment, looking off the ramparts and trying to seem casual, he added, "Me mum'll be there."

"Sod it. Lead the way." Constantine followed Bosky back, muttering. "This is mad. Going to a party. Fiddling while Rome burns."

Forty-eight hours . . .

———✦◉✦———

"Mr. Constantine," Maureen began, laying his clothes out on the cot. "I was wondering—"

"John."

"What?" She looked up at him, startled at the interruption; there was a peculiar, not unpleasant tension between them that made them both startle easily.

"My name is John, innit?" he said. "All right I call you Maureen, then?"

"Well . . . yes. Why not. I mean . . . certainly." They looked at one another; he in his robe, she in the slightly frayed old butter-yellow gown the queen had picked out for her. "Any gate, I was wondering—you aren't the John Constantine of Mucous Membrane, are you?"

The John Constantine of Mucous Membrane looked at her in frank astonishment. "Get on with you! You never heard of it!"

"I did. I had your 45—'Lies of My Own.'"

"You didn't! You're not old enough!"

"Oh I'm almost old enough. Anyway I was kind of obsessed with music from that era when I was young. Later on I got more into traditional music—Celtic folk, that kind of thing. Played some harmonium, sang with a little group that used to do pubs about Cornwall."

"Really? I'd . . . like to hear it. Sometime. I mean . . . when all this is, you know, sorted out."

In the unlikely event it's sorted out, he added, to himself.

Their gazes seemed to cling to one another. Then she quickly looked away, examining his folded clothing in an almost fiercely businesslike way. "Right. Anyway . . . I've found something like borax and managed to get your clothes something like clean, and if you're to get something like clean for the King's feast, you'd better hurry, you can wash behind that curtain there. Oh and here's a straight razor; the queen had several she uses for her legs and I nicked it, actually . . ."

"You nicked it? Not your legs, I'm guessing. I mean—not that they're—that is—"

She laughed softly. "Not for that no. I just don't like the way some of these twits have been looking at me."

Constantine smiled. She was ready to slash some bastard who tried to force himself on her; he liked her even better now.

He went behind the curtain, found a basin with water and a cloth, a crude sort of soap, managed something like a sponge bath, and scraped away his beard with the straight razor. He was fantasizing that Maureen would come in to give him his clothes and with him standing there naked she'd lose control, though nothing about him naked was likely to make a woman lose control. Except in the fantasy—with their chemistry overwhelming them both—she'd fling herself into his arms and . . .

And then she handed him the clothes, crooking her arm around the curtain without coming around.

What did you think, you childish oik, he told himself savagely.

Dressed in his old clothes and trench coat, feeling more human for being more presentable, and not minding that the pants weren't quite dry yet, he came out from the curtain, lit a celebratory cigarette, and offered her one.

"No thanks."

"You're smart not to smoke. Where's our likely lads?"

"They had some notion of trying to find out what happened to Finn, or someone they could ask. Some of the saner palace people."

He sighed, exhaling at the same time. "I'm afraid I've got bad news on that front, Maureen." Geoff had described Finn to him and he'd guessed whose dismembered body he'd glimpsed far below; whose hand it had been in the bowl. "That boy is as dead as a boy can be."

"Oh no. Are you sure?"

He nodded. He didn't want to tell her about how he knew. And he didn't think he should tell her what

Scofield had told him about the Universal Solvent. News like that, that there were two days till much of Britain would choke to death like a man in a gas chamber—in fact, less than that by now—could plunge Maureen into despair. And he didn't want to see Maureen despair.

She looked at him. "Funny to think of you in that rock band, and now up to your neck in magic. Down here."

"Funny to think of *you* with that rare 45 in your hands, and up to your neck in fairy blood."

"Oh. Bosky told you?"

"Yeah. Better keep it quiet, for now. Well . . ." He didn't want to leave her, to go off to the intrigues of the Underking's degenerate court. He tried to think of some reason to linger. "Not good, those boys wandering about this place. If you see them, tell them so, that's my advice. Don't want you to worry, but . . . better they stay out of sight in the gaff here. Geoff's supposed to be my apprentice; he'll babble something to the wrong person."

Stupid, you're just making her worry.

She glanced at the door. "I told Bosky to be back here, to stay away from that feast. But . . ." She shrugged. "He goes his own way nowadays. I've got to attend to the queen."

He looked at her; she looked back at him—then quickly away.

What is it that attracts me to her so bloody much? She's no great beauty, though she's pretty in an ordinary kind of way. Lot of character in her face, true. Intelligence. Sensitivity. But this feeling . . .

Is it the fairy thing?

It didn't feel that way, though. It wasn't magic, drawing him to her. Not that kind of magic. Making him linger like this . . .

He tapped his cigarette. Cleared his throat. Thought he ought to go. But somehow he didn't.

She hummed to herself. Glanced at him. Away. "Well . . ."

"Well . . ."

She started to laugh again, then, in a peculiarly pleasurable embarrassment, and he grinned. "Right, Maureen. I'm off."

She broke off laughing as their gazes caught again.

Her eyes.

Then he made himself turn away and look for the throne room.

⊷⊙⊷

"Curious 'tis, how seductive numbness is,"

. . . recited the courtier, Fallesco, a tall slender man, elegantly attired in a scarlet and silver coat and tails, accompanying himself on a lyre:

> *To insulate, to obfuscate,*
> *A strange way to elevate—but wait!*
> *What when benumbed, now resonates?*
> *The signals sent before, always more,*
> *Had muted what sung at the core;*
> *The clamor of the world, outside—*
> *Masked the rising of the inner tide;*
> *And not until I was stoned to dumbness,*

Not until I was smashed to numbness,
Not until I was crashed to dullness,
Not till I was choked with fullness,
Not till I had made my head ring—

Fallesco paused and everyone at the feast, sitting on the cushions about the smoky throne room floor listening to his recital, including the now-rejuvenated King and the queen, leaned forward on their reclining cushions to hear the conclusion of his musical poem, and he said:

—*"could I understand . . . the King!"*

And so saying he genuflected toward the King Underneath.

The room erupted in applause, which Constantine joined in, just as soon as he finished draining his glass. He looked at the young man who was evidently the King Underneath, Iain Culley. It took a moment to confirm that was indeed who it was; you could just make out something of the old man's features in this person who was outwardly a twenty-year-old.

A five-hundred-year-old twenty-year-old, he thought.

Easy to understand the King being morally seduced by regular restoration of youth, Constantine reckoned, signaling a servant girl who poured him some more from a stone jug. He tried to smile at her, but it came out a leer. She leered back showing a forked tongue and filed teeth. Or were they naturally a set of fangs all the way round? It looked as if the forked tongue had been done at some point with a knife, a crude surgery, the local version of having a

plate in your lips. She sashayed off to serve the King.
The queen was yawning beside Culley; their thrones
had been hidden behind decorative screens and the
sovereigns were now lounging luxuriantly on a raised
dais covered with opulent gold-trimmed silken cushions. Maureen sat a little behind the queen, and to
one side. It looked to Constantine like she was trying
to make herself seem small, inconspicuous. She
avoided the eyes of the male courtiers, and some of
the females, who looked at her with garishly candid
lust.

"Constantine?"

He looked up to see the urbane Fallesco hunkering
close beside his cushions. Constantine nodded, lighting a cigarette. "Fallesco, the court poet, yeah? I did
applaud, I think. Or did I? Not sure."

"May I intrude?"

"On me pillows, not me body."

Fallesco smiled; he was a fox-faced man with a del-
icate, braided beard, a sharp nose, and deceptively
sleepy green eyes. "A touch of wit. I do enjoy it." He
sat beside Constantine with a single graceful motion,
as several muscular black men who seemed to have
been captured somewhere, judging by the chains
linking their necks, and playing against their will,
judging by their sullenness, were now beating out
something like salsa on conga drums, just in front of
the King. And the now-younger King bobbed his head
to the beat.

The noise was such that Fallesco had to lean close
to Constantine to make himself heard. "I believe
we're both acquainted with Scofield?"

"Yes." Constantine spotted Bosky and Geoff drifting around the edges of the feast, snagging food from the trays, clearly looking for something else entirely. Bosky's mum had told them to stay away. *Little bastards going to steal some drink,* Constantine thought. He tried to organize his thoughts around Scofield so he could plan with Fallesco, but the strange green liquor seemed to make everything beyond the present moment, even the catastrophe waiting to claim the UK, so far away and unreal. "Ah. Scofield. Need to stop the King's machine so Scofield can do his mischief."

He seemed alarmed at Constantine's directness, and he looked at the glass Constantine was drinking from. "I can see this is not the time to talk of this. Fortunately the drums are muffling our conversation. Be careful what you say tonight, my friend; I beg you, trust no one. And speaking of caution, if I may take the liberty of observing it, that liqueur—which we call the Emerald Mead—is perhaps rather more powerful than you realize. You may lose all track of time, and all moral center, under the Emerald's crafty influence. Those who are new to the Underlands often find themselves undone by it, as when Scofield woke from a binge with the Emerald to find a collar about his neck . . ."

"Here, give it a rest. I've drunk enough alcohol to sterilize ten thousand liver transplants, mate," Constantine said, trying hard not to slur his words. "And that's on one good night."

"And good night is what I bid you, sir. If the gods permit it, we will have further intercourse anon."

"What's that you say? Intercourse with a nun? I'm in, mate! Bring 'er on! Kinky bitches, nuns!"

Fallesco rolled his eyes, and made his leave. Constantine thought: *Maybe he's right, maybe I've already taken a bit too much. Talking rather brassy . . . Stuff's strong, kind of like absinthe but far more so . . . Better watch meself. Better . . . get another.*

He signaled the woman with the darting forked tongue, and she brought him another drink. He was vaguely aware that some of the courtiers were dancing, the King was casually copulating with a flaxen-haired pasty-faced girl—shapely, though she had a fake nose—as the queen smiled indulgently; the King appearing to have a conversation with Spurlick while he shagged the girl; and other courtiers were drifting off into the shadows behind the columns, where a flagrant pansexual cruising was going on. Constantine was more interested in his drink. But he did notice the queen was making eye contact with one of the black drummers. *Shag me and I'll get you out of those chains and into a luxury cell,* her look seemed to say.

He took another long swallow of "the Emerald" and a pleasant wave of numbness carried a surge of dark purple neon hieroglyphics to Constantine so that seemed to see the cryptic, mutedly fluttering strings of glowing symbols, tracking by like glimmering ticker tape, everywhere he looked; twining around the feasters' faces, spiraling up the columns supporting the roof of the throne room, emanating from the big cluster of glowing crystals, big as a bonfire, in the middle of the floor.

This shit was stronger than he had supposed.

He felt himself carried back in memory, so that the present party was mingled with parties of the past: a night drunk and stoned at a sex club after a Mucous Membrane concert; an S&M club in California not so very long ago; two bimbos who'd come home with him in the punk rock era, with him and Sid Vicious but Sid had nodded out; a drunken party in Ireland, with the cops raiding it for the noise and ending up drinking with the rest of them, the drunk cops pinning a badge on him; a couple of girls in the bushes at a rock festival (was that one with the long straight brown hair a girl? He wasn't sure, he'd been so fucked up); a Wiccan orgy within sight of Stonehenge; several drunk meter maids in the back room of a specialized pub in Chelsea; an Irish girl in Dublin, who'd insisted on . . .

Irish girls. Kit. He could see Kit now, her face taking ghostly shape in the glow from the crystal, looking at him pityingly.

"Sod off," he muttered. "I don't need your condescension, Kit. Bloody world's probably coming to an end in a few days and you with it, so none of your judgmental bollocks mean anything . . ."

The drummers thumped; pipers threaded suggestive melodies through the drumbeats, the music seeming to crystallize into dancing figures in the smoke gathering overhead.

How'd the smoke get so thick? There were hookahs going around, the curious herbal smoke rising to coalesce, to shrug and swirl into the bodies of Hindu gods, Norse Valkyries, the face of the Green Man trying to tell him something . . .

"Would you like some?" asked a lady sitting beside him, a small hookah in her hands. She was a plump courtier, with all her features in more or less the right place, in contrast to some of the other inbred toffs stumbling about the room, her nose quite intact, long black hair falling in ringlets over her shoulders, making him think of Tchalai. He wished he had Tchalai's counsel. But how she'd chide him now . . .

He found he had taken the hookah's mouthpiece, was drawing in a great hit of the tarry, unfamiliar smoke. "What the devil is it?" he asked, the words coughing out with the smoke.

"Oh, we feed the bats certain mushrooms and certain herbs. We harvest and smoke their droppings . . ."

"What? I'm smoking bat shite?" He cackled, and somehow the idea was not unappealing. "Why not? Going 'bat shit' anyway." He took another hit, and another drink, and time melted away . . . until it ceased to exist entirely.

12

WHAT SWEETER DRINK THAN THE BLOOD OF THE FAIRY?

"What's the King want to talk to me about?" Bosky asked nervously.

"That is no concern of yours; your only concern is to obey and pray the King finds you a worthy servant."

The man looking dourly down on Bosky—he had introduced himself as "Lord Blung, the King's seneschal"—was a tall, stooped man with a gray mustache that seemed to stream from his nostrils to extend several inches from the edge of his face, as if rockets had just flown up his nose; he wore a black robe sewn with silver images of the King and the Phosphor Palace and he carried a walking stick made from what appeared to be a woman's arm that had been taxidermically preserved; its lower end was rounded off with ivory, capping the bone-end that stuck out; its upper end was her fingers, held open so that when he walked he could insert his fingers between hers, as if holding her hand. Magic must have been involved in its making as well as taxidermy, for the preserved fingers adjusted to his grip as he moved about, and sometimes one of the woman's preserved fingers caressed his.

"How come I haven't seen you before if you're such a big nob hereabouts?" Bosky asked.

"I'm not sure what you mean by a nob, but you haven't seen me before, boy, because I've been away on a mission for His Majesty."

The drums thumped, the pipes skirled, and the man in the black robe tugged at one of his mustache tips and looked at the boy with unconcealed distaste. They were standing behind the screen set up in front of the thrones; the images on the screen, backlit by the glow of the big luminous, warming crystal in the center of the throne room, seemed to move: A painted figure intended to represent King Culley seemed to actually fly along in an aerial chariot borne by three harnessed harpies, sending lightning bolts down at running trolls, men, scuttling goat-men, enemies scurrying away below him.

"I was just looking for me mate," Bosky said. "For Geoff. I turned my back and he wandered off with someone."

"Your friend will be fine. He is the magician's apprentice; the King has extended his protection to him. You must come with me to see His Majesty now."

"But I don't want to, you know, interfere with his party, like. I mean, he's having a bit of a blowout, and uh . . ." Bosky gulped, knowing none of this was going to convince Blung.

"The King has had his breakfast and his morning

copulation, and has had enough of the feast, which will continue without him, in his honor—and in the queen's honor, of course." Something about the way he added this last remark about the queen sounded as if he were indulging in a private irony. "Come this way."

Bosky wanted to run. But the Captain of the guards was walking up, frowning, as if wondering what the delay was, hand on the hilt of his short sword. The look in the Captain's eye convinced Bosky that running was not a good idea just now. Bosky had personally killed a number of the King's demonic pets with his rifle, and he knew himself to be treading thin ice in the Phosphor Palace.

"Right, lead the way, Lord Bung," said Bosky, trying to sound like he was merely having an exam at the dentist and if he didn't like the dentist he might still cancel the appointment.

"It's *Blung!* Just—come along." Lord Blung led the way to the door behind the throne room that opened onto the corridor down which Lord Smithson took his final journey as a living man. The Captain of the guards came along, close behind Bosky, who could feel the pallid warrior's gaze on the back of his neck.

The door was locked; Lord Blung had expected as much, and now he pounded on it with the lower end of his walking stick three times, one time, and then, after a pause, once more.

"I see you're staring at my walking stick," Blung said, with grim amusement. "It is my late wife's hand and arm. This way I can continue to hold her hand. I am a terribly sentimental man, in my way." His voice showed all the sentiment of a coroner remarking on the caliber of a bullet as he dug it from a wound.

There came a ponderous clicking and the door swung open, unlocked from within, and they entered the corridor, where two more guards awaited. Bosky turned to glance back at the still-open door, thinking he ought to at least try to escape. He might dodge the Captain's sword and run through the door before it shut, and then—

The door clanged shut, closed by no one visible. It went smugly *clickity-clack* as it locked. Bosky sighed in resignation.

They continued till they came to the library corridor where the King was waiting in one of the easy chairs. Beside him was a small table on which was a series of cutting tools on a black felt cloth; the tools were slim, and finely wrought of steel and diamond. They glinted with sharpness. On another, lower table was a crystal goblet, empty, and a crystalline beaker, also empty. Beside these vessels were two small vials of powder, one blue and one red.

Across from the King was another chair, of what looked to be petrified wood. On the arms of the chair were leather straps.

Now you're for it, Bosky thought, his heart sinking, looking desperately around. *Only thing to do is try to grab a sword, fight your way out of here someway. Better to get killed fighting than be tortured to death.*

The King smiled and raised a hand to forestall him. "I perceive you're about to bolt, or worse. It would do no good and isn't necessary; there's no need for you to be hurt. Ah, well . . . not much. You

were staring at the restraint chair and it would make
an alert, imaginative person understandably nervous. But there's no need for anxiety. Simply give up
a brimming goblet of your blood voluntarily and we
will forget all about restraints."

"A . . . goblet? You mean, like, for drinking from?"

The King and his seneschal shared a knowing
chuckle.

"Boy," Blung said, "you have misunderstood his
Majesty's nature . . . and his purpose."

"I am not a vampire," said the King, waving a hand
indulgently. "Occasionally we get them down here.
They like the 'sunless' part of the Sunless Realm, but I
find them out, quickly enough, and dispatch them. No
one is to feed off my people but . . . those I appoint.
No. It is in the nature of a scientific experiment. Now."
He selected a slender cutting instrument, like a more
elegant version of a surgeon's scalpel, and took the
goblet in his other hand. "If you will be so good . . ."

Bosky swallowed. The Captain watched him with
narrowed eyes, hand on his sword.

Bosky had no choice.

He drew back his sleeve and offered up his arm.

"Turn your arm over, boy," the King said, testing
the edge of his scalpel.

Bosky did so, and winced when the King made a
small slit in a vein on the back of his hand.

"Turn your hand again. Good . . ." The King filled
the goblet with Bosky's blood. It was just enough
that Bosky could feel its absence. The King took the
red vial and sprinkled some of its contents on the
wound; it instantly ceased bleeding. Then he took

the vial of blue powder and sprinkled a little into the cup of blood. A sparkling effervescence resulted; blue bubbles seethed in the crimson liquid. The bubbles gave off the smell of blood—or more precisely, essence of blood. Bosky's nostrils twitched and his stomach clenched rebelliously.

The King raised the goblet to his lips and sniffed at it. "Yes. It's genuine. Fairy blood! Diluted, but it is there. Ah. It is tempting. What sweeter drink than the blood of the fairy?" He grinned at Bosky. "But I would not waste it so." He poured it into the beaker, then stood, taking the beaker in his hand. "I shall experiment . . ." He turned to Blung and explained: "I will apply the liquid to my skin, just before my daily treatment under the projector, and, if I am right, the intrinsic fairy properties will improve the rejuvenation process when I bathe in the purple ray."

"I see! It is just possible!" Blung allowed.

"You have been wondering why I had you bring the boy yourself, Blung," the King said. "Perhaps now you understand."

Blung bowed. "I never doubted Your Majesty's wisdom."

The King turned to Bosky. "You see, Blung here has had experience with fairies. We specialize in capturing the unnatural creatures, the denizens of the Hidden World, in the Sunless Realm. He . . . performed some experiments on one of the treacherous rascals and found that the experiment led to a doubling of his own lifespan. Unfortunately it cost the fairy his life. Pity; it might have been of further use."

Feeling queasy, Bosky stared at the blood as the seneschal bandaged his arm. "So . . ."

"So yes, we shall require a 'donation' from you at regular intervals," the King said. Looking at Bosky's body critically, he added, "We might want to increase your blood pressure, give you a special diet . . ."

"Has he the mark, Your Majesty?" Blung inquired.

"Scofield says he has, there, upon that hip. Boy, show him the mark."

Bosky was feeling more and more like a beast poked and prodded after being fattened for someone else's feast, but he exposed the mark, and Blung made an *ahhh* of appreciation.

"You see, Your Majesty, how the upper and lower point of the star are the longer? This signifies—"

"Yes, yes, I know: air and water. The horizontal points are earth and fire. The four fundamental elements. So he has a greater connection to the spirits of air and water. Does it bear upon my methodology?"

"It does, perhaps, Your Majesty . . ." He spoke the rest in Latin and they conversed for a while in that language.

Bosky, after a time, took it on himself to ask, "Your, uh, Your Majesty? Just a question about all this . . ."

"Hm? Eh? Do you address me, child?"

"Um, yeah. Look here, you're the King and I've got no say, but don't you think it's kind of wicked and . . . and *evil* to be harvesting blood from people, for something like that? I mean, kinda like weakening their health to increase yours?"

"Evil?" The King seemed to think the question

droll. "You don't mean to say you believe in good and evil? But of course you are young; compared to me, even Blung here is young. Do you know how old I am? Coming onto five centuries. In the extremely unlikely eventuality you live to even half my age, you shall inexorably surrender up all notions of supposed right and wrong, good and evil, child. Utter nonsense, all that. All that remains, once those illusions are gone, are satisfaction, survival, and the lack of those things. You either get what you require, or you do not. That's all there is, boy. Take your cue from the voice of age, for with age comes wisdom, the wisdom of harsh truths."

"Age don't always bring wisdom," Bosky said, thinking he'd be wiser, himself, to keep his mouth shut. "My granddad said some lose their . . . what did he call it . . . their 'moral compass' when they get older. He said they can forget things they used to know. So I've got to wonder, how much could you forget, over five hundred years? That's a long time; you could forget a lot."

The King opened his mouth to make a glib reply; then he blinked and something flickered in his eyes, something that Lord Blung and the Captain of the guards were astonished to see. It was doubt.

"I . . . rubbish!" He turned angrily away. "Blung, take this boy out of here, put him in a guarded apartment, in reasonable comfort but without freedom to move about till I tell you otherwise, and see he's fed a good deal, *a very great deal,* of whatever food builds up the blood! I shall need as much blood from him as I can get and still keep him alive!"

"Very good, Your Majesty, My Lord and King."

The Captain close on his heels, Bosky followed the seneschal out of the corridors. He was relieved when the door opened to let them into the throne room, but he seemed to hear the King saying over and over again:

I shall need as much blood from him as I can get and still keep him alive.

⤙◦≡◦⤚

Constantine opened his eyes to find himself sprawled atop a naked woman, a rather plump one, who was snoring on a cot in a bleak, chilly cell carved of naked stone, her breath smelling of herb smoke and mead.

He climbed off her, got to his feet, tried blearily to take a step, and fell flat on his face. "Bloody Hell!" He realized he had his pants down around his ankles, and they'd tripped him. He was entirely dressed except for his pants and underwear being down. He turned over, pulled his pants up, and stood—and realized, as he closed his trousers, struggling to keep his feet, that he was still quite stoned and drunk.

And what was that nasty taste in his mouth? Then he was struck by a stomach-churning suspicion:

Bat shite.

The woman, the plump one with the hookah and the curly black hair, continued snoring, her mouth wide, wide open, the sound echoing about the bare chamber. An undernourished bluish light, and a very little warmth, came from a strip of luminous crystal flush with the floor.

Constantine glanced at his erstwhile sex partner and felt no desire to wake her. He thought for a moment the mead was making him see double, but no, in fact she *did* have a third breast growing just under her rib cage on her left side, a legacy of the genetic peculiarities of the palace's denizens. He remembered encountering the third bosom before he'd lost consciousness; he'd liked it then. But now, asymmetrically out of place, blue-veined and drooping in its loneliness, it looked like an excrescence, and he felt only revulsion.

He took a deep breath, centering himself as much as he might, got some semblance of balance back, and headed for the door. There was no actual door, just a doorway. He walked through and found he was in a long, straight stone corridor, with the crystal strip running to right and left. On both sides were other little chambers, like the one he'd come from, all with doorless doors, and, he discovered, as he set off to the right, people either sleeping or desultorily shagging in them.

Anyway some of it was shagging. Some of it was simply licking or whipping. And other things.

Head feeling like his brain was bouncing in his skull with every step, he stumbled down the hallway, passing door after door. He came to a place where the hallway cornered to the right. Down there, another long gallery of rooms. How was he to find his way out of here?

He tried to remember how he'd come here, but it was all a green blur. Had he shagged the plump woman? He thought he had, and rather thoroughly too, if he hadn't hallucinated all that.

It was difficult to say for sure, because he was indeed seeing things. There were dark places above the doorways where the shadows had a tendency to thicken and squirm, becoming shapes that one moment were great spiders and the next were six-legged dominatrices; he seemed to see a black anaconda snaking along up there near the ceiling, but when he blinked it turned into the tube train he took to get back to his flat in London from the card room. He thought he saw himself looking back from the train window.

He hurried on, passed another open room, glancing at the people inside, then came to a dead stop, and backed up to stare at two people who looked as if they'd just had a shag on their clothes, strewn like a nest on the floor. They were people he knew. Gary Lester, and Constantine's old friend Judith, the Tantrist from the Newcastle crew. Who'd burned to death.

That is, he *had* known them: they were both dead, long ago.

Now Constantine stared, trying to decide if they were ghosts or not. They looked just as if they were really there, but he was sure it must be more hallucination. Pretty sure, anyway.

"Well!" Gary crowed. "It's our old pal little Johnny Constantine."

Constantine knew he should walk on, but he couldn't quite look away. "Gary, how, uh . . ."

"Not going to ask how *we* are, then, me and Judith?" Gary snorted. He fumbled about in his clothes. "Got some H in here somewhere, Judith."

"That'd be lovely . . ."

"You want some, John?"

"Um, no thanks, mate, thanks ever so. Good to see you. Glad you're not . . . in a worse place."

"You mean Hell? Who says I'm not, mate? Who says you're not, you silly bastard, eh?"

"What about me, John?" Judith asked. "If you don't want drugs—do you want me? There was a time you weren't so proud."

She opened her mouth and stuck out her tongue; there was an eye on the tip of it that stared at him and blinked, before she sucked it back in.

Then they both burst into laughter.

Constantine backed away.

"Wait, John!" Gary called. "I wanted to ask why you let me end up like that, huh? Weren't we supposed to be friends? Weren't you supposed to watch my back?"

"I'm dead sorry, Gary," Constantine said, and meant it.

"Dead sorry! I'm sorry I'm dead, mate! I'm a fucking ghost, how about you? But then you'll be a ghost soon enough!"

They had another good laugh at that.

Constantine swayed and closed his eyes, shook his head. "They're not there. They're fucking *not* there.

Blue Sheikh . . . someone . . . send them to someplace peaceful!"

He looked, and the room was empty.

He turned and trudged down the hall. And heard ghostly laughter, again echoing to him, following him. From that empty room.

"I'm right off this Emerald Mead shite," Constantine muttered, picking up his pace to hurry down the hall. How the fuck *did* he get out of here?

"John Constantine," someone called, as he passed a doorway.

He set his jaw and ignored them.

"John Constantine!" More insistently, from behind him now.

Constantine reluctantly turned and saw Fallesco, dressed only in silken trousers, trotting up behind him. "Are you all right, my friend? You look lost."

Constantine glared. "You real?" He stuck a hand out and it stopped on Fallesco's chest. "Seem real. How the bloody fuck do I get out of here?"

"I did warn you about the mead. Seeing things, are you?"

"I hope so. I mean—"

"I know what you mean, my friend. The hallucinations will pass fairly soon. Let me put on some clothes and I'll take you back out. If you hear any screaming from the rooms we pass once we've gone around the corner, ignore it. It's not what it seems. They're facially mutilating, by prearrangement. It is nought but a faddish fashion statement."

"Oh bugger. I'm going to be sick."

"Right here against the wall, my friend. Do not concern yourself. The stewards will clean it up. That's it, get it all out."

◆━◉━◆

Geoff had gotten hold of some form of beer instead of mead, but it had done a job on him, all right. His head throbbed; his mouth tasted like a family of small rodents had made a nest in it. He remembered some geezer without much of a nose explaining, in patchy English mixed with two other languages, that there were crops grown in some great subterranean cavern with a magically generated sunlight, including grain for beer. He and the noseless geezer—Flegg, he'd called himself—had a beer-drinking contest and the geezer had fallen over, out cold, and then Geoff had fallen over beside him. Noseless was still there, snoring next to him on a cushion beside the column in the throne room. Other people were snoring around the edges of the room. Bosky was nowhere to be seen; nor the king and queen. Nor Constantine. Nor Maureen.

Geoff got up and looked around, hugging himself. He felt grievously alone and depressed and cold and hungry and he wondered if his friends were all dead, killed by the King on some whim. Look what had happened to the village, after all. He remembered when he'd been abducted, something prehensile winding about his neck and the terrifying journey through the air, then the soldiers grabbing him, tying him up, chucking him in a cell for a while. The agonizing wait, the torture of not knowing what would happen, then. After an unknown time, they'd come for him, taken him under armed guard to the shaft down to the crankers' workplace. It had looked like a bottomless pit to him. He'd thought they'd throw him down it, but they put him on that platform. Cranked him down, and down. And then Constantine . . .

Where *was* Constantine now?

"I should have listened to Bosky's mum," he muttered.

"Hello, my bright young fellow," said the spiky-chinned old perv, startling Geoff so that he jumped a bit, stumbling against a pillar.

"What the bloody . . . Spurlick, don't be sneaking up on a bloke like that. My head . . ."

"Would you like some water? I have a flagon here." He smiled, seeming less pervy than other times, and Geoff gratefully accepted.

The water was heavy with minerals, but Geoff felt a little better afterward drinking deep. "Um, Spurlick—"

"Lord Spurlick, if you please."

Geoff wiped his mouth. "Right. Lord Spurlick. Seen my . . . my master? Constantine?"

"I have not. He wandered off with some female many hours ago. But you look fatigued! Come with me to my chambers, I will draw you a bath, and see that you are . . . relaxed."

"Oh-h-h no thanks, guv, got to find me Master Magician and practice, like, turning people into Christmas crackers and whatnot, yeah? Ta for the water, talk to you soon."

"Wait! I have . . . a further inducement!"

Spurlick glanced around and drew a leather bag from his doublet. He opened it, jiggled it in his hands. Within glittered a good many precious gems. "These are of value on the surface, are they not? Here they are mere . . . that is to say, here they are also of great value. Here, hold the bag, examine it. Great wealth is yours!"

"Whoa, those look like rubies, emeralds . . . diamonds! Nice."

While he was looking at the gems, Spurlick was creeping closer, and Geoff felt his exploratory hands on his buttocks and crotch. "Yes, my boy . . . how you and I will cavort . . ."

Geoff stepped quickly back and, without hesitation, kicked Spurlick hard in the testicles. The courtier made a sound that was, more or less, *"Glee-eep!"* at a high pitch, and doubled over, clutching his groin. "You wicked little—"

"That's for *your* jewels, guv! You got your bag-of-gem's worth off me just now, and something to remember me by!"

So saying, Geoff turned and simply bolted, tucking the gems away in his coat as he went.

And almost ran headlong into the King.

"What's this?" King Culley exclaimed, as his guards rushed to stand between him and the skidding youth. "Where do you run from, boy?"

Come to a stop, Geoff was panting, looking from the King to the guards. The King was already late middle-aged at this time of his day, his face gone jowly, his eyes now edged with crow's feet, his hair and beard going gray, his hands showing age spots and a tremor.

But the King seemed amused to see Spurlick come shambling up, still clutching his groin. "Ho ho! I begin to see! You were fleeing Lord Spurlick, yes? He has made unwelcome advances, has he?"

"Your Majesty!" Spurlick said, bowing, and wincing as he did so. "This boy has struck me a vicious blow and robbed me! He has taken a bag of gems from me! It is a breach of Your Majesty's peace! I humbly request to be able to execute him personally, using the blunt, rusted sword traditional in the instances of terrible crime!" And he bowed again, this time with a courtly flourish.

"Blunt sword!" Geoff burst out. "Lord King, this bastard was trying to buy me with them gems and then he was fondling me up and down! I took the gems as a fee for fondling I never said he could have!"

The King chortled. "Ho, that sounds like the truer story, knowing you, Spurlick! Now sir, the boy has been paid for your fumblings, and you have been paid for your presumption! And I am pleased to have some amusement at a time of day when all seems bleak and dire! I decree that the boy shall keep the gems, and shall be held blameless. And if you object, Spurlick, you will indeed have access to the traditional blunt and rusty sword, but not as you had planned!"

Spurlick made a guttural sound, ground his teeth together, and then forced a smile and a very low bow. "I live to provide amusement for His Majesty. I can only thank my lucky ceiling lichen that I have been able to provide that amusement."

"Do I detect bitter irony in that pleasantry, Spurlick?" the King demanded, his eyes growing cold.

"Not at all sire! I am utterly sincere!"

"The only thing that is entire about you, Spurlick, is your insincerity . . . but as you are sometimes useful I will let it pass."

The King proceeded on his way, the guards tramping along behind, weapons rattling. Geoff turned to go, but not before hearing Spurlick mutter, "I will see to your downfall personally, boy. You may rest assured of that."

Geoff walked away, toward the servants' quarters to look for Constantine. But when he'd got to the door to the servants' hall, he glanced over his shoulder, and saw Spurlick still watching him. And smiling wickedly.

13

LONG LIVE THE QUEEN . . . TILL THIS AFTERNOON, LATEST

"*B*e thou my vision, O Lord of my heart," sang Maureen, sewing up a tear in one of the queen's gowns. "*Naught be all else to me save that thou art, thou my best thought by day or by night, waking or sleeping thy presence, my light . . .*"

"'O Lord of my heart'!" the King said, coming in, clapping his hands softly, beaming at her. "What a lovely sentiment, and what a lovely voice!"

"Oh, it's just an old Irish folk song, Your Majesty."

"Is it now? But do not think its meaning has eluded me, my lovely rusty-haired lady!"

"Its . . . *meaning*, Your Majesty?" she asked, looking nervously at the four guards who were there with him.

"Lord of my heart? Who else could it be but me! And of course I have been admiring you as well. But it was when I heard you sing that my mind—nay, my heart!—that my heart was made up!"

"What's this all about?" Megan asked, coming into the sitting room. "Your heart was all what?"

The King's face fell, seeing the queen. His eyes became flinty.

"You, lady, are under house arrest, until I have had a chance to declare our marriage annulled."

"What?" At first she looked dismayed; then a thought brought a flicker of hope to her eyes. "So, I can go home? If I'm not married anymore I can go back to Beverly Hills?"

"I fear not. I have a use for you, as you will see. You annoyed me last night. You're sickly and vulgar and I want you gone."

"And you'll marry this woman? She's older than me!"

"Yes, normally I would prefer someone younger, but she has charmed me. Besides, there is magical value to being married to a fairy!"

Maureen must have looked startled, for he continued. "Oh yes, Lady Maureen, Spurlick has been following, and listening, and has reported to me that you are the boy's mother and therefore of fairy blood! Thin the blood may be, but if your son bears the mark then the power is in it! I will have a great many uses for you, but first . . . the wedding night!"

The former queen turned to Maureen, her eyes full of tears. "You bitch! Don't you know what'll happen to me? What'd you do to get him all . . . all . . ."

"I didn't do anything, Your Majesty!"

"No need to call her 'Your Majesty' after this," said the King, yawning. "As for what you did, you sang! That beautiful voice, that meaningful song, and the fact of your ancestry . . . you are my destiny! For a time. And now . . ." He turned to the guards. "Take the queen to the Place of Bleak Pondering and lock her in. Give her a little water, that will be enough."

"No!" Megan shouted, turning to run. But the guards rushed to her without hesitation—she was not the first queen handled thus—and dragged her out of the room, sobbing.

"Oh no," Maureen said, her eyes filling with tears. "Poor Megan . . ."

"Yes, yes, poor Megan. Now, pretty yourself up. I will come later to arrange the ceremony; we will be married this very day!"

And the King turned on his heels and strode out, leaving Maureen simmering in a welter of emotion.

***

"How long did you say it's been?" Constantine asked Maureen, aghast. He had come in to the servants' quarters to find her sitting dejectedly on the cot and it didn't occur to him at first, with his head still throbbing, to ask what was troubling her. Being a prisoner far underground was, after all, reason enough to be troubled.

"You've been gone at least twenty hours," Maureen said, her voice betraying no reproach. "Maybe more."

"Oh Jesus, Mary, Joseph, and St. Paddy," Constantine said, sinking onto a cot, head in his hands.

I'm not worth the bog paper it takes to wipe me away, he thought. *The time's melting, nearly gone. Chas is fucked—Britain is fucked unless I can stop the bastard. It was all up to me and I dealt with it by getting pissed again.*

"I wish I had some tea to offer you," Maureen said, her voice hoarse, "but I've found a place to do a little cooking, and I'm told this lichen tea is rather like. It feels like it has caffeine in it."

She went to the cooking niche and returned with a crude clay-fired cup of the brew and he made himself drink it down. It was bitter, but it did seem to clear his head a little. Feeling angry at himself and along with that, inevitably, sorry for himself, would do no good. He sat up straighter, took a deep breath, and said, "Right. We've got to have a plan. We need to enlist the queen."

Maureen shook her head. "I don't think that's going to happen. She's confined to her quarters. And Geoff heard that Lord Blung say she was going to 'join the other queens!'"

"Long live the queen," Constantine muttered to himself. "Till this afternoon, latest, if I know that bastard Culley. He changes them more often than Chas changes tires on his cab." He looked at Maureen. "Who's the new sacrificial lamb, then?"

She rubbed tears away with the heel of her hand. "I'm afraid . . . it's me."

"What!"

Geoff came in then, with Fallesco. "I've found this rascal wandering about, looking for his friend," Fallesco said. "I believe Spurlick was following him. Lord Spurlick can be quite skilled at not being seen when he chooses to. You'd best keep the boy here."

"But where is Bosky?" his mother asked.

"Couldn't find him," Geoff said. "They've got him locked away somewhere, Mrs."

"Locked away!"

Fallesco sighed. "The King has learned of his fairy blood. He's to be kept prisoner and bled for its magical properties, a little at a time."

His mother put a hand over her mouth, horrified. "Oh God. He's going to bleed my boy dry!"

"No, Maureen, he ain't," Constantine assured her. "Wait—Fallesco, best check to see if Spurlick's out there."

Fallesco went outside their rooms and indeed found Spurlick lurking in the hall, trying to hear something he could use against them. Constantine, coming to the doorway, heard their confrontation.

"Spurlick, you have offended me," Fallesco said. "This lurking at my back implies you think I'm up to no good!"

"What? Oh nonsense, I was merely, ah, that is—"

"Spurlick, as is my right, I now issue an oath-challenge! I challenge you to mortal combat, sword against sword, pike against pike, for the entertainment of the court! I hold my left hand in the air and call the world as my witness, and I hereby—"

"Wait! No need for haste! I apologize, and I will withdraw!"

Fallesco and Constantine watched as Spurlick scuttled down the hallway and was gone. They waited to be sure and then returned to the servants' quarters; Constantine looked curiously at Fallesco. "Now you've made Spurlick your enemy too, Fallesco. Just wondering, mate, what's spurrin' you on to risk what you've risked: death, or a right-nasty living-death. You could cruise along at your orgies till you fall over dead from drink . . ."

Fallesco sniffed contemptuously at the word *orgies*. "I only indulge in that foolishness so that I will be there to listen! People talk more freely in their cups. I know where the bodies are buried, so to speak, Master Magus. As for what spurs me, one moment." He checked, once more, to see that no one was listening at the door, before returning, closing the door carefully behind him, to continue: "It is simple; I wish to escape the Underlands. True, I was born here, but I have always wandered as far as I might in the Underlands, in the realm of the Sunless and beyond it. I have learned as much as I could. I am, you know, also the King's librarian, and when I read of the surface world, I long to see it, to be part of it. But Culley will not allow me to go to the surface to fetch books; this is done through surface intermediaries, lately the associates of the unfortunate MacCrawley. It is they, also, who deliver the King's wives to him, in exchange for gems . . . and certain magical favors. Those of us who were born below, stay below. Mine is the heart of a poet, sir! My spirit longs to soar through the blue sky of the surface world! So long as the King commands this realm, I am a prisoner here. He knows of my longing to be away, and his shadow watchers, his harpies, his Il-Sorg, his gripplers, all know I am not to be allowed to escape."

"Right," Constantine said. "Then let's give you your chance to bust out. And Maureen"—his voice became subtly tender when he turned to her—"the King won't bleed your boy dry; we're going to bleed the King dry. And we're going to get your son out of the lockup. We've got to put a stopper to the King's plans and get ourselves out from underground. I think I've got it worked out, but we've got to move fast. There's a great big bloody job to do and not much time for it. Fallesco, can you contact Scofield for me? He's going to have to meet with a troll."

"A troll! If the King finds out he'll regard it as treason."

"Aye. And so it is, the best sort of treason. Treason against a bloody damned tyrant! I also need for you to find out where MacCrawley is being kept. If he's still alive, I'm going to need him too."

"What!" Geoff couldn't believe his ears. "MacCrawley! He wanted you dead, mate!"

"Oh I know; he wanted me brought here and probably put to work right where he is now. A job that'll kill a man, sure. But I'm going to need him if what I suspect is true—if it's Fludd's Spell of Dire Containment we've got to crack—and I'll have to make use of him without turning me back. I'll just wait for him to turn his."

"Anything to get us out of this bloody place," Geoff declared, shrugging.

"Now, the King's strengths are ritual magic and alchemy, but he has a contempt for folk magic, and the bastard despises the elder spirits of the world. So I reckon we can con him when it comes to folk magic. Maureen, can you go along with the wedding night, up to a point?"

"I can do whatever's necessary, John," she said simply. Implying, without stating it, that she was willing to give herself entirely to the King if she had to, if that's what it took to save them all.

"We'll try to see that what's necessary is as little as can be," Constantine said, inwardly tensing at the thought of the King touching Maureen intimately. No one should touch her intimately, come to that. Except . . .

"There is a certain sleeping potion I keep about me," Fallesco said, taking a small vial from an inside pocket. "Many times it has subdued those who would have cut my throat otherwise. Take it and slip it to the King in the privacy of your wedding night, Maureen, so that he loses consciousness before he can force himself on you. But he is no fool, and when he wakes, he will know he was drugged and his vengeance will be terrible. Unless . . ."

Fallesco broke off, then went to the door, looked out a third time, checking once more for eavesdroppers, before returning and going on, "Unless the King never wakes. I see a straight razor on yon table . . ."

"I might be able to do it," Maureen said, pulling a face. "But there's the problem of that magic bed of his. The queen's told me some creature lives in it, who watches them as they . . . watches them in bed. And the creature won't allow any attack on the King, or anything taken from his person. The King trapped it there to protect him."

"Trapped it, did he?" Constantine said. "Interesting. That suggests . . ."

"The creature might be neutralized somehow,"

Fallesco said, stroking his beard. "How, I don't know. That would be more Constantine's purview. But if it could be done, you might well be free to dispatch the King. A blessed turn of events; I live for the day the King Underneath lives no more!"

"But if Culley were to have his throat cut in the night, his faithful would know it was Maureen who did it," Constantine said, thinking it through as he spoke. "Too many of the local gits regard him as a god; that evil-eyed Captain of the guards would scour the place for Maureen. And there's summat else: it seems likely to me the King's spell of control includes vengeance on whoever killed him—more like on the whole kingdom, if he's done away with. He's got to be alive and kicking when the spell's undone. Just killing him won't release it. We'll use the potion; it'll keep him asleep just long enough to do what needs to be done. I hope."

"And we'll be no better than him, if we go around cutting people's throats to get them out of the way," Geoff said, surprising the others.

Constantine nodded. "Got no argument, there, kid. We'll fight the King Underneath with his own sorcery, and let karma take its course . . ."

⋯⋯◉⋯⋯

"Are you quite sure these preliminaries are necessary, my queen?" asked King Culley, licking his lips as he looked Maureen over, at the threshold of their honeymoon chamber.

"Oh but my darling, it is quite necessary, if the

blossom is to open willingly to the bee!" said Queen Maureen, drooping her eyelashes bashfully.

The Royal Wedding, held in the throne room that morning, had been an abbreviated affair, swift on the heels of the annulment of the King's previous marriage. A few words sonorously intoned by the seneschal, a quick invocation to some forgotten gods, too deeply asleep in limbo to know they'd been invoked, and the ritual kiss, and it was done, with the courtiers, summoned by gong, dutifully applauding, crying Hosanna, and trying not to yawn at this latest in the endless string of royal nuptials.

Now the King stood just inside the door. Constantine, looking quite politely neutral, stood outside it with Maureen, who yet wore her sheer blue-white wedding gown, slit up both sides to the hips.

Constantine had to work at it not to stare at her in the gown. It wouldn't do to let the King know how he felt.

"Explain again the nature of this, ah, invocation?" the King asked, taking off his crown to flip it about impatiently in his hand as he looked at her.

Maureen, who had in fact not grown up in Ireland, had no Irish accent, but she now fell into one for psychological effect as she said, "Sure it is that in my village—throughout Ireland in fact—we had to have the local Priest of the Fields in to drive out the Little People, who will follow anywhere, even to the bowels of the Earth it is said, so as to inhabit the . . . well, the private places of the bride, waiting for the groom's intrusion, so that they might strike his tenderest places with small pins, much to their amusement."

The King blinked. "Small pins . . . striking his . . ."

"Yes, Your Majesty."

"Superstition, surely."

"No doubt, Your Majesty. But why take a chance?"

Constantine cleared his throat. "If you'd go ahead into the bridal chamber, Maureen, I'll just have a word with His Majesty . . ."

She curtsied and slipped past the King, who stepped into the hallway. "Yes, Constantine? Well?"

"It's all the psychology of the Irish, Your Majesty. Rubbish, this Little People thing, I suppose, but they just don't like to marry without the ritual. It happens I'm a certified Priest of the Field—"

"What is that, some sort of Celtic shaman?"

"Yes, sire. I'll just enter the room, spend a few minutes alone with the queen; the two of us, according to the ancient rites of olde Eire, will set about banishing the Little People."

"If there were any Little People following her into the chamber, the guardian in the headboard of the bed would have warned me."

"No doubt, Your Majesty. It is indeed psychological. The lady will give of herself freely afterward."

"Constantine, are you practicing upon me?"

"Practicing upon you, sire?"

"Ah, it's an old expression. It means deceiving. Often for another's amusement."

"No, Your Majesty!"

"I warn you: If you are playing a game with me, I'll know it—if not tonight, tomorrow. I'll consult certain magical beings, who will tell me so. As it is, I feel a certain uneasiness . . . but it might be attributable to nerves. I have never bedded a fairy before, or one with fairy blood. I am aquiver with excitement! I have always wanted to despoil one of the creatures and this is as close as I shall come until I can catch one of the few remaining fairies."

"Your Majesty," Constantine said, clear-eyed, his whole mind playing the role perfectly, in case of psychic probe, "you may look into my heart with all your arts, if you like, to see if I am deceiving you." It was a risky bluff, but Constantine was counting on the King's impatience.

"No, no, that would take preparation and I wish to be at it. Very well. You shall enter the room without me for a few minutes only. Then I must be about my wedding night."

Constantine bowed and entered the room, closing the door. He immediately began droning loudly in the few random Gaelic words he knew. The King, he had ascertained, spoke many languages, but Gaelic was not one of them. *"Erin go Bragh!"* he cried, stomping about the room. *"Ní cleas é go ndéantar trí huaire í!"* Kit had taught him that one: *It isn't a trick till it's done three times.*

It was a circular room, with a circular bed in the midst of it. The oaken headboard was a semicircle carved with images of the King, and topped with a wooden five-pointed crown. At the center of the headboard was a scowling, puffy-cheeked face, which looked carved of the wood itself, until one looked closer and saw its eyes moving, following Constantine about the room. To either side of this face were its arms, the fingers twiddling, ever so slightly, with the tedium of its life.

The new queen, Her Majesty Maureen the First, was sitting at the mirror at the other end of the room, brushing her hair and now and then wailing in Gaelic, as if doing her part of the ritual.

Constantine noticed a table near the bed on which stood a decanter filled with mead and two goblets.

He crossed to Maureen, bent close to her ear, and whispered, "Set to a great caterwauling now, and then sing a song in Gaelic, any song, to cover up the talk I've got to make with the imp."

She nodded and began, so piercingly he clapped his hands over his ears and grinned at her.

He crossed to the imp in the headboard, sitting down on the edge of the bed, leaning back on his elbow, looking it in its wooden eyes. Wooden they were but mobile, just as its face, the scowl deepening, seemed flexible, as if hard wood had softened to the constancy of flesh.

"Look here, mate," Constantine said, "you and me've got to talk."

"Do you speak to me?" the creature said in Latin. "I don't understand your language."

Constantine repeated his opening gambit in Latin, going on in that language: "I'm John Constantine, friend of imps everywhere."

"I have never heard of you. What is it you wish? A boon? You shall not have it, because if I do aught but the King's bidding, he'll throw me into a fire. And since I am not wooden truly and yet I am, because of his magic, I will burn forever, never consumed, always suffering!"

"Oh, the cruel irony of it!" Constantine said, clucking his tongue sympathetically. "It's your sort who should be subjecting his kind to torments in Hell, but here you are afraid to be burned in his Hell!"

"Too true! It is good to have a little sympathy; for centuries I've been here, with no freedom to move about, no diversion but watching him spasticate with his wenches . . ."

"How difficult it must have been not to laugh at the ridiculous expressions on his face!"

"It is as if you were there!" the imp said, sulkily. "But if I mock him, he plays a flame about on my face, for a while!"

"It's a wonder you can bear such cruelty," Constantine observed, in wonder, shaking his head.

"What choice have I?"

"Are you willing to take a chance in the hopes you might at last be set free? If you are, I believe I can provide you with a real hope. You can be set free! You have only to do one thing for me, or more precisely, choose to do nothing for the King, for one night, and I will remove him from power! Once he is rendered null, I will be free to cast a spell and set you free from your wooden prison!"

"What! Do you take me for a fool? You would never return to set me free!"

"Do you know the Oath to the Depths of Hell?"

"Do I know it? My spawn-kin helped write it!"

"Then you know that if I speak it I am bound! I will speak the Oath and will set you free or suffer the consequences—immediate banishment to the utter-most depths of Hell!"

"But how do I know you have the power to render the King's power over me null?"

Constantine sighed. Then he leaned closer and spoke for two full minutes, naming names he had encountered in his journeys to Hell, speaking names of power, extolling the secrets of the Hidden World. He had to hurry; he could sense the King growing impatient, even as Maureen, still chanting, was growing hoarse. She threw in every Gaelic phrase she'd learned from her mother: *"Ná a glac pioc comhairle gan comhairle ban!"* she cried. *Never take advice without a woman's guidance.*

"Only a true magician could know such things," the imp admitted, as Constantine ended his recital of the Hidden World's secrets. "I will take the chance; at least burning forever in his furnaces would be a change!"

"Good. You have only to do nothing when the queen steals something from his person. Do not wake him, do not touch her . . ."

"Hmmm . . . normally I would be required to seize her about the neck and throttle her, while alerting the King. One of the few aspects of the job I enjoy. However, I'll hold off this time. If you give me the Oath!"

Constantine spoke the Oath, which cannot be repeated, even in print, without he who unlawfully repeats it vanishing from the world in a jet of sulfurous flame.

The imp in the headboard nodded. "So be it."

Constantine signaled Maureen; she ran to the decanter and poured the tasteless sleeping potion into the cup etched with the King's crown, then filled both cups with mead.

"Constantine!" the King shouted, from outside the door. "I have waited long enough! I ache for relief!"

"Erin go Bragh!" Constantine shouted, again. "There, 'tis done!" He strode to the door and flung it triumphantly open. "Your Majesty, I take my leave! My task is done! The room is cleared of baleful influences! Your queen awaits; the blossom will open to the bee!"

"Yes, yes, begone with you!"

Constantine bowed and left the King alone with Maureen. The door was closed behind him. He took two steps, then stopped in the hallway, chewing a knuckle and looking back at the door, where a guard had taken up position.

What if the King thought it suspicious that she offered him a drink the moment he arrived? Like all long-lived Kings, he was a suspicious man.

But the die had been cast. He walked onward, around a corner, and stopped to wait.

Within the bridal chamber, the King was approaching his new queen with a wolfish smile, his youth, so powerfully restored at this hour, burgeoning, aching to express itself in the most direct way possible.

His new queen turned to him, smiling, her eyes shining—tears of joy!—and offered him his goblet, already brimming with mead. His smile faded as he looked at the glass. She'd been alone in here with this glass. Suppose the witch had slipped poison in it?

He looked at the imp in the headboard. "Well?"

The imp shook its wooden head and said, in Latin: "She put nothing in the goblet, Your Majesty. It is quite safe to drink."

The King nodded, grinned, and took the goblet. He drank a great deal in one draught, and then set the glass down and took a step toward her. "Now, my dear, let us have few preliminaries. I am only young for a portion of the day. I am like a steel sword under my clothing already, just looking at you . . ."

Maureen blew him a kiss, but took a coy step back. "It excites me to gaze at Your Majesty; if I might just fill my eyes with your glory for a few moments—"

"Come, my dear, you're stalling! No need to be shy, you are no virgin, and so much the better. I value experience!"

She crawled onto the bed. "Perhaps I might strike a pose for Your Majesty, to heighten your excitement!"

"And enough of this 'Your Majesty' business, except when we are in public. Call me Iain, my dear! I am only a King, after all, because I seized power here. And that power I would show you—when I seize *you!*"

And as he said it he made a grab for her—a rather clumsy one, as the potion was beginning to affect him despite his supernatural vitality. Maureen slipped from his grasp, rolled away, but he lunged and caught her, clasped her to him, fumbling at her.

Turning her face, she let his hands wander across her bum, up her back . . . and then his eyes crossed as the drug claimed him and he fell back onto the bed, out cold, instantly snoring. *"Dochtúir na sláinte an codladh!"* she muttered. *Health's doctor is sleep.*

And the imp in the headboard chortled in malicious delight.

She drew the chain, with its keys, from around the King's neck, as Constantine had instructed her, concealing it in the bosom of her dress. Then she picked up the royal goblet and went to the door, opened it, and smiled winsomely at the Fallen Roman standing guard, doing her best Marilyn Monroe imitation.

She spoke the words in Latin, as Constantine had taught her. "The King wishes you to have a drink, to celebrate his wedding! And then, if he is of a mind . . . well, you know how free he is with his queens."

The guard, artless and bored, looked pleased and took the goblet, drained it straightaway, and moments later fell with a clatter in the hallway, snoring.

Constantine hurried up to the door, grasped the guard under his armpits, and dragged the unconscious man inside, laying him on the bed beside Culley. After a moment's thought he quickly arranged King and guard on the bed in positions that made the imp chortle once more.

Then Constantine and Maureen, closing the door of the bedchamber, hurried down the stone corridor to begin a process that would either save them, or kill them.

14

A MAN CANNOT BE TOO CAREFUL IN THE CHOICE
OF HIS ENEMIES

Carrying a light-crystal in his hand to illuminate the way, Scofield was muttering to himself as he strode along the path beside Stabbing Falls in search of the troll. "I'm a damn fool to trust Constantine, and I'm a damn fool to be trusting myself to a damned, damned, double-damned troll."

The double-damned troll grabbed him from behind just then, encircling him with a massive arm, and drew him into a deep hollow in the rocky wall to one side, clamping a hand over his mouth. "Hist!" whispered the troll. "Keep quiet—they come!" He smothered the light-crystal with his other hand. Scofield froze, more afraid of the troll than of whoever was coming; he could feel the enormous manlike being's looming presence, the heat from his body hunched over him in the hollow.

A few seconds more, then Scofield heard the tramp of boots, and beheld a patrol of six Fallen Romans, marching two abreast up the path toward its end at the falls. The Fallen Romans marched obliviously past.

"They are searching for you, Scofield," Balf whispered. "Constantine has spoken to me through a calling crystal; he had the tale from Fallesco: you were not at your post when the seneschal Blung went to supervise you there. You are scarcely within the boundaries of the realm here. Look!"

He pointed at a fluttering dark shape, bat-like but made of shadow-stuff, just outside their concealment in the cliff. "There, you are being watched by that fell creature. Hence, the guards know where to find you."

Scofield nodded and Balf took his hand from his mouth. "What of the guards?" Scofield whispered.

"I will deal with them."

Balf took a curiously shaped cutting instrument from a belt of tools about his massive waist. He turned to the stone wall, felt about on it till he located a big knob of stone, then tapped it with a crystal held in his other hand. He listened to the crystal, nodded, then struck at the edge of the knob in the exact right spot with the cutting tool, and a crack spread around the knob, encircling it, till a bushel-sized boulder simply dropped from the wall. Balf caught it easily in his big left hand and, carrying it tucked against him and returning the tool to his belt, he stepped out into the path, in clear view of the Fallen Romans at the other end beside the falls.

They shouted in Latin, and a crossbow arrow

flashed past Balf's ear. He was already throwing the
boulder, like a man pitching an enormous softball.
Scofield peeked out of concealment and saw the
boulder smashing into the front two soldiers in the
rows starting toward Balf, striking them so hard they
flew backwards, one into another, and all the pale
soldiers pitched backwards, wailing, off the cliff,
down into the pit under Stabbing Falls.

"That's done," said Balf. "But others will come soon
enough. There is no time to think of your dignity."

"What do you mean by that?" Scofield asked, holding the light-crystal up to see better, but he had his
answer in the next moment as Balf lifted him onto his
shoulder, in a fireman's carry, and climbed up the
wall, using handholds only he could see.

"Damn you, troll!"

"Do not call me 'troll,' my name is Balf Corunsiggert Stonecracker of the Icy Black Unseen River
Which Seeks the North Sea, or just Balf if you prefer.
And as for my nature, I am an Azki-Hak. The term *troll*
has such unpleasant connotations."

A few moments later he put Scofield down at the
entrance to his cave. "Where are we . . . Balf?"

"My hiding place and work chamber. Come around
this way . . . up this shaft . . . and you will find yourself in a tunnel that I do not believe the King knows
about."

"But the shadows will follow us, and then he will
know, when he awakes."

"Give me that crystal."

Scofield handed it over and Balf tucked it into a
pouch, dousing its light. They were in deep black-

ness. "The shadows need light to see, and to be. They will wander, lost, now. Hold on to my neck from behind, and I will carry you."

Scofield obeyed and, growing used to the rank smell of troll at close range, allowed himself to be carried up a cliff, through a tunnel, and then another, in pitch blackness. Two miles at least they went, wending this way and that in cold, damp, echoing darkness.

At last Balf declared them free of the following shadows and brought out the crystal. It showed a hemispherical chamber, only about thirty feet in diameter, and just high enough to admit Balf's head without his stooping.

"Hullo, Balf, you great Azki-Hak bastard, how are you?" Constantine cried, coming into the chamber from another entrance.

"I am well enough," Balf rumbled. "Anything is better than chains, even life as a fugitive."

"Constantine!" Scofield cried. "What have you been about?"

"Putting the King to nighty-night," Constantine said, lighting a cigarette. "Maureen's done it, really, with Fallesco's potion. She's waiting down below; I've got to get back to her, soon as I confirm the con with ol' Balf here. Running low on these," he added, looking at the Silk Cut critically. "You want one, Scofield?" Scofield nodded, and Constantine handed him one and the lighter, as Balf, on calloused hands and knees, searched about the floor for something neither of them could see. "May as well smoke the buggers," Constantine went on. "There's so little time left. We'll either get out right smart or die like dogs, soon enough; I'm not surrendering to the King's men. Too many nasty ways to die . . . or worse, down here." He blew smoke at the ceiling. "Right. What have you got for us, Balf?"

"You will see." Balf was tapping the stone floor experimentally with a crystal, muttering to himself in some language Scofield didn't understand.

And at last the troll grunted in satisfaction. "Ah. Here we are."

He tapped the floor carefully with his tool, and a chunk of stone four feet across fell away, to crash in some hollow below. Light shafted up from the break in the floor.

Scofield knelt beside the hole and saw with surprise he was looking down at his own work cavern; the toxic sump, the Universal Solvent, bubbling away in its cauldron, held in chains over the waiting pit of toxins.

"That is where you and the King have been doing your mischief, is it not, Magus Scofield?" Balf asked. "Constantine told me of the place, and the deed."

"It is," Scofield admitted, looking away from the troll's baleful stare, wondering if Balf intended to kill him for cooperating with Culley. Easy enough for the troll to pitch him down through the hole into the cauldron . . .

"How does the cauldron hold this Solvent?" Balf asked. "Why does not the cauldron melt away?"

"It will," Scofield said, "when the final ingredient is added, which will be done when the solution you see has completed its transmutation. And that is, by my reckoning, in less than three hours. If I don't put it in, or the King, Blung the seneschal will do it, and he'll be heavily guarded."

"And then the Solvent will eat a hole through the cauldron, and the container of the sump, and thus into the underground river, which will take it to the sea?"

"That is the King's plan. Thus destroying the upper world."

"But suppose we were to move the cauldron?"

"We cannot reach it from here. It is guarded by Il-Sorg! No flung boulder will stop them!"

"But if Constantine can get them out of the way . . ."

"It could be done; the destruction of Britain would then be delayed, I suppose."

"Could be stopped completely," Constantine said, "if we wreak enough havoc down here. Sort of a specialty of mine, wreaking havoc. It's a gift." He blew smoke at the ceiling. "Some have it, some don't."

"You see," Balf said, his star-spoked head illuminated by the glaucous light from below as he gazed down into the sump cavern, "I know these caves as no human does. There is a place we might move the cauldron to; when it is poured, something interesting will result. Very interesting indeed . . ."

"Scofield," Constantine said, "you've got to go back to work; tell them it was all a misunderstanding, you're eager to work. Talk fast if you have to but get into that room. And wait for the signal."

⋆═◉═⋆

The guard stationed in front of Bosky's luxury cell, alone in the barren stone hallway with nothing to look at but the strip of glowing crystal at his feet, was yawning with boredom when Constantine sauntered up and asked, in Latin, "How'd he get away, friend? I'm just curious."

The Fallen Roman compressed his lipless mouth. "How did who get away, magician?"

"The boy you're supposed to be guarding. Can't imagine how he escaped." He shouted the last two words in English so Bosky would get it. Then translated in Latin: *"He escaped!"*

"What? Nonsense!" The guard turned, unlocked the door, and looked in . . . and Bosky was nowhere to be seen.

Constantine, meanwhile, was concentrating, visualizing Bosky, sending the image telepathically—for telepathy worked here still if ritual magic didn't—and the guard turned back to the hallway only to see Bosky scurrying around a corner, taunting, "Fuck you, noseless!" the illusory Bosky shouted.

The Fallen Roman shouted in fury and sprinted in pursuit of the phantom, drawing his sword, leaving the door open behind him.

"Come on out, kid!" Constantine hissed into the apartment. The real Bosky emerged from the apartment's privy where he'd been hiding, prompted by Constantine's cue, and rushed grinning into the corridor.

"Crikey but I'm glad to see you; they're draining me dry, the bastards!"

"Come on, your mum's waiting around the corner,

the other way, with Geoff. We've got to hurry before
that gormless skull-face gets back here."

⊷≡◉≡⊶

There were two Fallen Romans posted on either side
of the threshold of the corridor behind the throne,
when Constantine and friends trooped up to it.

The skull-faced guards scowled at them: one very
tall and the other very short, the difference comi-
cally extreme. They made a slight obeisance, the
mere inclination of their heads, to the new queen.
Queens weren't taken very seriously in the kingdom
of the King Underneath.

"No one is to pass!" said the shorter of the two.

"Two of them, thank the King's wisdom, somehow
still alive!" Constantine said, in Latin. "With so many
others in the King's army dead, we were afraid the
contagion had reached you too!"

"Contagion?" asked the shorter of the two guards,
in Latin. "Of what do you speak?"

"You have not heard? A madness afflicts your
men, sent by the rival sorcerer, to destroy the army
from within! The victims become rabid and attack
one another murderously!"

"I have heard nothing of this. What sorcerer sends
this killing madness?"

"Why, ah . . . Mer . . . flermian. The . . . third."

"Who?"

"Merflermian the Third! You must have heard of
him. But look—your partner is afflicted!"

And as he said this Constantine projected a tele-

pathic image to the shorter guard; his true compan-
ion was blotted out, opaqued by the false image of
the same man drawing his sword, snarling, foaming
at the mouth, swinging the sword at the littler man.
"Die, scum!" the image shrieked, though it was heard
by no one but the littler guard, who instinctively
drew his sword and swung it at the other.

The taller guard, having heard fearfully of the contagion, turned to see the shorter one swinging his
blade at him. He leaped back, drew his sword, and
the two men set about fighting, furiously, back and
forth, their attention consumed with the life-and-
death struggle.

Constantine nodded to Maureen, who drew out
the King's keys and passed the chain to him. He
sorted through the keys, found the one that unlocked the door, and they hurried through, leaving
the guards, still clashing swords, behind them. Constantine closed and locked the door, once they were
through, and they hurried on through the several intervening doors, unlocking each in turn, until they
came to the portal that emanated a sinister cold.

"This'll be a bit of a shock, Maureen," Constantine
warned her, unlocking the door.

They entered the icy corridor and Maureen covered her open mouth with her hand, staring at the
frozen women in the farther chamber. "Oh God."

"Oh Christ on a bloody bike," Constantine muttered, "there she is, too."

They all saw her then, Queen Megan of Beverly
Hills. Frozen through and through, she was dressed
in a white gown, standing in front of a mirror, arrang-

ing her hair, her mouth open as if she were talking, eternally talking, talking . . .

"Oh poor Megan!" Maureen said, bursting into tears. "That monster Culley!" Bosky put his arm around her and escorted his sobbing mother down the corridor.

At long last they reached the room with the rejuvenation projector. Constantine made the others wait outside; Maureen had seen enough.

He unlocked the door, went through, quickly closing it behind him, and passed under the babbling prisoners of the mold, through the purple glow of the projector. Ignoring Lord Smithson's high-pitched pleading, giggling, and more pleading, Constantine crossed hastily to the farther door, the one the King hadn't wanted to talk about.

He tried all the keys in the lock but one, murmuring, "This last one better be it, or me whole theory's fucked and we are too."

The key seemed reluctant to work, but at last the tumblers clicked over and he swung the door open.

Inside he found a cavern, about a hundred feet in diameter, its upper reaches lost in shadow, its floor illuminated by the glow of a giant's eyes.

The giant was four times bigger than Balf, a massive, man-shaped creature apparently of stone and crystal, granite marbled with quartz; yet where stone would be inflexible and hard, for the giant it bent without breaking, merely creaking in the bends of his arms and legs as he shifted restlessly about in the faintly glimmering transparent magic sphere that entombed him alive. The sphere stood on a foot-high raised dais of stone, with just room to walk around the rocky platform's circle.

This was the chieftain of earth and stone Constantine had suspected would be here—a powerful elemental, as kingly a figure as the Lady of Waters was queenly. His head, indeed, was surmounted with alternating spikes of ruby and emerald: a crown that grew from his granite brow. His broad, inscrutable face was a craggy carving; his glowing eyes, flames licking from them, were formed of molten stone, and they beamed out like red-bulbed lamps. Their rays now fell on Constantine, with an unnerving warmth, both of the heat of his internal being, and the tingling of his psychic inspection.

He spoke to Constantine with his mind:

Who comes now to mock me in my imprisonment? Another puny sorcerer? Someday I will make it my business to seek out sorcerers and dismember them, taking my time about it.

The walls of the cavern seemed to rumble inwardly with the reverberation of his words, though they were expressed only in thought.

"I have come to relieve you of your imprisonment, if I can, squire," Constantine said, bowing. "I perceive you to be royalty amongst elementals, a lord of the stones! It isn't right you should be cooped up, and I assure you, your enemies are mine, great king of the earth!"

You speak with unctuous flattery but not without truth. I have foreseen your coming. Water drips here, sometimes, and one with whom I mated of old, whom you know as the Lady of Waters, has

spoken to me here, drip by drip, telling me you would come if you could. But you cannot open Fludd's trap alone.

"So that is what Iain Culley used to jug you here, squire? 'Fludd's Spell of Dire Containment'?"

That is the spell that was used, but the wretch Culley was not the invoker of it. Fludd himself entrapped me, saying he wished only to hold me a single day and night so that he might question me in safety. I did not honor him for the entrapment, but he did me no harm, and since he was a servant of the Overgod, I would have gone my way without punishing him for his impudence. But the wretch Culley informed on Fludd to the little minds who held the reins of the worldly church, and they took him away to demand answers from him for what they supposed was heresy, though it was they who were the heretics. With Fludd gone, Culley took command of me, tormenting me with corrosive acids until I did his bidding. I may send certain emanations from this containment—only such as he stipulates, and with one of these I caused the earth to open up and swallow the magical cage, and Culley, so that we were lowered together into this cave. He said that he would release me once we were here. But it soon became evident that he intends to keep me in the cage forever. My elemental emanation is the source of his control over his kingdom, suppressing all sorcery but his, shackling the harpies and gray demons to his will. Woe to you if you do not release me and he learns of your enmity! For my power, so long as I am trapped, is his power!

Constantine approached the cage—the sphere of containment—and put out his hand, feeling its power . . . and drew his hand back quickly. It felt as if the energy bubble was conscious, aware of him, warning him spitefully to stay away.

He closed his eyes and extended his psychic prescience, instantly perceiving that the spell drew on the elemental's own power, against the Lord of Stone's will, and turned it against him; a thorny problem in spell-busting.

Do you now perceive the difficulty? the elemental asked. **The spell was created by two men, Fludd and Culley, incanting together. It must incorporate both light and dark energies from two magicians at once to be complete, even as a cage of steel must contain yielding space as well as unyielding metal. Fludd provided the light energies, Culley the dark—for Fludd knew Iain Culley to be formed for the Left-Hand Path. He hoped to convert him to see the wisdom of the Overgod through the intervention of the Crucified One, but Culley would not have it. He betrayed Fludd and hid me away from him.**

Constantine nodded. "I get you, squire. I suspected it was Fludd's Dire Containment, and I know the spell. But I can't see how to end the spell without magic." He rubbed his jaw in puzzlement, gazing at the pulsing sphere of power trapping the elemental. "And I can't use ritual magic because Culley's using your power to control magic around his kingdom. No other magic but his works, so we're buggered, far as I can see."

Some of your terminology is puzzling to me, but

I comprehend the meaning. There is a way to circumvent his restraint on magic. If you can bring another magician, I will tell you then how it might be done.

"Right, then. I think I know another who'll help me dispel it in exchange for a release from his own prison. I'd better see to it."

Hurry! I go mad in confinement!

"You've been patient for hundreds of years, Lord of Stone! Be patient an hour further! And listen, there's something else we have to clear up. There's one thing more I need to arrange with you if I'm to let you go . . ."

⊷═◉═⊷

One of the King's grimoires tucked under his arm, Constantine pushed the door open into the throne room, expecting to be arrested . . . but no one was waiting for them but two dead men.

Outside the door, behind the throne, they found the two guards Constantine had tricked into fighting collapsed in a pool of blood, the smaller atop the larger, having bled to death from multiple sword cuts. They'd killed each other.

"Oh, how awful," Maureen said.

"They're all assholes, those skull-faced bastards," Geoff muttered, remembering his capture.

"They couldn't all be," Maureen said, as they hurried past the dead men. "Anyway they'll be found soon. There'll be an alarm raised . . ."

"Come down this way," Constantine said. "Down at

the end of this hall there's a cell. In the back, the wall's been knocked down just today, thanks to our Balf. The tunnel back of the cell is one of Balf's secret ways, and it'll lead us to that bastard MacCrawley."

They were relieved when they got into the cell, found the new entrance to the cave at the back, and, using a crystal of illumination, made their way through a half mile of tunnel to the corridor outside the cell where Bosky had been kept in chains.

"God I hate coming back here," Bosky muttered.

On the threshold of the slave cavern they found another Fallen Roman; Scofield had killed this one, Constantine supposed, stabbed him in the back.

Comes more naturally to Scofield than me, Constantine thought.

The door was unlocked, and inside he found Mac-Crawley sprawled in chains, alone in the room, looking old and weary and sullenly angry.

When Constantine came in, MacCrawley leaped to his feet and lunged for him, stopping just short of being able to reach him when he came to the end of his chains. His outstretched arms, the fingers clutching, clawlike, swiped the air just an inch from Constantine's nose.

"Kill you!" MacCrawley snarled, spittle running from between his clenched teeth. "Kill . . . *you!*"

Constantine blithely lit a cigarette. "Hello, Mac-Crawley! Comfortable little gaff you have here."

"When I get out of here, Constantine, I'm going to kill that bastard King, end his magical suppression, and then I'll call up the nastiest, lowest, foulest-smelling, ugliest, cruelest demons from Hell and I'm

going to give you to them! And I'm going to see that
they're the laziest too, so that they take at least a
century tearing you into bits! But I'll see to it, Constantine, that once they've torn you to bits those bits
will live, will suffer, each bloody shred still invested
with your mind! And after a decade or so of that I'll
see you're reconstituted so you can be torn slowly
apart again and then, once again, I'll see to it that—"

"Yeah, yeah," Constantine said, blowing smoke in
MacCrawley's face, "brilliant, mate, lovely, looking
forward to it. But in the meantime, how'd you like to
get out of them chains and come up with me to set
the elemental free, eh? What do you say? Seems I
can't do it myself."

MacCrawley gaped at him. "What's that you say?"

"You heard me. Haven't you wondered why you're
here alone today, and not out there humping barrels?
I've got this place wired, mate. We're going to over-
throw the King; you just said you wanted to do it
yourself. And I don't think he's told you he's planning
to poison most of Britain. Might throw a spanner into
the works for your SOT boys—I'm guessing London
is your home base, yeah? Shortly destined to be unlivable if the King has his way."

"What are you babbling about?"

"The Universal Solvent; the King's going to use it
to spread toxins through the seas, destroy the air
around Britain. Survivors come down here and he
enslaves them."

"Why that's utter . . ." But then MacCrawley, broke
off, frowning. "Then again . . . it would explain certain
things . . ."

Constantine nodded. "You've seen he's been keeping something from you, I reckon, and now you know what it was. King's power comes from keeping the Lord of Stone in lockup: the king of Britain's earth elementals. But I can't release the Lord of Stone myself. Fludd's Spell of Dire Containment needs two opposite types to do the job. I reckon I've got just enough light in me to do the trick, and we bloody well know you've got enough dark. Well? What do you say? But you can't be strangling mé after I've let you go, nor turning me over to demons to tear apart—disappointing as it'll be for you to do without it—as the King won't stand for you to be running about free. So you need to take him down, and you need me alive and in one piece to do that, as much as I need you. Right: What do you say, old cock?"

MacCrawley's hands clenched and unclenched. He glared. He breathed hard, in and out, staring. But at last he grunted and said, "Very well. I give you my word, I will cooperate with you to free the Lord of Stone."

Constantine chuckled, reaching for the King's keys, to unlock the chains.

"What's so funny, Constantine?" MacCrawley growled. "Your sense of humor makes me bloody nervous."

"Just thinking of something Oscar Wilde wrote," Constantine told him, turning the key in the lock. "'A man cannot be too careful in his choice of enemies . . .'"

15

THE STAMPEDE OF VULCAN'S HORSES

The hourglass was trickling the last of its sand from higher to lower when Lord Blung, the King's seneschal, arrived with the final ingredient for the Universal Solvent. He turned the big hourglass on its shelf himself; when the sand ran out, after an hour, it would be time to introduce the final ingredient into the solution.

Face wrapped in water-soaked cloths against the fumes, Scofield stood on the top of the rusty iron scaffolding that rose up to overlook the cauldron. He was alarmed, seeing the seneschal arrive. The time for the troll to act was near and there had been no word.

And he could see the Il-Sorg—transparent but maleficent demons like the ones guarding the alchemical transfusor of the great machine—watching him from their balconies of stone on the walls near the scaffolding. They kept a close scrutiny on him as if they suspected he might be about to betray their master. He could do nothing to advance Constantine's scheme with the Il-Sorg there.

Constantine wanted him to delay the final step in the transmutation of the Universal Solvent until "everything is in place." Perhaps he should not do as Constantine asked, even if the chance came. After all, it was all likely to fail. The King's scheme would take its inexorable course, the country above would be destroyed in all probability, no matter what he did. Why destroy himself as well by becoming involved in useless conspiracies? If he played along with the King he might become seneschal himself one day, if he could contrive to get rid of Blung.

The present seneschal climbed the stairs to the top of the scaffolding, reaching the railed-off top where Scofield waited. The old man coughed as he looked into the enormous cauldron: a seething stone pot, banded with iron, forty feet across. Blung nodded, satisfied with the progress of the transmutation, but his expression was troubled.

"Is there something amiss, Seneschal Blung?" Scofield asked with all the innocence he could muster.

Blung tugged thoughtfully on his sweeping mustaches. "The King is still sequestered with his new wench. He should have finished his sport with her long ago. He should be here! I am loathe to interrupt his honeymoon . . . but suppose something has gone awry? Suppose the wench is treacherous?"

"Impossible; his imp protects him."

"Yes . . . true . . . But if he does not come soon, I must investigate . . ."

Scofield nodded, looking at the vial containing the final ingredient, held in Blung's hand. He glanced at the vial, and at the Il-Sorg. Who continued their baleful observation of him.

Perhaps, indeed, he should not play Constantine's game.

◆━━◦◉◦━━◆

Fallesco was glad he'd decided to turn the tables on Spurlick by following the underhanded courtier. Now he watched from the shadows of a nearby doorway as Spurlick shouted for the guards at the door to the rooms Bosky had been in. The Captain of the guards himself, leading a six-man patrol passing by, stalked up at the outcry. "Well? What is it?"

"Can you not see?" Spurlick demanded. "Look, the door is open! Your guard is gone! And the boy with the fairy blood is not here! Something is afoot! We must go to the King; these interlopers are interfering with his plans!"

"Just so!" Fallesco declared, striding up, his manner all authority and confidence. "Let us go to the King's apartments!"

Spurlick glared at Fallesco. "Who are you to take charge here? I've long suspected your loyalty . . ."

"What's that? I am the King's librarian! I am the court poet! What role do you play, pray tell? Court Buggerer?"

The guards laughed and elbowed one another.

Before the sputtering Spurlick could continue, Fallesco said, "Come, let us go together to see about the King's well-being! He shall decide what to do! Your keen observation here will not go unrewarded!"

"Very well!" Spurlick said sullenly.

Fallesco led the deputation through the corridors to the King's apartments at the other side of the palace.

"No guard is in place here!" observed the Captain, nonplussed, as they arrived at the royal bedroom. "Something must be afoot indeed! Why haven't I been informed?"

He rapped on the door. "Your Majesty! Forgive the intrusion, but mysteries abound! Is all well within?"

There was no response from within. "Why does he not respond, if only to tell us to be on our way?" Spurlick asked. "Captain—you have a key!"

"Only for use in emergencies . . ."

"This is emergency enough! Open the door!"

The guard shrugged and unlocked the door, as Fallesco toyed with his braided beard. "Hmmm . . . as King's librarian and court poet, I am the highest dignitary here. I shall go in to see that all is well. Wait here!"

"What?" Spurlick shook his head. "By no means! We will go together! The King will know it was I who came to his aid!"

"Just as you like . . . Captain, we'll call you if we need you."

Fallesco opened the door—not too widely—and held it as Spurlick sidled in.

"Fallesco, open the door wider!"

"The King's privacy must be preserved insofar as it can be!"

Grumbling, Spurlick entered, Fallesco coming behind him. He closed the door on the anxious, paper-
colored faces of the guards, and turned to see
Spurlick staring at the bed, where the King had apparently fallen asleep during coitus with one of the
guards. Both men snored softly, the King with his
arm thrown around the other man, his trousers
about his knees.

Fallesco chuckled. "It appears the King's tastes are
more eclectic than I had supposed."

Spurlick sensed something was further askew
than a change in sexual preference. He approached
the King. "My King, I'm sorry to disturb you, but I
have reason to believe a conspiracy is afoot. There
have been secret meetings, there are missing guards,
and . . . My King? Why, I believe he has been dru—"

He never quite finished the word, his last sound
being an *eep* noise, as Fallesco, clapping a hand over
Spurlick's mouth, used his other hand to drive a dagger into the courtier's heart. Spurlick quivered,
struggled flailingly for but a moment, and then went
limp. "That should keep you out of mischief, Lord
Spurlick."

Fallesco let the dead man's body fall over the
sleeping men on the bed. The King stirred as
Spurlick's blood spurted onto him. The tyrant Culley
would wake soon . . .

Fingering the edge of the dagger, Fallesco told
himself that he ought to kill the King now. He badly
wanted to, and it would be so very easy. But Constantine had said the King must be alive for the spell
to be safely undone.

Sighing, he wiped the blade, returned it to its sheath, and went out to speak to the guards. "Gentlemen, the King is deep in conversation with M'Lord Spurlick. He wishes you to guard the door, and no one is to enter for at least an hour!" And Fallesco strode self-assuredly away.

The Captain stared after him suspiciously. Finally he said, "You two, guard the door. The rest of you, come with me. I wish to decide for myself what is going on. We will check the corridor behind the throne."

⤙⇒◎⇐⤚

Constantine and MacCrawley were just arriving at the door to the corridor behind the thrones when the Captain of the guards and four soldiers rushed up from the opposite way. They stopped, gawking at the two bloodied bodies of the sentries sprawled at Constantine's feet. They looked at the dead men and they looked at Constantine. "Take them!" the Captain of the guards shouted in Latin.

"Well that's just brilliant, Constantine," MacCrawley said with disgust, as the guards started toward them, drawing their swords. "You've brought me here only to get us both killed."

"Psychic attack, perhaps . . . telepathy," Constantine suggested, wondering if it would do any good to run.

"What, all five of them? Don't be stupid. Gentlemen—" MacCrawley put up his hands like a felon caught by the police as the guards surrounded them, raising their swords. "I submit to arrest, but I advise you to kill this conniving con artist. It is he who's behind the deaths of these good sentries, not me! He's tricked me into—"

Then a looming presence, a thud of heavy feet . . .

And Balf was there, rushing in from behind the guards, swinging a poleax made of petrified wood. He swung right and left, smashing bodies aside like a man with a machete cutting through undergrowth. Two of the guards screamed and panicked, stumbled into one another, and went down with a single brutal, bone-crunching crack of the poleax. The Captain of the guards managed to fire a single bolt from his crossbow, which stuck in Balf's right shoulder a moment before the Fallen Roman's crossbow and his bones were shattered by a single sweep of the troll's great weapon. The Captain went tumbling, shattered within himself.

Balf casually plucked the arrow from his shoulder as a man would remove a thorn, and turned to Constantine. "I was looking for you in your quarters. The woman of fairy blood sent me; she said I should watch your back, and though the term is somewhat confusing I divined her meaning. Now . . ."

Balf turned and swung the poleax once more, smashing in the door.

"I do have a key," Constantine muttered. He shot a sharp look at MacCrawley. "And you; I thought we agreed no treachery?"

"Well, in the circum—"

"Never mind, let's get on with it. The noise of the fight's been heard. More of those skull-faced bastards coming. Balf, off with you, take up your post near Scofield, if you would, squire."

He led the way into the corridor, toward the last room, where the Lord of Stone waited.

◆──◎──◆

Scofield was growing increasingly nervous. Coughing sporadically from fumes, Lord Blung was again examining the seething brew, the gigantic cauldron of preparatory solution for the Universal Solvent, and it seemed to Scofield that Blung's satisfaction with the proceedings suggested he was about to pour the final ingredient into the mix. Whereupon the land above was doomed. And Scofield had not yet made up his mind about his part in all this.

His hope that his sabotage here would turn out for the best was based entirely on the word of a stranger, a man with an unsavory reputation: John Constantine. Many had come a cropper, relying on Constantine's word. True, they'd mostly been right bastards. But still, even if Constantine was trustworthy, he might bungle the whole thing. The odds, after all, were against him. On the King's side was the King's power and his minions, numbering in the hundreds and thousands: the harpies, the gripplers, the army. Not to mention a number of sleazy backstabbing eavesdroppers, like Spurlick, who hoped to curry favor with their sovereign, though of course they secretly hated him.

On Constantine's side were one vain poet, two teenage boys, a woman far out of her depth, and an

unpredictable troll. And there was Constantine himself, a notorious con artist.

The odds for success in the rebellion against King
Culley simply didn't seem good. And at any moment
Blung might notice the hole in the ceiling, punched
through from the chamber above by the troll. It was
hidden in mist rising from the cauldron . . . most of
the time.

Blung glanced at the hourglass. "It is just about
ready to pour. There is no use in waiting for the King.
Let us pour the final ingredient."

"But it's not yet a full hour."

"You seem to be laboring under a misunderstanding," Blung declared, with pompous condescension.
"The final ingredient can be applied at any time in
the last hour, Magus Scofield, once the solution
seems ready. And clearly it is. Notice the flecks of
mercury making tiny bobbing pellets at the edges;
notice the strong smell of iron, alternating with sul-
fur. Notice the increase in corrosion at the edge of
the cauldron. These are infallible signs!"

"No, no, I disagree," said Scofield, hoping he
wasn't too obvious in his stalling. "Look, there are
really very few mercury pellets, and the corrosion is
left over, it is old, it is not of recent origin—"

"Nonsense! Look at that pitting! The solution eating away at the cauldron is hungry for the final ingredient! Once we pour in the tincture, the full solvency,
the *universal* solvency, will transmutate into highest
potency, and the solution will eat through the cauldron in seconds!"

"But . . ." Scofield pretended to have a coughing fit. He made it last as long as possible.

"Perhaps you haven taken ill; I advise you to go to the infirmary. I can handle this."

"Respectfully, seneschal, I am the more experienced with the Solvent, I must stay, and I do believe we must not put the final ingredient in too soon, or . . ." Here he managed another reasonably believable coughing fit. With the fumes there, it wasn't hard to do.

Blung cocked his head and looked at him skeptically. Clearly becoming suspicious. "I'll wait a few minutes, but already the last stream of sand falls through the hourglass, Scofield! We must do the King's bidding, and soon!"

Scofield thought: *I'm being a fool to try and stop him. I must let him do as he wants, or I'll die with all the rest . . .*

⊷═╼

"The Lord of Stone is the real key to his power, then?" MacCrawley asked musingly.

"He is," Constantine said, taking out the key to the final room beyond the rejuvenation projector chamber. Both of them ignored the pleas and babblings coming pathetically from behind them. "The great machine run by the crankers gives him rejuvenation and some of the energy running the palace—heat and light. But his magical control extends from right bleedin' here."

"However did you manage to get the key to this room?" MacCrawley asked. "I've been looking for a way to get at it these many months."

"Sex opens doors," Constantine said, opening the door.

"Oh I see. You used the new queen . . . cunning of you." MacCrawley irritated Constantine hugely with this remark. "I just hope, Constantine, that you've not got us in deeper than . . ." MacCrawley broke off as they entered the chamber, gazing with awe up at the Lord of Stone. He remembered himself and bowed low to the elemental. "Great Lord of Stone, king of earth elementals, I honor you."

The Lord of Stone's reply rumbled through their minds, and grumbled in the walls, the floor underneath . . .

Honor me by ending my captivity—a captivity brought about by one of your own ephemeral, deceitful, underhanded kind. I hold all your perfidious species responsible. But if you release me, magician, you have nothing to fear! Someone must pay the price, but it will not be you.

MacCrawley bowed again. "But there is the matter of the suppression of ritual magic; your own magic power is siphoned off to stop anyone's magic but the King's. If it takes magic to release you . . ."

There is a way. John Constantine, go you to the wall, behind me. There you will see the bones of two men, and the tools they brought with them here to enlarge this chamber, so that the Gloomlord could steal my magic the more effectively.

Constantine walked around behind the sphere and

found the bones of two men, both with their skulls severed from their necks. They'd been executed here, it appeared.

Culley did not want anyone to know what was in this room, and he killed the two after they completed their work to keep the secret. Now take up the chisel and hammer you see lying there, and take three steps in the way of your left hand ...

Constantine picked up the rusty tools, which had lain there undisturbed for generations, and took the three steps, to stand before the back wall where water was trickling thinly down from a crack.

Now raise the chisel and strike, three times, just under the place where the water drips.

Constantine did as he was bid, striking hard, and on the third blow the crack widened with a creaking sound and water sprayed out, hitting him in the chest. He stepped hastily out of the way. "Bloody hell that's cold."

The water was about the same as might run from a garden hose with the spigot fully open. It gushed toward the dais and began encircling it, making a pool on the floor around it.

Constantine put the chisel down and returned to MacCrawley, as the Lord of Stone rumbled, **Thus the Lady of Waters is freed to surround the stone on which stands my cage. The power the Gloomlord uses is the elemental power of stone, darkly transubstantiated for his purposes. The power of the Lady of Waters is another manner of energy which blocks his power within the pool. Here you may now perform ritual magic without the inter-**

ference of his spell of suppression . . . but always staying on the stone platform, within the circling water.

"Splendid!" MacCrawley chuckled. "Let's be at it."

Constantine was already at work, hunched over on the dais, murmuring magical formulae as he set about marking the dais's floor—a foot above the water, dry but enclosed by it—with the chalk he had brought, inscribing sacred signs, names of power, runes of invocation, and relevant alchemical symbols within a circle around the sphere. He worked quickly, concentrating intensely, not allowing himself the luxury of the slightest lessening of close attention to the work, still angry with himself for the time he'd wasted after the feast.

He finished circumambulating the caging sphere, but hadn't yet closed the magic circle.

He looked significantly at MacCrawley. "The blood," Constantine said. Simple as that.

MacCrawley nodded and drew a magical dagger from his waistband: a lucky find in the King's library, picked up on the way here. Its slim silver blade was incised with magical symbols, its handle made of human bone carved into the shape of a seraphim. He used its point to prick his arm, dipped the blade in the blood and completed the circle with it; Constantine, after cleaning the blade, did the same with his own blood, so that the circle was completed by blood from both men. Then he laid the magic dagger across the edges of the circle, pointing outward.

The two magicians then walked around the spherical cage of energy, going in opposite directions, passing one another three times, chanting sonorously in Latin: *"Libertas consummatio, regio silex!"*

Liberate completely the King of Stone!

"Libertas consummatio, regio silex!" Not merely saying the words, but making them resonate through their whole being, thinking their meaning, projecting that meaning through the clearly formed mental picture of the magic circle, like directing light through a magnifying glass to sharpen its power. And magical energies thrummed in the air, making Constantine's mouth go dry, his pulse pound, his eyes misty . . .

They heard boot steps drumming from the corridor. The King's men had found Balf's victims. They were coming . . .

Constantine felt an impulse to panic, to despair. It was too late! But he focused his mind, the current from above flowing through it, once more, and he chanted more forcefully than ever, his voice merging with MacCrawley's:

"Libertas consummatio, regio silex!"

And so saying the two men met face-to-face, chanting certain names of power which cannot be repeated here, that consummated the *consummatio* . . .

The Fallen Romans crowded into the doorway, raising their weapons. A crossbow bolt flew past Constantine's nose; another went between his legs, punching a hole through his coat. The soldiers charged.

And were met by a stone fist.

The spherical cage, till now powerful enough to keep a giant made of stone trapped for centuries, had simply popped like a soap bubble, banished by the spell Constantine and MacCrawley had performed, and the giant was wading through the soldiers, knocking them to the left and right, like a man smacking cockroaches off his table.

Vermin! the Lord of Stone thundered, making the surviving Fallen Romans stagger with the psychic intrusion. **Your kind have kept me pent long enough! You are the servants of the vile one who put me here! I will kill all who stand before me!** He smashed his fist on the floor, which opened under four of the soldiers, swallowing them up. They scarcely had time to cry out before it closed up over them.

Constantine cleared his throat. "I say, great guv'nor of stone, I wonder if I could persuade you to hold back a bit; most of these silly bastards don't know any other life. And there are other people out there who need to be protected."

I promise nothing, John Constantine, except that I will kill neither you nor the man MacCrawley! This is the bargain! Any others you wish to protect keep out of my way!

So saying, the Lord of Stone turned and stepped on two surviving Fallen Romans who were trying to crawl away. Crushing them, indeed, like cockroaches.

Constantine winced and looked away. *I did the right thing here. Millions will die up above unless I carry on with this. Still . . .*

The Lord of Stone smashed the doorway to widen it for his mighty frame and hunched to go through in pursuit of the fleeing soldiers.

Constantine turned and saw MacCrawley grinning,

the dagger in hand, stalking toward him. Constantine backed away.

"And now, Constantine, it's your turn to die," Mac-Crawley said, relishing each word. "The Lord of Stone may choose not to kill you, but I promised only to forbear until His Lordship here was liberated! Now be a good fellow and die, you bastard. A special corner of Hell is waiting just for you!" He slashed the knife artfully at Constantine, cutting through a corner of his trench coat's collar. The little triangle of cloth fell away as Constantine, backing off, tripped and fell on his arse. MacCrawley stood over him, grinning. "Just toying with you; I'm good with a knife, Constantine!" He raised the knife, preparing to throw himself at Constantine, shouting his curse—and then froze, looking down in horror.

The floor had opened up under him, and he was sinking down into it; the stone seemed to have gone soft around his feet, and he sank till it closed up around his waist. Constantine got to his feet and backed just out of reach, coolly lighting a cigarette. "I forgot to mention the other bits of my deal for arranging to release his nibs. First the Lord of Stone's got to swear to use his power over stone to lift the village of Tonsell back up to the surface. Second, he's got to keep you contained after his release, seeing as I knew you'd try to kill me right out of the box, soon as the ritual was done. He's been watching you—can watch from any rock or stone."

"Constantine!" MacCrawley roared, flipping the knife around and throwing it, trying to transfix him from a distance. "Goddammit, die!"

It was a clumsy attempt. Constantine easily side-stepped the knife and went to pick it up off the floor. "Right, I'm off. Enjoy your new digs."

"What? You can't leave me here!"

"You're not entirely alone. Door's open now, you can hear Smithson babbling in the next room. You two can gabble a while together, in harmony. It could be quite entertaining. I'm sorry"—he blew smoke at MacCrawley, making him cough—"that I won't be here to enjoy it."

Then he turned on his heel and walked out, whistling, stepping over the broken bodies of Fallen Romans as he went.

He knew that MacCrawley would think he was stuck there forever, was going to die of starvation trapped in rock. But the Lord of Stone wouldn't have permitted that, since MacCrawley was one of those who'd freed him. He'd release him, in good time. Maybe he'd survive the ruination of this place, afterward, and maybe he wouldn't.

It was easy to see where the Lord of Stone had been. There were the bodies of pallid soldiers strewn in his wake. There were big holes smashed through intervening walls; there was rubble everywhere, the walls and floor rumbled, and screams were heard in the distance.

Out in the throne room two of the pillars had been knocked over, one of them having smashed across the thrones. The ceiling had collapsed in many places, but he was able to pick his way through the smoking rubble to cross the room. He hurried down the side hallway, ever faster, till his breath came in rasps, trying to get to Maureen and the boys.

They were huddled together in a corner of the servants' quarters, frightened by the intermittent shaking of the walls and the screams, though the boys were trying to look heroically unconcerned.

"Come on, then!" Constantine shouted at them as the floor shook and more screams came from without.

"What's going on out there?" Bosky demanded.

"The Lord of Stone is taking his vengeance! Now come on and follow me; we've got to scarper out of here and make sure Scofield does his job!"

Maureen nodded, smiling with new hope, leading the boys as they all followed Constantine out the door. "Does this mean we get out of this place, back to the world up above?"

The ground shook; someone, not far away, wailed in despair.

"With luck, that's just what it means," Constantine said. Trying to sound as if he was sure of it himself.

He just hoped it was true.

✦══◉══✦

The King woke to find a dead man draped across him.

He groaned and rolled aside, letting Spurlick's body slump away, and sat up, looking woozily around. His head throbbed, and the room seemed to tilt first to one side, then to the other. This was no mere hangover—he had been drugged!

He took a deep breath, and drew a little magical energy from the air, making himself steadier, and then looked around . . .

She was gone. The queen had drugged him—had

tricked him with the help of that ungrateful wretch, John Constantine. He had been taken in like a country bumpkin. They'd murdered that wanton old bastard Spurlick too, he saw. And there—one of his guards, struck unconconscious.

But surely the imp in his headboard had done something about all this?

He turned to stare in shock at the headboard. It was gone! Released from its prison! The imp, too, had colluded against him!

So now—where to find the conspirators?

But what was the time? Was it not time for the Universal Solvent to be poured? That must take precedent.

Afterward, there would be countless ages in which to exercise an exquisite vengeance . . .

◆━◉━◆

"Lumptydumptyhorry, I shall make him sorry," sang the troll to himself, striding into the bubble-shaped alchemical transfusion chamber. *"Lumptydumptygleep, I shall make him weep!"* The great central shaft was here; the five vanes turned and crackled their purple energy to their electrodes. But the Il-Sorg, as expected, were gone. Only the power of the Lord of Stone had kept them here; with the Lord of Stone set free, they had returned to their hell-realms, to caper in celebration, Balf supposed, dancing upon lost souls like a winemaker stomping grapes.

"Lumptydumptyskreek, I shall make him shriek," Balf sang, as he took the tools from his belt, the tools he had fashioned in his hiding place, near the Stab-

bing Falls. There were just two. One was shaped exactly like a Phillips head screwdriver, the other like a flathead screwdriver. He was unaware of the existence of these tools in the upper world; these just happened to be the shapes he needed.

He took one in each hand now, as he dodged under the electrodes, slipped past the discharge of dark electricity, and stepped up to the adjustment box on the central shaft. He pried it open with the flathead tool and with the other, turned a single screw inside it.

The shaft squealed . . .

And stopped turning.

Far below, the crankers, those gray, scabrous laborers in absolute darkness, suddenly found themselves straining to turn their cranks. The cranks would not respond. Continuous pressure only made them snap off.

The crankers, fearful and confused, gathered in their place of resting, except one who, more enterprising than the rest, snuffled around the edges of the base of the machine, expecting to be driven back by the gripplers . . . only to find the gripplers were not there. Instead his probing fingers found a six-inch-thick slick of paste on the stone floor. Sustained in this world only by the power of the Lord of Stone, the gripplers had melted away, their base souls returned to Hell.

Several levels above, hurrying on his way to the secret tunnel that would take him the short way up to the cauldron of the Universal Solvent, Balf sang, *"Lumptydumptyslimper, I shall make him whimper . . ."*

"You have been trying to stall me, Scofield," Blung declared. "Admit it! Something is going on; I sense a diminution of the King's power, and look! The Il-Sorg are gone!"

Scofield looked and was relieved to see that the balefully glaring demons were gone. "Thank God for that. Constantine's succeeded!"

"Has he indeed?" asked King Culley, coming onto the top of the scaffolding. In his hand was a sword and just behind him were two Fallen Romans, one with a crossbow, the other a pike. The King, Scofield noticed, was growing elderly at this time of day.

"My King!" the seneschal exclaimed, bowing. "I have been concerned—"

"And well you should be!" Culley growled. "I woke but minutes ago—drugged by that treasonous witch I made my queen! My power is diminished for now—but I can kill you, Scofield! 'Thank God Constantine's succeeded' you said? Traitor!"

Culley raised his sword to strike. Scofield shouted, "No!" and rushed past him, leaping off the scaffold toward the stone floor edging the sump. He struck with blinding pain, realizing he'd shattered his ankle. He tried to hobble on the other foot but a stabbing hurt came a moment later, as an arrow from a crossbow struck him in the back.

He fell onto his face, feeling pinned like a butterfly, every small movement redoubling his pain.

"Good shot, soldier!" Culley crowed. "When I regain control, you shall be Captain of the guards!"

"But with the Lord of Stone released, my King . . ." the seneschal said fearfully, looking toward the doorway below.

"He will soon tire of killing the Fallen Romans!" Culley declared confidently, taking the vial of the final ingredient from Blung. "I will conceal myself from him, and when he has at last returned to his vast realm, I will lead my armies to capture the thousands of new slaves who will descend to us! I will restore my youth, and summon other magics to support my reign! Now, Blung, pour in the final ingredient! Let those greedy slugs crawling the upper world begin their suffering!"

"Here, 'greedy slugs'? That's rather an unfair generality," said Constantine, coming in down below with Maureen and the boys behind him.

"You dare to come here!" Culley shouted, gazing down at him, amazed. "I should have listened to MacCrawley!"

"I reckon MacCrawley could be right, once in a while," Constantine said, lighting the last cigarette in his pack as he sauntered closer to the scaffold. "Not that I've checked to see if the moon's blue lately." He crumpled up the empty pack and tossed it nonchalantly in the sump.

"Is it done?" asked Fallesco eagerly, as he hurried into the room beside Geoff and Bosky. "There was pandemonium outside. The palace is dimming; surely his power is diminished?"

"You!" Culley roared. "Fallesco! You have betrayed me too! Another backstabbing conspirator against me!"

Fallesco gave his courtliest bow. "Your Majesty flatters me."

The King turned to his guards. "Kill Constantine first!" he ordered. A Fallen Roman leveled his weapon.

"John, they're aiming a crossbow at you!" Maureen warned him. "Get back!"

Constantine smiled and held out the magical dagger he'd used in setting the Lord of Stone free. *"Advolo flagro!"* he shouted, and a spear of flame shot from the blade to consume the crossbow in the soldier's hand. The soldier yelped and flung the burning crossbow away.

Maureen was dragging Scofield out of the way, with Bosky and Geoff helping her. The hooded magician groaned. Fallesco helped him to stand. "Lean on me, Magus. We'll see the surface world yet! How I long to see the sky!"

"You notice anything, Gloomlord?" Constantine said, blowing a smoke ring, keeping the King's attention turned toward him. "Your spell suppressing other people's magic ends with the release of the Lord of Stone! And with the machine down, you're weak, far weaker than ever before! Don't you feel it?"

"You—you have sabotaged my machine!"

"Me and Balf! You won't rejuvenate, Culley, and your magic is limper than a eunuch's John Thomas!"

"Is it? We'll see!" Culley began to make magical passes in the air, muttering names of power. His power was ebbing, but he was still a master of ritual magic.

Constantine turned to Fallesco. "Get them out of

here! Wait down that corridor for me, but not if it
gets dodgy!"

Fallesco nodded and took Scofield, Maureen, and
the boys out with him as Constantine collected his
prana within himself. He felt the King's enchantment
building up in the room, more feebly than it would
have before this day, but perhaps strong enough.

Constantine projected a psychic image at the
guard standing closest to Culley; the man began to
shriek, seeing a harpy flapping at him, clawing at his
face, though none was truly there. He flailed about,
knocking into the King. Weakened and off balance,
the King lost control of his spell. It went awry, and it
was Lord Blung, not Constantine, who was caught up
in the enchantment, sucked up into a compressing
ball of energy, and then flung shrieking into the cauldron where he vanished in a red gush of steam.

"No!" Culley shouted, turning to stare into the
cauldron. "Blung!" Then he remembered the vial in
his hand; he popped the cork from its top and
poured the final ingredient into the cauldron.

The solution reacted instantly. It spouted, geyser-
ing up, then commenced roiling furiously within itself . . .

And the cauldron began to show cracks. It quivered, clearly about to fall apart.

Constantine looked desperately up at the ceiling
and saw that he had delayed the King long enough:
Balf had gotten into position. Through the mists
Constantine could just make out the troll's arm
reaching down through the hole in the ceiling to the

pulley holding the chains attached to the cauldron. With an engineer's precision he tugged at a cable and swung the pulley around so that it moved away from the sump, toward the stone floor on the side opposite Constantine, and as the cauldron disintegrated, the Universal Solvent fell not on the sump of toxins, but on the shelf of stone beside it. Instantly the solution began to eat through the stone, close to the wall and away from the sump, making an oblong hole that deepened, deepened, the alchemical Solvent sizzling granite away faster than boiling water consuming ice . . .

"Who has done this thing!" Culley asked, looking at the ceiling.

Balf's face showed in the hole, grinning down at him. "Greetings, O 'King'!" Balf cried, sneering the word *King*. "Now you will know punishment for enslaving your betters! You shall behold the stampede of Vulcan's horses!"

Constantine didn't care to hang about and find out exactly what Balf meant by Vulcan's horses. He ran from the room, into the corridor, where Fallesco had been having difficulty keeping Maureen and the boys from going to look for him. "Get out of here!" Constantine shouted at them. "Go!"

⊷══◍══⊶

Balf watched with deepening satisfaction, and Culley watched in enthralled dread, as the Solvent ate its way toward the underlying lava that the troll knew to be only one hundred eighty-five feet under the chamber, beneath the level of the underground river. The shaft cut by the Universal Solvent passed the underground river with eight feet to spare and continued down, down, to the cyst of lava. The magma's heat neutralized the Universal Solvent, but not before it had opened the way for the molten rock.

The King was chanting a spell of summoning as a vast rumbling noise, like thousands of horses riding down on them, racketed through the room, and then the magma erupted upward along the shaft cut by the Solvent to burst up in spurts of red and yellow, only to fall back and ooze over the sump, capping it forever. It began to seep out toward the door that Constantine had gone through, on its way engulfing the base of the scaffold, which began to dissolve, collapsing, the soldiers on it tumbling, wailing as they fell to be consumed by the molten rock.

But the King, concentrating the last of his energy, had levitated and was hovering unsteadily over the lava. Almost panicking, he cried out a series of commands, summoning his harpies, who flew in through the door and lifted him into the air, carrying him out through the tunnel, just above the magma.

Their claws dug rather forcefully into his shoulders. "Careful you oafs!" he cried to no avail as they went.

Balf retreated up through the hidden chamber over the sump, down the tunnel that led to the gigantic main cavern containing the darkening palace. Here he found Constantine and friends on a stone balcony, Fallesco, Bosky, and Geoff carrying Scofield between them. Scofield groaned and twitched, still living.

Arriving on the parapet, Constantine glanced at the
Palace of Phosphor and saw the surviving courtiers
lined up on its ramparts, looking at the destruction
wrought by the Lord of Stone on the Fallen Romans.

Fallesco had plucked the arrow from Scofield's
back and leaned him on the stone wall. He muttered
inaudibly to himself.

"Where now, John?" Maureen asked.

"Uhhh . . . right . . ." He hadn't quite thought as far
as that.

"What's to happen to the village?" Geoff asked.

"It'll be raised back up already," Constantine said.
"The Lord of Stone gave his word. You can count on
him to do as he says. But as for the ones who were
taken . . ."

He turned to Scofield. "What about those the King
had working at the cauldron? The people from the
village?"

"They . . ." Scofield licked his lips. He took a deep
breath and managed to say, ". . . when they were of
no more use, they were—slaughtered. Food for . . .
those below . . ."

"Oh God," Maureen said, squeezing her eyes shut.

Bosky put his arm around his mum's shoulder.
"Right. Then we've got to get back to the surface."

Constantine looked inquiringly at Balf, who nodded. "The tr . . . that is, our Azki-Hak friend will show
us the way!"

But they hesitated upon the parapet, the very one
where Bosky had fought, and from which Garth had

fallen, gazing in fascination at the palace and the colony of the Fallen Romans.

There was little left of the colony. The Lord of Stone was still ravaging through it, up to his knees in rubble and brick and blood and body parts, flinging screaming Fallen Romans through the air, stepping on those who tried to creep away, roaring his hatred.

"Look!" Geoff shouted, pointing at two harpies flying out through the tunnel opening, carrying the King Underneath between them. "He's getting away!"

They could just hear Iain Culley shouting orders at the harpies. They seemed uncertain as to whether to obey him, Constantine thought.

The Lord of Stone stopped his ravaging and gazed up at the King flying by. And the elemental called out an order to the harpies.

No longer enslaved to the King except by habit, they responded, doing as the Lord of Stone told them. They flew in opposite directions, one taking Culley's right arm with it, the other taking his left.

Spouting blood, Culley fell, his body turning end over end—to be caught by the Lord of Stone. Broken and armless but alive, the King lay groaning in the Lord of Stone's big granite hands. The giant used his powerful stone fingers to pinch the King's torn arteries shut. Culley let loose a scream that echoed across the cavern.

Now, said the Lord of Stone, **let us preserve your miserable life . . .**

Constantine thought he knew what the elemental meant by that, and he shuddered as he watched the

Lord of Stone carry Culley away, toward the Palace of Phosphor. The great elemental strode to the palace and, as the courtiers scattered before him, he gestured, opening a new fissure in the walls.

Then the Lord of Stone stepped into the fissure, carrying the King Underneath with him. And they were gone from sight.

Constantine glanced upward in time to catch the harpies flapping for the higher tunnel entrances, vanishing into them, seeking some covert roosting place where they could resume their ancient sleep.

"Constantine . . ." Scofield called, weakly.

Constantine knelt beside him. "Not much I can do, mate; you're pretty far gone. I'll try to slow it down." He stretched out a hand, and emanating a restorative energy into Scofield, muttered a magical spell that might preserve him a while.

"Just . . . long enough to . . ." Scofield whispered huskily, his eyes seeming to look beyond the stone ceiling, "to . . ."

"We can linger no more!" Balf declared, picking Scofield up in his arms. He led the way down the stairs and into a tunnel that sloped upward. Constantine paused after Balf, Fallesco, and the others had gone up the tunnel, and looked back to see the magma coursing from the tunnel he'd come through to get to the cavern, spewing and sizzling out over the ruins of the Fallen Romans' colony. The palace quivered in place and began to fall to pieces, tumbling in on itself. The courtiers on its ramparts howled in a mixture of terror and perverse delight, and died in its wreckage as the lava flowed over their bodies. Then a new fissure opened, deep and wide, the lava pouring down into it to fall all the way, Constantine knew, down to the cavern of the crankers. Their long degradation would be blessedly ended in a quick death.

"John, come on!" Maureen called back to him.

Feeling sick, Constantine turned away and hurried up the tunnel.

16

... AND SUICIDE IS CONFESSION

In the rejuvenation chamber, Smithson was talking to the mold that had invaded his brain, was telling the mold a story about the time his nanny stuck her finger up his arse, and warned him not to tell his mum, and how . . .

But who's this? Visitors?

The Lord of Stone carried the former King Underneath into the chamber, cradled in his massive left arm like a baby. Nearly as white-faced as his Fallen Romans, now aged the equivalent of about seventy-five, Iain Culley ogled frantically about, looking for egress where there would never be any.

The room was only dimly lit by crystals in the corners; the purple rays had ceased when the great machine had ceased functioning, and in the dimness the King numbly watched as the Lord of Stone reached to the man trapped in a socket of metal and invasive mold beside Smithson and plucked him out whole, killing him in the process, to the man's infinite relief.

But the growth, like a giant artichoke stuffed with dirty cotton, was still alive around the edges of the vessel, and the Lord of Stone dropped the King into this. Having no arms, he fit quite neatly. The mold instantly sealed up around him, closing off his wounds and penetrating his pores, working its way toward his brain . . .

The King, realizing what the Lord of Stone was about, screamed and screamed, to no avail.

The Lord of Stone considered the other men trapped in their vessels, and took pity on all but one of them. He killed them with casual flicks of his fingers.

Then he went to the contiguous room, where he released MacCrawley from his trap. **Go now . . . I have opened a channel for you to reach the surface, there! Enter that fissure, find a tunnel, enter and climb! These rooms I have preserved from the flowing stone, but there will be no other way to escape! Go!**

MacCrawley bowed deeply, taking the opportunity to reach to the floor to grab the little triangle of Constantine's coat he had cut away, and then rushed hastily to the exit the Lord of Stone had opened for him. He began to climb doggedly toward the surface through a narrow tunnel lit by flecks of phosphorescence on the wall. As he climbed, he had but two thoughts, alternating: *Get to the surface. Destroy John Constantine.* He thought nothing else.

The Lord of Stone returned to the rejuvenation chamber, and here he spoke to Iain Culley, the erstwhile Gloomlord, the King no more. **This room will** by degrees grow darker and darker. You will be Gloomlord indeed!

"Don't leave me here!" Culley begged. "Kill me, I beg you!"

Perhaps if I grow bored, I'll check on you—in five or six centuries, said the Lord of Stone.

Then the kingly elemental made a gesture, opening a fissure in the floor, and dropped into it. The fissure closed up behind him. He was gone.

"No!" screamed the King. "Don't leave me here!"

But it was done. The other surviving man gaped at him in idiotic delight. "Hullo, hullo old King old boy! Hullo! I know some songs! I'll sing you one my Uncle Clive taught me!"

"Shut up! Shut up, you!" Culley bellowed.

But Smithson ignored him, as he always would, and began to sing, *"It's a long road, to Tipperary . . ."*

"No no no no! Shut up!"

But the former Lord Smithson sang to the former King Culley; sang the same song, over and over and over again. And then he sang it some more, and some more after that, and after that some more too, and rather more after that and . . .

And then he sang it again.

⊷═◉═⊷

"Can it be?" Fallesco asked. "At last I'm to see the sun, the sky! We're nearly there, I can feel it!"

"Are we . . . almost to the surface?" Scofield asked weakly as Balf set him down just inside the doorway to the barrow. Sunlight was streaming into the tunnel from outside, and with it came the smell of woods and water and the sounds of birds singing . . .

"You are there," Balf said. "Your friends must take you outside. I will return to the realms of my people now, under the mountain range you call the Himalayas. I may yet find another living Azki-Hak. I bid you all farewell."

Constantine wanted to shake Balf's hand, but he was afraid the troll might accidentally crush his fingers. He compromised by nodding. "Ta, mate! Cheers, and good luck finding your kind! They're out there somewhere!"

The others thanked the troll and then, hunched over, Balf slipped away down the tunnel, moving with astonishing grace and facility, vanishing into the subterranean darkness.

"The sun . . . the sky . . ." Scofield groaned. "Please . . . take me outside . . ."

"Is that you, sor?" came a rusty old voice from without. It was Old Duff.

He entered the tunnel and helped them carry his master out into the sunlight. He laid him down on a patch of grass, in the shade of a standing stone. "Duff . . . good old . . . Duff . . ." Scofield said feebly. "Knew you'd be here . . ."

"Threw the bones, sor! Divined it was here I'd wait and here I am!"

"Stand aside," Scofield said croakingly. "Let me see . . ." They moved out of the way, and Scofield gazed up at the blue sky, the clouds. A hawk flew past. "At last, after all these years . . . to see it again . . . to become a part of it . . ." And then his eyelids fluttered and he died.

Constantine was aware of a moaning near the entrance to the tunnel, and turned to see Fallesco on his knees, face hidden in his hands. "What is it! What *is* that dreadful thing!"

Constantine walked over to him. "What dreadful thing?"

"That burning face above, that ball of fury in the endless blue! It sends arrows into my eyes!"

"Oh. That's the sun, mate. You've read about it."

"But how can you bear it? It's so fierce, so harsh! It stabs the eyes! It burns the skin!"

"Well, you're not to look right at it. Takes some adjusting. That blue there, you take a skeg at that? That's the sky you wanted to see!"

"I looked . . . it goes on and on and on! Who could bear it? You might be sucked up into it! And what a color! That giddy blue—a color for infants! And the riot of growths out here, the smells! The shrieking, shrieking of animals!"

"I don't hear any screaming—you mean the birds? Just a little singing is all. You'll get used to it."

"No, no!" And shading his eyes with his arm he got up and lurched back toward the entrance to the cave. "I'm going home to the Underlands! I'll find one of the other kingdoms! Balf! Wait for me! I cannot bear this place! It has no top to it! Balf, wait!"

There came an answering call, grumpily reluctant, from deep in the tunnel. "Very well, but hurry up, if you must come!"

And Fallesco nearly dove back into the cave, scuttling to the dark places that were his homeland.

Constantine was about to try to push the boulder

in place to block the entrance when it began to quiver, then rolled on its own, blocking the tunnel off with a *clomp* of finality. The Lord of Stone's doing, he supposed.

He returned to the group standing around Scofield and found Maureen softly singing an Irish dirge over the magician. Old Duff was on his knees, weeping. "I'll bury you under that great oak we spoke of, the druid's oak; I'll bury you as you asked me to, I will, and your spirit, master, it'll go to the druid lords in the high place . . ."

Bosky and Geoff were looking around, trying not to smile too much, since a man had just died, but beamingly happy to be outside.

━━◦◯◦━━

Constantine stood on the outer edge of the crowd in front of the ruins of the pub in Tonsell-by-the-Stream, smoking, watching as a red-faced Royal Army General with tufted eyebrows scowled around at the crowd, then read from a typewritten sheet of paper, proclaiming, "We have determined that this place and many of the soldiers who were sent to investigate have suffered from argot poisoning. This natural hallucinogen, which finds its way into the food supply, has caused a number of communities, over the centuries, to hallucinate—"

"But what about those faces on the sticks people seen, at the edge of the village?" demanded Butterworth, whiskey glass in hand. "How do you explain them!"

"They're gone!" Skupper declared. "I've just been to look. Just . . . gone!"

"But the people who're missing . . ."

The General shrugged. "There will be a missing person report for each of them; doubtless they wandered off in a haze of hallucinogenic—"

He was interrupted by cries of protest and disbelief. He raised his hands, palms outward, and shook his head. "That is the official position, do you understand? Nothing else is to be said to anyone!"

Constantine smiled. He expected something of the sort.

Geoff hurried up to him, tugging at his elbow. "We've got the car you wanted; took some doing to hire a car in all the chaos here, but Maureen's got it."

"Good. I've got to see to Chas . . ."

"We're going with you, me and Bosky!"

"With me? What about your family?"

"My uncle was taking care of me. My family's in Sheffield; I couldn't stick them and came out here to live. Never liked my uncle either. I stayed with Bosky as often as with him. Maureen's like me own mum. And she doesn't want to stay in Tonsell—not knowing what's underneath it! Well come on, then! We're all going!"

⊷═◉═⊷

It took another hour to drive to the stream, find the path in the woods, and retrace their way. The boys waited in the car as Maureen and Constantine hiked to the cave in the hillside.

Constantine was tired, deeply tired, after all that had happened. Much of it seemed unreal now, in retrospect. He had to believe in it, and he had to find Chas. But it was as if the weight of the world was settling on his shoulders. Traipsing along beside a stream, with a woman he very much liked, about to bring his journey to its consummation, he should be happy, or at least relieved to be out in the open after being shut up underground. But it was as if he were still down in the pit with the crankers. In utter blackness. Anything else seemed distant—the song of birds, the whir of bees, the wind in the trees, the fluffy clouds overhead, the moss underfoot. It was as if all those things, though clearly visible, were imaginary. They were all in his mind. The darkness, the cave, the bones on the floor. That was reality. And wasn't it? Wasn't mankind like that, really, scrabbling, most of them, in the black, black darkness of ignorance, preying on one another, the stronger exploiting the weaker, parasites in a pit? A nightmare to go on in a world like that. Better to end it, really. Consider, after all, all the harm he'd brought on his friends in the past. On Chas and Kit, on Gary Lester and Judith. He deserved to die for that, really, didn't he? Suicide; freedom from guilt, at last. A way of confession, was suicide, as Daniel Webster had said. He ought to get Chas out of his prison of ice and then . . . and then . . .

The habit of inner self-observation had become strong with Constantine after his time in Iran with the Blue Sheikh, and he noticed something then, turning his attention to his inner world . . .

A certain feeling. As if the dread, the whisperings of despair, were not coming from inside him. As if . . .

"Strewth!" he burst out, stopping on the path. "It could be him."

"What?" Maureen asked, catching up with him, breathing hard. "It could be who?"

He told her what he suspected, and how the problem might offer its own solution. Death was a kind of solution. Maureen was gratifyingly appalled at the thought.

Then they went onward, Constantine feeling like he was getting heavier with every step. But at last they arrived at the hillside, another entrance to the world under the world.

"This isn't on, at all, John. You couldn't get in there!" Maureen said as they pushed through the brush to the crevice in the hillside that fed the little creek. Water trickled out, but nothing could get in.

But then the stone barrier shuddered, seemed to mutter to itself, and fell away. The water that had pushed it aside gushed out, roaring past them. After a while the surge of water abated enough so that they could go in.

"You sure you want to come?" Constantine asked. "I have to go. But you just got out from underground."

"You're pretty sure she'll let us leave?"

"Pretty sure."

"Then I'm coming too."

Still, Maureen couldn't mask her reluctance as she followed Constantine into the cave. They waded along the chilly stream in the dim phosphorescent light, deep, deep into the hills, until at last they came to the cave of the waterfall.

"You've cocked it up again, Constantine," someone was saying in the shadows beside the pool. "This can't be right, me waking up in a fucking pile of ice . . ."

Constantine came closer to find Chas sitting on the edge of the stream, blinking around in confusion, kicking bits of ice away, brushing it from his shoulders.

"Where'm I, John?" He seemed dazed, dreamy.

"You'll be all right, mate. You've been somewhere, a few days. Asleep, in a way."

You have done what you pledged to do, said the voice of the Lady of Waters, issuing from the pool.

Constantine and Maureen looked into the pool and saw the Lady's face there, like a reflection, rippling with the surface of the water.

And I have released your friend, she went on. **Now go your way and trouble this sacred place no more.**

"There is one thing more I would ask of you, Lady," Constantine said.

I owe you nothing! You made an oath to me, but I had to force you to fulfill that oath! You are fortunate I do not drown you for that impudence!

Maureen knelt by the water and gently put her hand in it. "Lady, I'm one of those of old who knew you. Many times I have heard you singing to me. I am of the fairy blood, and we are the servants of the elements of air and water. I ask you to do this for us, to honor that ancient pact! And in turn I will honor you all my days, and sing your glory . . ."

"I can't believe how much the bastards charged me to get me cab out of tow!" Chas groused as they drove up to the shabby brick building where Constantine kept a flat. "The sodding pricks!" In the backseat, Geoff elbowed Bosky, grinning. Chas amused them. Maureen shook her head at them. "Bleedin' Christ," Chas went on. "Five days in some bloody limbo, as bad a cold as ever I"—he paused to sneeze—"and three hundred pound to get me cab back. Last little bit of credit I had of me plastic. Fuck the sodding lot of them. And as for you, John—"

Constantine, sitting beside him, reached over and put his hand on Chas's arm.

The look on Constantine's sadly smiling face struck Chas dumb for once: that smile flitting from an expression of abject despair, like a swallow flying from a cave. He had never seen Constantine so sunken-eyed, so gray. Though unbruised, Constantine looked worse than he had that morning he'd bailed him out of jail.

"I'm sorry you went through all that, mate," Constantine said. "No worries, after this. I promise you."

He started to get out of the cab, Maureen and Geoff and Bosky getting out of the back. On impulse—feeling strangely like he'd never see Constantine again, and, even more strangely, regretting it—Chas reached over and grabbed Constantine's hand. "After . . . after I've had a chance to get over this cold, mate, let's have a pint."

Constantine only nodded, the ghost of a smile on his lips, and climbed out, closing the door.

◦⊷═◉═⊶◦

The cab drove away. Constantine watched it go. *Chas.* At least he'd got him out of the ice and back to London.

He turned to Geoff and Bosky, handing Geoff his keys. "The gaff's top of the stairs. Go on in. It's not much; maybe it's better than Culley's dungeons. Make yourself some tea, watch some telly, Maureen'll be back soonest."

Misunderstanding what Constantine had in mind—thinking he wanted time alone with Maureen for romance—they ran upstairs, hooting.

Constantine and Maureen walked silently along the street for a while. It had clouded over and a thin rain was misting down, just like the rain that had fallen on Constantine that day in Ireland, when he'd run into Kit.

"You sure you have to do this?" Maureen asked, her voice thick.

"I do," he said. "I have to. It's the only way. The SOT will be on me forever otherwise, and they'll connect you with me. They'll go after you if I'm around. For Bosky . . . for you and Geoff and Chas . . . it's got to be done."

"There has to be another way. It . . . I don't know . . ." She shook her head.

"No. I've got to die. Or there'll be no end to it. It's that simple. He's watching me right now."

He was. MacCrawley was half a block behind them,
quite comfortable in the back of a limousine driven
by a low-level Servants of Transfiguration functionary.
MacCrawley was watching Constantine like an owl
watching its prey, and he had the triangle of cloth he'd
cut from Constantine's trench coat in his hand.

"Just follow at a distance, sir?" the driver asked.

"Yes. Slowly. If he looks back, move on ahead,
round the corner, and we'll go on as if we're on our
way someplace else. We'll pick him up a few minutes
later. I've got my link to the bastard; I won't lose
him."

Then MacCrawley went back to concentrating.
Over and over he rubbed the triangle of cloth, a bit
of cloth from a trench coat saturated with Constantine's vibrations. A magical link to the Scouse magician. He rubbed the cloth and pictured Constantine.
He watched him through the window of the limo to
enhance the connection. And slowly he built up to a
full psychic attack; a renewed attack, really. He had
commenced when Constantine was walking to the
grotto of the Lady of Waters with Maureen.

Gradually, that was the best way to carry out a
psychic attack. You started slowly. You hit him hard
and then cease. Let a little time pass. Then you do it
again, a little longer this time. Then again. The attack
gained momentum, and once you'd planted enough
thoughts of self-destruction in his mind, you went all
out. You went for the kill.

MacCrawley had killed a number of men this way.

He relished it. Loved to make his enemies kill themselves.

It wasn't difficult, once you had entry to their minds. Men were strangely unaware of their own minds. They were always looking outward at the world, never inward, never knowing themselves. That made them vulnerable to manipulation by politicians, by propaganda, by television commercials . . . and vulnerable to psychic attack. Most men didn't question the impulses that arose from their subconscious. And it was MacCrawley's particular skill to make the psychic attack seem to rise from the victim's own mind.

His research on Constantine had convinced him that psychic attack would kill the Scouse magus despite his efforts at self-knowledge, because Constantine was front-loaded for self-destruction. His drinking binges, his barely disguised self-loathing, his bouts of depression, all pointed to a man who secretly hungered for death. MacCrawley felt sure that Constantine would play along, would unconsciously collaborate with the psychic attack . . .

So it seemed to be. The echoes coming back to him from Constantine's mind, though fuzzy, intermittent, and fragmentary, were redolent of a man in despair. A man hungry for the peace of death.

MacCrawley had a moment of doubt. Might it not be smarter to simply call one of the SOT's assassins and have a bullet snapped into the sneaky little bastard's skull?

But that was too easy. Constantine had tricked him, twice. He had to pay for that. Assassinate him and there was no guarantee he'd go to Hell. But make him commit suicide and down he'd go . . . Not that God would send him there. Suicides, except for the Kevorkian variety, had turned their backs on life, so they drifted into the outer darkness and were prey to whatever was there. And there were demons out there just waiting for John Constantine to drift into reach . . .

Constantine was stopping on the corner up ahead. Talking to the woman, an air of resignation in his posture, his sagging shoulders, the way he held his cigarette. Now she was turning away, walking back toward Constantine's place.

He was getting rid of her, so maybe now was the moment to press the attack.

MacCrawley rubbed the cloth the more firmly, murmuring to Constantine's mind through the psychic link, making him feel that these thoughts were his own:

The world is shite, isn't it? You save people by killing people. Does that make sense? How many died down there, killed by the Lord of Stone? How many in the village were fed to the crankers? All people I failed to save. And that's the kind of world it is. The Americans had stopped the second world war by nuking Hiroshima and Nagasaki. Death to stop death? Satan's little joke on us. And how long does anyone live anyway? Maybe eighty years? A drop in the bucket of time; then you were churned back into the sea of consciousness. It was all meaningless. Why not just leap headfirst into that sea? Suicide will be confession, confession of my failures, my complicity in the

*deaths of my friends . . . It is an ugly world, after all.
It's reckoned that by 2010 half of the children in the
UK and USA will be obese, while more than half of all
children in India are malnourished. What delicious
irony; how Satan must enjoy it. Horror after horror
stalks the planet . . . so why stay and take part in the
horrors? Look at that stinking bum in the doorway—
that's my soul, really, that's John Constantine's soul, a
rotting pissed-up tramp at heart, that's me . . .*

It was working. Constantine was heading for the
River Thames. And a foggy echo came back from him:
Constantine envisioning throwing himself in the river.

Drowning.

Not bad. Not as pleasing to MacCrawley as poison
would be, but not bad.

⊷⊚⊷

The rank old Thames. A high concrete bank in this
place, mottled by graffiti. One bit of graffiti read DIE
YOU PIGS. The jade-colored water, sluggish and dark.

The ancient artery of London. It'd be perfect to
die there. Perfect. Join his ancestors . . .

Constantine took off his trench coat, folded it up,
laid it on the ground. He smoked a final cigarette,
watching a tugboat chug by. He'd bought the pack of
cigarettes on the way to London. Still twelve left.
Seemed a shame to waste them. A bearded tramp,
toothless mouth hanging open, shambled past, wearing a trench coat himself. Gray hair but hints of
blond remaining. Like a ghost of the future Constantine, maybe, if he was fool enough not to kill himself.

The tramp gaped at Constantine, then made a two-fingered gesture, the universal sign for "Got a smoke?"

Constantine threw him the whole pack. "Keep 'em, mate." The tramp nodded to him and moved on, lighting a Silk Cut.

John Constantine took a final, long hit on his smoke, and blew that last plume into the air; it drifted over the Thames, quickly lost in the drizzly wind . . .

Just like me. A puff of smoke, blown away. And good riddance.

"Good-bye you bastards," he said aloud, flicking his cigarette butt into the river.

And then he backed up, got a running jump, and flung himself into the River Thames, his mouth wide open to make sure he got water into his lungs as quickly as possible.

The dirty, cold, dark water closed around him. He sucked water in, and kept his body rigid so he'd sink faster. *Get it over with . . .*

—=◎=—

MacCrawley cackled to himself, watching from the limo pulled up on the side street leading to the river. He got out and rushed to the river side, and watched with deepening satisfaction as Constantine sank into the water, the bubbles rising where he'd gone under. But he was no fool. He was going to wait and be sure . . .

The minutes passed. More than enough. Then the body bobbed to the surface, facedown.

There it was. John Constantine's body, unmistakable, floating facedown.

MacCrawley kept watching, just to be absolutely sure.

The body floated slowly down the Thames, not far from the bank, where the current is slower. Turning slowly, slowly, like an autumn leaf on the water.

MacCrawley rubbed the triangle of cloth, tried to connect with Constantine psychically. Got a few faint reverberations from some dark place. Constantine's lost soul. *Where am I . . . darkness . . . There are things here . . . coming for me . . .*

Not wanting to be damaged by the psychic feedback from a soul being eaten by a demon, MacCrawley broke the connection. He chuckled and skimmed the little triangle of trench coat cloth into the river.

That was it. John Constantine was dead.

Humming a Scottish ballad, MacCrawley turned and walked back to the limo. "To my club," he told the driver, climbing in. "I'm going to celebrate."

✦═◦○◦═✦

Seeing the limo drive away, Maureen emerged from the dark doorway she'd been hiding in and hurried to the concrete bank. She saw the old rusted ladder that went down to the water and she climbed down it, stopped on the bottom rung, hung low and trailed one hand in the river.

"Lady," she said, "return him to me, as you promised."

I have preserved him, giving him the air he

needed, in my river, came the reply. **He returns to you, the breath preserved in him. This boon I give you in honor of your ancient bloodline, child of fairies.**

"Bless you, Lady!"

The body floating down the river suddenly stopped floating, and a current that shouldn't have been there carried it back, against the main current of the river, to the rusted ladder. The body began to thrash, the head lifting free of the water, sputtering, spitting. Maureen grabbed Constantine's hand and pulled him to the ladder.

He gasped and spat more water. "Christ on a Vespa but that's foul! Pull me in closer, darlin', will you?"

She helped him up on the ladder. They climbed to the concrete bank. "Bloody hell, that was unpleasant," he said, putting on his trench coat, teeth chattering. "Cold. The Lady came through, though. Kept enough air moving into my lungs, all the time I was under. I want a shower."

"Do you think it'll work?"

"I think he was convinced. I sent him a little message there at the end to complete the illusion. If the Servants of Transfiguration reckon me for dead, they'll leave us alone. Only, I've got to leave town for a while. Lay low somewhere to make sure. Can't even tell Chas, for now. Let them think my body wasn't recovered . . . Shite I'm cold . . . Wish I hadn't given away me smokes . . ."

Constantine reeked of the river, and he was cold and wet, but he was feeling lighthearted, quite uncharacteristically cheerful. Like a world of weight had been lifted off his shoulders. As if his "suicide" had actually been a kind of ritual enactment of death—a kind of cathartic death. And his coming back, an enactment of rebirth.

He glanced at Maureen—thought about Kit for a moment. He made up his mind he wasn't going to write to her, after all. Sometimes the omens spoke loud in a man's ear. And somehow—he didn't miss her so much now. Not with Maureen here.

Not so very many minutes later, with Constantine huddled in his trench coat, they were climbing the stairs to his flat. Geoff and Bosky were just coming out, and looked "busted" when they saw Maureen and Constantine.

"How'd you get all wet, John?" Geoff asked.

"Never mind that," Maureen said sternly. "Where do you two think you're off to after I told you to stay here?"

"We were just going to a jeweler's, see if they could give us a, what do you call it, an assay or whatever it is," Geoff said, "on these . . ." And he showed them the bag of jewels he'd taken from Spurlick.

"Well!" Constantine laughed. "Look at that, Geoff! You're rich, boy! Funny old world, innit?"

"I'm rich? *We're* rich! You saved my life, John. We all did our part. We'll share equal, like. This is enough for all of us!" Geoff declared. "And I'll need someplace to live; don't want to be a sponge. What do you say, we can go on a road trip for starts."

"Yeah!" Bosky said. "We can buy a van! Or one of them big American SUV things!"

"Funnily enough, a road trip, the four of us, is just

what I had in mind," Constantine said, looking at
Maureen.

She looked at him coolly. "So, you think I'm just
going to go off with you on a road trip, do you? A
man I barely know . . ."

"Oh, right, I shouldn't have—"

". . . but then again, that'd be a pretty bloody good
way to get to know you. Now wouldn't it, John?" She
smiled and put out her hand.

He cleared his throat. Put on a look of cool detach-
ment. And said, "Yeah. It would."

And then he took her hand in his, and they went
into the flat together.

About the Author

JOHN SHIRLEY is the author of many novels, including *Demons, Crawlers, In Darkness Waiting, City Come A-Walkin'*, and *Eclipse*, as well as collections of stories, which include *Really, Really, Really, Really, Weird Stories* and the Bram Stoker Award–winning collection *Black Butterflies*. His newest novels are *John Constantine: Hellblazer—War Lord* and, for Cemetary Dance books, *The Other End*. Also a television and movie scripter, Shirley was co-screenwriter of *The Crow*. Most recently he has adapted Edgar Allan Poe's *Ligeia* for the screen. The authorized fan-created Web site is www.darkecho.com/JohnShirley and official blog is www.JohnShirley.net.